while the sun is above us

while the sun is above us

a novel

MELANIE SCHNELL

 freehand books

Freehand Books gratefully acknowledges the support of the Canada Council
for the Arts for its publishing program. ¶ Freehand Books, an imprint of Broadview
Press Inc., acknowledges the financial support for its publishing program provided
by the Government of Canada through the Canada Book Fund.

Freehand Books
515 – 815 1st Street SW Calgary, Alberta T2P 1N3
www.freehand-books.com

Book orders: LitDistCo
100 Armstrong Avenue Georgetown, Ontario L7G 5S4
Telephone: 1-800-591-6250 Fax: 1-800-591-6251
orders@litdistco.ca
www.litdistco.ca

LIBRARY AND ARCHIVES CANADA CATALOGUING IN PUBLICATION

Schnell, Melanie
While the sun is above us / Melanie Schnell.

ISBN 978-1-55481-061-1

1. Title.

PS8637.C5545W55 2012   C813'.6   C2012-900304-2

Edited by Don LePan
Book design by Natalie Olsen, kisscutdesign.com
Cover photo by Françoise Lacroix, panoptika.net
Author photo © 2011 Graham Powell | Photography, photo.grahampowell.com

Printed on FSC recycled paper and bound in Canada

For the women of South Sudan

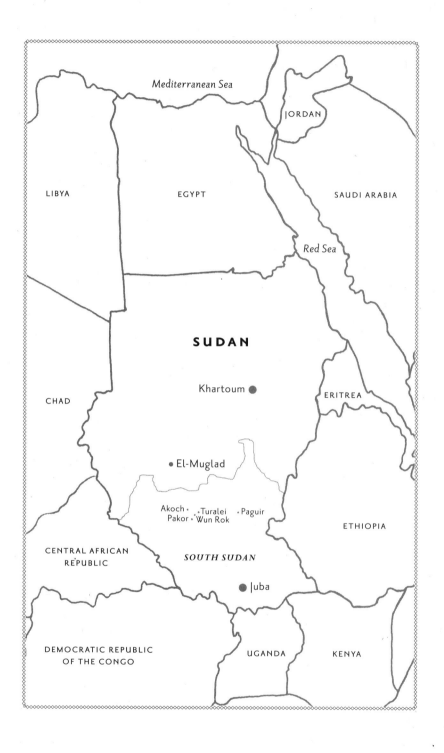

Mediterranean Sea

JORDAN

LIBYA

EGYPT

SAUDI ARABIA

Red Sea

SUDAN

CHAD

ERITREA

Khartoum ●

● El-Muglad

Akoch ·
Pakor · ·Turalei · Paguir
·Wun Rok

ETHIOPIA

SOUTH SUDAN

CENTRAL AFRICAN
REPUBLIC

● Juba

DEMOCRATIC REPUBLIC
OF THE CONGO

UGANDA

KENYA

WE TELL OURSELVES STORIES

IN ORDER TO LIVE.

JOAN DIDION, from "The White Album"

Adut

A long, long time ago, Heaven and Earth were connected by a strong, thick rope that allowed Man to walk into Heaven and God to walk onto Earth amongst His people. It was during this time that Man knew what Heaven felt like under his feet. But one day, because of Man's greed, God became angry and He sent a bird to cut this rope with its beak, severing the tie and forever imprisoning Man on Earth and God in Heaven. With no access to Heaven, and no pathway to God, Man began to suffer from hunger, illness, and death. Soon after, the weather began to change, the seasons became strange, and the animals and trees began to die. We only knew what Heaven was like from our memories, from our stories. Slowly, we Dinka people turned into mere mortals, and Earth became a kind of hell. Not long after this happened, Mama told me, the war began. She told me bad things were happening to our neighbours all around us because of this war. I asked her what these bad things were, but she refused to talk of it further, no matter how much I whined and prodded her. But here we are safe, she said, and she stroked my cheek. Her fingers were rough from tilling the soil. Nobody can get to us here. These rivers that surround us are like deep occans for the enemy of the north. They cannot cross over, no matter how hard they try.

The story you will hear is a strange one. Perhaps you will choose not to believe it. But I am certain you will believe it, you must believe it. I know you have seen things you never thought you would see in your entire life. You have learned things you did not want to learn. You have stepped on these lands, alongside my people, and so you have lived some of this war, *khawaja*. I am sorry for this.

This story may answer some questions for you, if you are still with us, *Insha'Allah*. Before you arrived here, perhaps you had heard of terrible things happening in a faraway place, from your newspapers and your television sets. This faraway place is my home, and our stories bear a different kind of burden from what your own land holds.

I am not proud to admit I knew nothing of the outside world before I was captured. I was a simple village girl, married only four years when I was forced to leave my home. One afternoon, not long after I arrived, I wandered into a room I did not yet know I was not allowed in. I was shocked to see a box with colourful moving images. I had heard of television sets, but none had yet arrived to our small village.

Saleh's Head Wife laughed when she saw the look on my face, and she said to me, "Do you not know what that is, *abida*? I suppose they do not have television sets in your mud huts, where you live with the monkeys!"

She hated me all the time I was there, and I believe she was happy on that morning eight years later when she found me gone, though it meant she would have to buy another slave to replace me. She did not like the way her husband looked at me. Even when he tried to hide it from her, anyone could see his eyes follow my body in ways they should not. Soon after I arrived I was kept far away from the others, so I would also be far from Saleh's prowling eyes.

I am much older now. There are days when I feel like an ancient one, my life already spent from my body. There are days when I feel empty inside, and it is as though I can hear the sound of a faint wind blowing through my bones, made thin from all these years past. And there are many dark nights I cannot breathe, for the turbaned horsemen chase me in my dreams.

Since our return home to the south I have been taking care of my father and my two children. We live with my auntie Nyakiir and her daughters in this village, who remain alive and together after it all. We are a good day's walk from the village in which I was born and raised. Auntie makes the *marissa* and sells it to the men in the market who want to forget about the war. My job here in these two *tukals*, which live side by side and hold all of us, is cooking and washing clothes. It is not so different than what I was made to do in Saleh's house. Though here, of course, I am free.

My father is not well. I tend to him every day. His skin hangs from his bones. He has diseases in his stomach that will not cure. He will no longer eat the food I make for him and I am worried he has little time left. This war has been too hard on him. But my daughter knows her baba now; she knows who came to save her.

A cleansing ceremony was given for my children and me, just after Rith was born, not long after we arrived at Auntie Nyakiir's place. To thank the ancestors for keeping us alive, with Adhar's small hand clutched in mine and with Rith swaddled in my arms, we jumped over a goat that Auntie Nyakiir had bought in the market. Afterwards he was slaughtered and became the meat for our feast. There was much dancing and a big fire, and our neighbours came to join us, to welcome us home. On this night my father blessed my children with their proper Dinka names, Rith Arop and Adhar Arop, after their ancestors. Even though they have lighter skin, our people now consider them to be pure Dinka. With our one fire burning bright under the many small fires in the night sky, I thanked the Women, secretly.

I still believe this circle of Women were my ancestors, *khawaja*. For how could anyone else but those of my blood clan have pushed me through what I had to endure?

The war is almost over, they tell us. The agreement of peace between the leaders of the north and the south will soon be signed. The ones who were lucky enough to flee the madness of all these years past are returning, to help build the country back up again. But alongside this new talk of peace, there is more talk of war. Every day we hear these whispers. They speak of fresh battles occurring not so far away; we hear of people dying by the enemy's hands in neighbouring villages; we hear of guns stored in the homes of our relatives and friends. Just in case it all begins again. It is too difficult to release this war from our blood, when it long ago shaped who we are, how we live, how we move, how we breathe. Blood has filled this earth up; it has made God angry. We must be forgiven or nothing will change; these wars will continue forever. But we continue to push forward in the name of peace, even though there is still this fear in our hearts, like an open mouth with a hunger that cannot be satisfied.

It seems like so long ago now, but it is only two seasons that have passed since we made the long trek back from Saleh's big farm in the north to my auntie Nyakiir's home here in Turalei. For almost one week we had moved at night and hid during the day in the bush and the reeds of the river so as to avoid the raiders. Rith was kicking against my insides at his own hunger and thirst, as for days we had only eaten bits of bread from Father's sack. Adhar stopped crying after the first day of that trek and became silent and listless, stricken with her own heat and hunger. But once we were past the river Kiir I knew we were on safe ground, and lucky to be so. Many people who tried this route from the north did not make it.

Along the route was the spot where my village used to live. My father told me he did not want me to see it. There were too many deaths there, he said, and it was nothing but dust; floating ghosts would creep up on you, sit on your shoulders, and attach themselves

13 while the sun is above us

to your life. Perhaps they would, but still I insisted, though we were exhausted and hungry from the long trek. I said to Father what Mama had said to me when I was small, that those who die become our angels. They stay here to protect us, to make certain our people do not get wiped off the earth. But then, as I stood in the dusty place that was once my home, and as I felt the ghosts who still lived there, I was only sick and fearful inside.

There was a time not so long ago when the earth's heart beat strong in this place. There were scatterings of *tukals,* gardens, crops of sorghum, goats bleating, children playing. Now there remained only red dust and rings of black scars where *tukals* used to stand. Some outer walls still stood, roofless, crumbling and yellow with years of loneliness. Only two *tukals* remained intact. The wind whistled through the old, bleached straw of their roofs, with only the sun and the trees to hear its keening song.

My father stood in the entrance of one of these *tukals.* A flat board hung by one nail beside its door. On the other side were two planks that looked as though they were meant to hold this board. I thought this very strange — who had come and put this here? My father had leaned his walking stick against the outer wall and was peering through the doorway. It sounded as though he were talking to someone. As I moved closer, I heard that what he was doing was giving his prayers to this *tukal,* his head tucked inside the dark entry, with just the back of his body visible. I wondered why he chose to say a prayer for this one *tukal* that was left whole, when most of the others were broken and open to the sky.

This was the place I had reached for in my mind every night for the eight years I was kept as a slave — but I had seen it standing and alive, just as it was before the men came on their horses. Now I saw it was gone, the life of it burnt away. The red dust blew, swirled around my feet. I tried to find the places where I slept as a child, where I was married, where my husband and I conceived Khajami. I looked for the spot of earth that held the memory of my screams when my eldest son was born. My heart fell to my stomach in that moment. I listened to the echoes of this hollow place, and finally I understood what was lost. I looked down and watched the white sunlight play with the whirling dust in its own dance with God.

The huge old acacia tree where we used to hold our ceremonies, where the elders met to discuss marriages, the cattle movements, the planting of crops, still remained, but now it guarded nothing. It was dry and creaking, alone in the wind. I held back my tears. I had not cried in so very long; I did not want my father to think I was ungrateful to be here, ungrateful to finally be free.

I think of you often, *khawaja*. My father told me what you were like. Perhaps you were too frightened to notice, but he observed you well, knowing he would need to send his prayers up to *Nhialic* later to forgive him for what he had to do. He thought that by observing and seeking to understand your character, the prayers he sent up to the sky would be more easily received. He said you were kind but young and misguided. He said you did not understand who we are, or the real reason for this war. But how could you? Forgive me, but life was not difficult for you. And there are things that I have wondered since that brief moment when we met, when you touched me on the wrist as you helped me to my feet, your white fingers brushing my scar, and I was shocked by the colour of your hair, like the sun: did you think you could escape the debt of grief that this land carries? Did you think you could come here and then leave, untouched? Did you believe the colour of your skin would keep you safe? Are there monsters hiding in your own land that you needed to escape? How could they have been more frightening than the monsters you encountered here?

When my father prays to *Nhialic* for forgiveness, he sends prayers for you too, *khawaja*. He prays that you are free from danger, wherever you are.

I can hear him just outside his *tukal* now; his steady river of words floats through the door and calms me. I can see him as though the mud wall were made of thin, woven cotton — his slender knees on the hard floor, palms touching, long fingers splayed, as he bends his forehead to his crooked fingertips. He has been praying a lot these days past. He does not want his grandchildren to carry the burden of his guilt. He must be forgiven by the ancestors, and by all the spirits above who look down on us, so that this heavy life of ours can be made lighter for Rith and Adhar.

I hope you made it out alive, *khawaja*. I hope you are back home with your family and your people. I hope you have found a husband to marry, and that you will bear him children. If you had a child who was taken, would you do the same as my father did? I hope you think of the answer to that, and can forgive us.

The stubborn sun is setting across the low huts, fat and bright, still shining. We share the same sun and moon, you and me, and I think of this while I hope you are safe. Sometimes I look into the sky, and sometimes, God help me, I pray for those clouds to reach down with their light fingers and lift me up to that space behind them, so I will not have to wash these clothes, watch my father die, tell my children there is not enough food to eat today, again. But it is a beautiful sunset; there are waves of light turning purple and gold, floating down into the ground behind the huts of this village.

I believe we will not meet again in this lifetime, *khawaja*. But it is my hope that we will meet in Heaven someday, *Insha'Allah,* perhaps beyond the clouds. And then, I promise you, I will thank you properly. I have a dream of my family and I making a proper ceremony for you there to thank you for your sacrifice. We will slaughter the largest bull and bring for you the sweetest part of it; we will build a large fire; we will give to you gifts and jewels, pretty things; and we will sing and dance all night, under Heaven's close stars. When we show you how grateful we are, it will make you smile.

I

Sandra

APRIL 21, 2003, EL-MUGLAD, NORTH SUDAN

I can't believe it's all come down to this.

I keep seeing you in the tiny spaces that have opened up in between my thoughts, a tuft of grass from a jagged crack — your long, sloped forehead, your plaited hair. Your sad face. And the man, the one who brought me to you, ancient, his face etched with rivers of tiny lines.

Perhaps you do not think of me. Perhaps once you left this place you wouldn't let yourself think of me. My only company is this snake and a one-armed boy who doesn't understand me. But it's you that flits in and out of my mind, as though you are waiting to hear me speak.

The snake in this stall — who else can I tell what he said to me? I swear to you, I heard him say my name. He said it slowly, began with a heavy "s." He said, "Sssssssssandra . . ." Only one time. Then he slithered away.

This snake wanted to tell me something. I think he has a secret for me. I think he is holding key information. He wants to help me get out of here. He would've bitten me by now if he wanted to kill me, right? His fangs would've sunk through my flesh, clean and deep, his efficient poison mixing with my blood. He could've done this when we first spotted each other last week. But he didn't. Instead, he lifted his head up and down in tiny jerks, and then he trailed away, all soft and quiet, a curving line through the dust.

He's a black cobra, long and sleek, with a small, diamond-shaped head that continually pulses, looking for a current to follow, sniffing at rivers of air. He exits and enters through a small hole in the ground in the corner of this stall, where the servant boy put me one week ago. The boy, tall, thin, and dressed in only ripped cotton pants held up by a piece of rope, looked shocked at the colour of my skin, horrified, perhaps, to see a white girl — dirty, bleeding, with skin darkened and blistered by the sun, but a white girl nonetheless. He threw me in here, a horse stall with a low ceiling and thick wood slats for walls. Through the spaces between the slats I can see into the empty stalls on either side of me. The ground on both sides is covered with hay and horse manure. After he fastened the chains through the wooden door and around the post beside it with an iron lock, he left me in here all night and all the next day, alone.

Another man came into the barn the next evening, and peered at me through the slats in the door. His eyes grew huge at the sight of me. He took his face away and I heard yelling in Arabic. It went on for a long time. I was sure I heard him hit the boy, many times, loud smacks on skin with the palm of a hand. But the boy didn't complain, didn't cry out. I peeked through the slats to see the boy and this man leading all the horses away from the other stalls, leaving the entire barn empty, save for me and Mr. Cobra.

I was left alone again for another day and night. Just when I was sure they were going to leave me to die of thirst and hunger, the servant boy came back and pushed a bowl of rice and a bowl of water toward me through a hole made by the broken slats in the bottom of the door. When I moved to the hole to look at him, I saw his eyes blown wide open with fear. Then I saw where his right arm had been. There was a piece of gauze tied tight around the stump, soaked in bright red blood. The man who had peered in at me and slapped the boy — had he chopped that boy's arm off? I looked back up at the boy's eyes, still wide. I don't think he even blinked. His eyes were red and wet. His breath was rapid, strained. He turned away and screwed up his face, pressing his eyes shut, against the pain, I imagine. Then he pushed himself up with his good arm and walked out the main door.

Since then, the boy has come back about five times with food. I'll hear the barn door slide open, and then through the hole in the door the boy will push a bowl of rice and a bowl of water, sometimes a piece of white bread. Then he'll leave. When I finish, I set the bowls outside the door of the stall, squeeze them through the hole, one at a time. Usually he comes back the next day to retrieve them. But he doesn't come every day. I found a stick on the floor and last night, when the boy didn't come with food, I used it to try to coax some pieces of straw from next door through a space between the slats. I needed some moisture in my mouth, something to chew on. After what seemed like an hour, I finally managed to pull one piece through. When it landed on the dirt of my floor, light as a feather, I noticed a speck of horse manure on one end of it. My stomach turned, and I pushed it into the corner with the toe of my sandal.

I also found a small rock in here. I thought it was quite something, this smooth pebble lying in the dust, like a gift. There are few rocks of any kind here in the north of the country, land of dust and wind. It was as though someone had left it for me.

The last few mornings, as soon as the sun filters in through the cracks in the walls of the barn, I've taken the magazine article out of my pocket, unfolded it, and lain it on the floor. Then I've closed

while the sun is above us

my eyes and thrown the pebble onto the paper. Where it lands offers me some kind of sign for the day. This morning, it landed on the young black boy, a slave who had just returned home to the south. Missionaries had bought him back for fifty dollars. The pebble landed right on his head, near his mouth. I think this means the one-armed servant will bring me food today.

I am waiting for it to land on the final word of the article. "Freedom."

I need to talk to you. I want you to hear me. I don't blame you. I wonder if you know that.

If I had to blame someone for how I got into this mess, it would be easy to blame Graham. Though that just seems pathetic now. In this country, everyone knows life is hell; no one expects anything else. You don't complain about your lives. Not the way we do. You seem to accept it all, the horrors of war, your own broken lives, your dead families. And yet I have met some people here who have this shining happiness about them; it beams out clear and alive against the crumbling mess around them, a searchlight in the dark.

But my soul has shrivelled, this I know: a small, mewling fetus turning its back to the light and going to sleep. I'm not who I was before I came here. And the truth is I don't want to go home. I mean, I need to get out of here. But I don't want to go back to Toronto. I'm scared my light went out, my eyes look different, and people at home will notice.

Dad phoned just before I left Toronto for Africa. I'll never forget his words: "What the hell are you doing? Do you think going over there is going to make you feel alive again? Do you think going off to some godforsaken place is going to heal your broken heart?" Stung, I hung up the phone. The day after landing in Nairobi, I found an Internet café and wrote him an email telling him I had arrived safely. He wrote back immediately, telling me to write him often. As is our habit with each other, neither of us mentioned our previous phone conversation. We've always been all about avoiding what needs to be said, Dad and me. It's somehow been easier that way. I knew I was never in danger of any heart-to-hearts with him, not like whenever Mom called, trying to force words out of my throat that wouldn't budge.

Right after Mom left us, she asked me to write her letters. Her voice crackling over the phone, she asked me to write down "all the slipstreamy thoughts from the pocket of my soul" and send them to her. That's exactly what she said: "slipstreamy thoughts from the pocket of my soul." I was ten years old then, and I didn't have a clue what she meant. I didn't speak her New Age-y language. Perhaps it was when she asked me to do this that everything began to close in. Whenever Graham and I fought, he would throw words like "remote" and "stoic" at me because I refused to let my anger out in a dramatic, spewing caterwaul. Knowing that he would have preferred the drama made me more resolute; I would keep myself in check even if he stumbled home drunk at three in the morning. How could I explain to Graham that I didn't want my mother, or him, or the world, to have my thoughts? My thoughts were the one thing nobody could take away from me.

My mother was always moving. She constantly complained to me, from wherever she had moved to, her voice whining through the phone I held in my hand, about how I refused to "open up." She still expected some kind of mother-daughter intimacy, impossible since she had put thousands of miles between us. All I knew was that I needed to keep my thoughts hidden from her, inside my bones, alive and shouting in secret.

I can picture them both now, Dad on the phone with the embassy, his face all screwed up, trying to figure out what they're telling him. "Your daughter is missing, Mr. Bilinsky. Somewhere in Sudan. There was an accident, a mishap of sorts, sir, and we don't know exactly where your daughter is." I can see him, taking out his life's savings to hire someone to find me, while Mom says some hokey prayer and then taps a crystal with a wand from the alternative therapy corner store or some shit. Dad will figure it out; Mom will stay in the dark. That's how it's always been with those two. I don't think she'd even want to know this story — it would upset her carefully constructed world. But I have a feeling that you, the girl whose name I'll never know, will want to know my story. Maybe it's nothing more than the way your deep black eyes looked at me. Not angry, not pitiful, not even curious. But like you knew me. We shared something that night, something permanent, the turn of a green leaf to red. And I think you would listen if I told you a story, even if it takes a very long time to tell. I must talk to you as though you are someone who can bear witness to this life. I must do this before it's all too late.

Adut

2003, TURALEI, SOUTH SUDAN, IN THE MONTH OF OCTOBER,

THE SEASON OF *RULE*

I wake from the nightmare and feel for the scar on my wrist. It is always when the sun falls that they chase me now. It is strange that I did not have these nightmares up north in Saleh's house; they came to me upon my return home. These dark pictures keep me from sleeping, and in the daytime I drag myself around like a ghost. Father yells at me sometimes, because I am not being careful. Last week I spilled his morning tea on him, leaving a red welt on his arm. I did not tell him that I do not sleep at nights, that this is the reason for my clumsiness.

Just before I woke, I heard hooves galloping on the ground. It sounded like hundreds of horses racing toward me. Closer and closer the terrible sound came until it filled my ears and my brain, a thunderstorm inside my head. Then this sound sunk down into me and became a hard drumming along my spine, shaking my whole body. And then everywhere there was the blood, all over me, and all over the inside of the *tukal,* and all over my mother and father, and Khajami.

What was strange about this dream was that I was a small child, and yet Khajami was there, and still alive.

Then my father's eyes were before me, wide and wild. It was as if his eyes were screaming at me in a language I could not understand. It was not your language, *khawaja,* but another one. It sounded as though it came from another planet in the sky. Grunting words strung together to sound like terrified nonsense. And then, I awoke to the darkness, and to the sleeping bodies of my children.

It is only to you I speak of these dreams. I do not talk of them to those around me. I do not scream when I awaken from these terrors; the screams keep themselves locked away inside my dreams only.

I allow my breathing to slow while I lie still on my narrow mattress. My children are nestled against me. I listen to their breath, put my hand on each of their chests, feel their rising and falling rhythm. Their sleeping, small innocence calms my mind. What a deep place they travel to so easily every night. Adhar curls around Rith like a shell. In the day she carries him around and coos to him, just as she did with the make-believe dolls she made from cloth up north.

Please forgive this talk of my dreams, *khawaja*. It is simply that once I awaken from a dream, there is nothing but the night to face, and nothing to tend to but my own rapid thoughts and this heart that hammers. The black night taunts me as it looks in at me through the small window above this bed. It tells me I will find no more sleep this night.

It was only in the nights that my beloved grandmother would tell me the stories I begged for as a child. She swore to me that telling stories while the sun was above us was a sin. It is most necessary for the proper telling of these stories that the night be alive in its darkness, when they can float down unseen from the powers.

My grandmother told me stories for moral lessons, for learning about my people. She told me stories of love and struggle, stories that made me understand that everything in the universe is together as one, that even the animals are our brothers and sisters. Always in these stories the good overcame the bad. I would rush through my day's errands to come back to the hut and listen to her deep, old voice planting within me her stories I will never forget. Often she would repeat stories, telling them in different ways. Every once in awhile she would tell me a new story, and I would listen very closely, wanting to remember it always, because I knew I would never hear it the same way again.

My grandmother told me that a story has the power to travel to distant lands and float into the ears of others, so they too can hear it, even if they cannot see the storyteller. I hope this story reaches you, *khawaja,* wherever you are, so that you may understand. I am thankful my grandmother died before our village was raided; she did not have to endure what so many of the other elders had to, watching everything they had built their lives toward burn and die away, with only their own withered bodies remaining upon the earth.

And so I will begin, here in this dark night with you. I fear I have so much to say, so many words that have waited too long to spill out from me. I fear I will not stop even when the sun comes to break up my song. This story is my gift to you. Perhaps when we come to the end of it, we will learn that the good has overcome the bad. Perhaps.

"Adut. Adut! Wake up." Mama's voice was raspy, scared.

I groaned. Mama heaved me up by my shoulders.

"Get up now, *man dia,* my child. We have to move again."

It felt like I had only just fallen asleep moments ago. It was still dark. I peered into Mama's face, just inches away, and saw the deep furrow between her brows, like a worried scar. The familiar heaviness spilled into my heart, as I re-entered the awakened world and forced myself through the last thin threads of the veil of sleep.

Mama left the hut to go outside and serve the men their tea. I shifted quietly around Khajami so as not to awaken him. My body was still warm from where he had curled into me during the night, clutching at my breast with his small fingers. I began folding the thin, rumpled blankets into four neat quarters, leaving the heaviest one to cover sleeping Khajami. I laid them at the end of the narrow cot, just as Mama had shown me to do when I was a girl, before I became Tobias's wife. I had noticed that Tobias's mother folded her blankets differently; she rolled them up into the shape of a young tree trunk and laid them sideways in the middle of the bed, so that when you glanced at it, it might look like a tall, swaddled child. But I was in my mother's house now, and so I knew I must be careful to follow the way she had shown me to do things. Otherwise she would chastise me, tell me my way was wrong.

I knew Mama was jealous, though it would not be right for her to admit that. She was jealous because I had learned my new ways from Tobias's mother. I was Mama's only daughter, and now I lived in another woman's hut, a woman who already had an abundance of daughters not yet married. They were there to help her cook, to help her build new huts for her growing family, to help her cut down *durra* in the fields and pound it into meal for food. It was Tobias who suggested I move into Mama's hut for a while to help her.

Like me, he could see the extra lines on her thin face as she worked all alone. Sweet Tobias. I remember how thankful I was, thankful to him for noticing, for considering Mama's burden at this time.

I stood on Mama's cot and felt with my hands on top of the wooden beam for the tin box that held the cloths. I took out the red one, held it in my hands. This was the cloth onto which I had sewn the shiny beads Mama had given me as a gift, just before I was married. Mama had returned from the market one afternoon, her face stretched into a small, rare smile. She told me she had a secret in her closed fist. After I pleaded with her, she opened up her hand to display the multicoloured beads that lay in her palm. They were so beautiful, glinting their red and gold against the sun, as though they could talk to it, as though they had dropped from the sun and were asking to come home again. She told me the beads were a gift from my very own female ancestors, to celebrate my moon time.

Just the week before Mama gave me the beads, I had been squatting in the trees behind the *tukal*. It was evening and the sky was beginning to light up with its tiny fires. Under the new starlight, I found streaks of brown between my legs. I screamed, bringing my mother and Auntie Nyakiir running. When I showed them my thighs, they just laughed, told me I was a woman now, that my time had finally come. The next day Mama sent me to Auntie Nyakiir's house. I spent the week there with her, helping her with her chores, while the new blood continued to come out of me. Auntie Nyakiir sat me down in the evenings and told me this strange blood was good, it spoke to me of being ready for a new life. After several days Mama brought Grandmother and Auntie Amath over to Auntie Nyakiir's hut. My grandmother spread sticky red clay onto my nose and cheeks. A neighbour brought her small daughter and sat her on my lap in front of the fire. That night we ate the meat from the goat and danced under the moon, the songs that arose from the women's throats quivering and shrill. And not long after, Tobias took me as his wife. In my youthful ignorance, I had not known that finding those marks would be something so important as to cause two people to wed.

I carefully placed the tin cups full of *durra* and small bags of tea and sugar in the beaded cloth, tied it together, placed it in our pot. I would carry this on my head and carry Khajami in a sling on my back as we travelled into the bush. This food would sustain us for the night, or possibly longer; we did not know when Deng Dit would tell us we could move back home. I wondered if Mama would scold me for using the fine cloth for this purpose. I did not know why, but something inside of me wanted to touch those beads, wanted at this time especially to feel in my hands what had led me to Tobias.

I lifted up the branches of firewood I had cut the night before, just a few hours ago, it seemed, and patted the damp earth beneath with my fingers. Below this spot was buried the rest of our food stores, so that if the *murahaleen* came and burnt down our homes, we would still have our food to dig up underneath the scorched ground.

My heart raced in this early hour, and I strained to hear what was being said in the murmur of voices of the men and women outside. There was a quiet desperation and confusion in their whispers. I poked my head between the rainbow-patterned sheets hanging in the doorway. I breathed in the cool dawn, and I watched the pink light just beginning to slip over the hills. Sometimes when I breathed that light into my body, it softened the fear that ate at my heart. But that morning the hammering of my heart would not stop, as though it was already running from what chased it.

Khajami had been especially tired lately, exhausted from the night movements, like all of us. I stopped for a moment to look down at his long eyelashes and his smooth face as he lay on our mat on the floor. He had three years only, and always he was asking questions of his father and the elders. But his questions sounded different now. "Why are we moving again, Mama? Are the night animals hunting us?" His questions were born from the night-time stories Mama had told him of the animals that go hunting when the darkness falls down, looking for the youngest ones.

Khajami was spoiled, Tobias often told me with a playful smile. Before the night movements began, he had been used to sitting in his

MCNALLY ROBINSON
3130 8TH ST E
SASKATOON, SK

Term ID: 28356224

Purchase

xxxxxxxxxxxx4918

VISA   Entry Method: C

Total: $ 23.05

2014/04/12   19:45:40
Seq #:   0013581820
Appr Code: 062123
Resp Code: 01/027

VISA CREDIT
A0000000031010
85 8F 14 5F 93 F3 06 1U
00 80 00 80 00
F8 00
D7 1F FE 75 DB 60 00 86

APPROVED
Thank You:

Customer Copy

- IMPORTANT -
retain this copy for your records

Purchase

xxxxxxxxxx4518
VISA   Entry Method: C

Total: $ 23.05

2014-04-12   19:45:40
Seq #:   08135818?0
Appr Code: 062123
Resp Code: 01-A027

APPROVED
Thank You

359758 Reg23 7:39 pm 12/04/14

S WHILE THE SUN IS   1 @ 21.95   21.95
S 9781554810611
SUBTOTAL   21.95
TAX: GST - 5%   1.10
TOTAL SALES TAX   1.10
TOTAL   23.05
VISA PAYMENT   23.05

grandfather's lap at the head of the men's circle in the evenings. My father would patiently answer, one by one, the mountain of questions that Khajami asked him. He would laugh in wonder at the boy, at his young head filled with a strong need to know everything about this world, so new to him. He was the first male grandchild born to my father, the chief of our village, and so my father coddled him. But lately, burdened with fear and fatigue, my father had fallen silent and Khajami's questions became fewer. Even little Khajami was quickly learning that silence and danger lived side by side.

A war had been raging around us for too long. Since I was a child, my people had hoped the fighting would somehow miss us. Some believed the answer to our fear was to flee, and left for the north or the south. But most of us stayed. Many messages came to us over the years of clan and family members or neighbours killed or taken. But for some reason, our village had not been touched. Deng Dit, our diviner, insisted it was because we know to pray to the river Kiir, the totem of our Padylang clan. Mama told me something different: our village was too small for the enemy to bother with.

For the past few years, the stories of death around us had decreased, and we had begun once again planting our crops without fear and grazing our cattle further north. Just as things seemed to be returning to our normal way of life, Ajeng, Deng Dit's eldest daughter, disappeared. She had gone alone to the market one morning and had not returned. Two days later, Deng Dit's cousin from the neighbouring village came to tell us there were rumours she had been seen taken away on the back of an Arab's horse to be made a slave up north. Lovely Ajeng, so tall and strong, hardworking. She would have made a good wife to one of our men. And always she had a smile for Khajami, even when he was being mischievous. Perhaps it was at that time Deng Dit began going mad. Soon after Ajeng's disappearance, more messages began to reach our ears every day of villages around us being destroyed, people we knew killed or taken away.

And so our night movements had increased. Fleeing from the

enemy in the night was now part of our lives. These journeys, where we would leave in the night to go hide in the bush, sometimes for days, leaving our village a ghost town, became as common as going to the market for sorghum or rice. We had left our strongest bull as a sacrifice to the lion on the last moon, but the ancestors took no heed of this, for the enemy came one night two weeks later when we were hiding in the bush and set our fields on fire. We were unable to harvest, and our food stores were almost gone. They were getting closer.

Deng Dit listened to the earth's heartbeat and watched the sky at night. We trusted him to translate these magic things to us, and to tell us when it was time to move. His urgings for movement had become more forceful than usual this past moon. For every night we spent in our village, we spent two nights in the bush. And there was now a wildness in his eyes that had not been there before.

When I stepped outside to tell Mama everything was ready, I breathed the chill into me. It swirled around my heart and into my stomach. The women were hurriedly packing, gathering water from the well, stuffing cups of rice and packets of tea into cloth, placing them in pots and gourds to carry on their heads, preparing for our journey. The elders were crouched around a small fire, smoking shared cigarettes given to them by the soldiers who came through our village yesterday. My father had asked one of the soldiers if they could send some men to protect us. This soldier looked tired. His eyes were small and held no light. He told my father most of the men were fighting at the front lines, beyond the river Kiir, and there were not enough to protect the villagers as well. It would be best if we kept fleeing to the bush as we had been doing, he said. He had offered cigarettes, from his pocket, to my father. My father had accepted them silently into his open palm, the valleys of his sunken cheeks carving shadows in the dawn light.

I looked over at my father, squatting on his haunches, staring blankly into the fire, cradling a cup of sweet black tea in his hands. His elbows rested on his knees, and his long fingers tipped the cup to his lips. He looked small and thin. He was hunched under the weight of this new fear that was infecting his people. The man I used to see at village council meetings under the big tree had a calm face, with eyes powerful and fierce like a lion's. He spoke with authority about what should be done about the cattle, the harvests, and how we should move, in these dangerous times.

As our chief, my father had made the decision to send out the boys who had recently gone through their rites to become men to lead our cattle to the river. The cattle needed water in this dry season, but my father also wanted to move the cattle away from our village so the *murahaleen* could not steal them in the night, while we were hiding. The boys set out last week toward the river, a few of them in a small pack, with their long cattle prods and spears. They would hide in the forest at night, and drink the milk from the cows for their strength. Aluel, the eldest daughter of my father's second wife, told me that these enemy tribesmen had horses and many guns. And that they also used machetes. The women clucked their tongues behind Father's back at his decision to send off the younger boys toward the front lines with little protection. It was dangerous for us to be broken during this time, they said. "He is doing just what the enemy wants," Mama told me angrily one evening, unusually defiant against her husband. "They want to disperse us and then gather us all to them. And he is granting them their very wish."

This very same night, Aluel had told me these men would take a child's virginity, they would try to impregnate an old woman, they would cut off the limbs of a man, and kill him as they would any animal. She said it in a low whisper and her eyes shone by the light of the fire, wet with fear. In this moment, I felt as though my heart had come free from its beating place and spilled out some of its contents into my throat. I remember being secretly scared to speak for a long time afterward, being fearful that my heart would come out of my mouth altogether.

And so the routine of our lives changed. We would stay in the village in the day but not always at night. Whenever we heard from

Deng Dit that the *murahaleen* were nearing our tiny village, our people would set out to spend the night in the wild. At least if we came back to a burnt village, we still had our lives, and each other, Mama said. I knew it was difficult for these *murahaleen* to get to us, the walking people. My people have lived on this land since the beginning, and we know every hill, every tree, every rock. Our children are taught at a young age to know this earth well. These raiders come from the north, and they do not know this land. To their eyes we become invisible, as if we know how to turn into the trees or the rocks themselves.

I looked out to the dawn light coming over the horizon and thought it strange we were moving in the early morning. We had not done this before. One evening not so long ago, I had overheard Deng Dit talking to Father in front of our *tukal*. He told Father that the earth weeps for what these men are doing. I lingered behind the hut to listen. A hot burning travelled through my body to my scalp when I heard Deng Dit tell my father, in his cracked voice, that the earth told him dark secrets and he would not share these stories with anyone, for such horrors were making the earth herself fall silent with grief and would make mute anyone who heard. Some people in our village called Deng Dit a madman behind his back. And that is how he looked that night. I saw by the light of the fire his hair matted and long, his eyes like red suns, spittle flying from his mouth when he spoke.

Who were the gods of these people from the north? Certainly gods we knew nothing of. Deng Dit told my father that the earth was terrified. And so are we, I thought, as I listened to them talking, crouched behind the hut.

I never told Mama or my aunts about the circle of Women in the sky. I remember our first meeting, the very night I found the blood on my thighs that came from inside of me. The night was too hot, and so Mama and I set up her cot outside the hut and slept under the dark, wide sky. I remember staring up at the stars, unable to sleep, with Mama's arm tucked safely beneath my neck. That was when I saw them — a circle of elder women, with plump, lively faces, sitting on their haunches round a ghostly fire. Their billowy skirts brushed their bare feet. The circle they sat in looked as large as the earth. They were huge, and all of them were smiling down at me. With Mama's breath deep and steady in my ear, I rubbed my eyes and looked again, but they remained there. While I stared up at them, my stomach felt quiet and happy. I did not want them to leave, so I tried to stay awake all night with this new feeling.

The next morning things happened as usual: we woke up when the sun did and began our chores. I promised myself not to tell anyone what I had seen, for fear they would think me crazy, like Deng Dit. For some time after I was afraid that perhaps the Women came from bad powers in the sky, and I had been wrong not to have made some ceremonies to protect myself from their spells the moment I had laid my eyes upon them. I told myself that I had been dreaming that night, and tried to put them out of my mind.

And yet, I continued to remember how they sang all at once on that night, the chorus of their voices echoing down and pulsing through me. In their song they spoke of the long, challenging journey that lay ahead. At that time, of course, I did not know what they meant. But there was joy in their singsong voices, joy in the circle they shared, which shone out from their fire of stars and beamed down directly to my tiny point of life on the ground outside our hut. I looked up at the sky often after that, searching them out, and I began to hope that it had not been a dream after all, especially when things became much worse.

I did not see them again until years later, in the midst of all the chaos. Still, I did not tell anyone about them. It is only you that I tell now. You are the only one who knows of these Women in the sky. You may think me mad, but I tell you this: they are the ones who truly saved me.

II

Sandra

I wake up to a shushing sound. At first I think it is the snake, but when I open my eyes I see a glimpse of the servant through the hole in the bottom of the door. He is coming to get the dishes I set outside yesterday. I scramble up and crawl to the hole, peer out at him. He looks right at me. His eyes are huge, still lit up with fear. He is bent down and moves quickly back at the sight of me, but stays squatting, staring. His bare feet are gnarled and dusty, toes like crumpled tree trunks. I catch a glimpse of his stump, severed above the elbow. The bandage is coming apart a bit, with pieces hanging down that are caked with blood, now turning a russet colour.

I call out, "Hey!"

He starts back some more, clambers to his feet, his one hand planted in the dirt beside him to help get him vertical. Then he bends down at the waist, sticks his hand through the hole, makes a quick motion. Index finger up, a small wave back and forth. *Don't talk* — is that what he is saying to me?

I stay quiet. There is a long silence. I can't even hear his breath. Then he picks up the bowls and leaves. The main door slides open and then closed. The morning light falls through the slats in the wall onto my black toes, my dirty sandals. It takes everything in me not to yell at him: *Come back here! Talk to me!*

I crawl back to the corner, hug my knees to my chest. Shivering. Cold in here. I see now that the pebble is gone. Did the servant boy take it? How could he have gotten to it? I didn't hear the lock open. Did he somehow retrieve it with a stick through the hole? I search for the pebble in the corners, feel for it in the dust, the splintered wood. Maybe the snake took it. Maybe the snake is not so good after all. I need to do this ritual. I need to know what today is going to be.

Things being taken from me. Important things. When Graham left, he took the necklace he had given me as a wedding present. As though the gift had been his all along. As though he could annul our marriage with a swipe of his hand across my chest of drawers, wipe it clean of the gold chain and blue pendant.

That first morning I awoke and found him absent from our bed, his pillow untouched and risen like a hill, I jumped up, dizzy, my heart and throat catching the queasy wave of what I already knew. I padded out of the room to silence. No smell of coffee, no shower running, no whistling or strumming guitar. Nothing but a vacuum of air, sucked inwards.

Had he been in an accident? Had he had too much to drink after his gig and decided to stay at his bandmate's place rather than risk the drive home? Had he tried to call and I hadn't heard the phone? I ran to the living room to check the call display, and that was when I saw it. The note was stuck to the receiver with a piece of Scotch tape.

Sandy — I need to straighten a few things out in my head and I don't want to burden you. Please live your own life and don't worry about me. I'm sorry. L. Graham.

I sat down on the couch and read it again. And again. What was he talking about? I called his bandmate's apartment. No answer. I called again, left a message asking Jason to tell Graham to call me. I fingered the Scotch tape, wondered where he had found it. He had to have snuck in while I was sleeping and stuck the note to the phone. It hadn't been there when I reached up and kissed him goodbye at the door the night before, his guitar case banging against my shins, nor when I crawled into bed later. Why wouldn't he call? What was he hiding? I peered at the ink on the paper. Ballpoint pen. I searched the apartment for a ballpoint, found one in the back of the kitchen drawer, behind the phone book. Then I began looking for the Scotch tape. I looked everywhere — in all the drawers, the closets in the hall and the bedroom, the bathroom cabinet, behind the fridge. We didn't have Scotch tape in our apartment.

The clock said 4:00 p.m. when I heard a key turn in the lock of the main door of the apartment building, and then Graham's heavy footsteps on the thinly carpeted hallway. When he opened our door, he looked terrified. And guilty. I thought afterwards of how he also looked guilty.

When he sat down on the couch beside me he put his hand on my knee, very carefully, as though it were his first time touching me. I slapped him then, slapped him in the face. I wanted him to remember who I was, who we were. Without a word he stood. Then he grabbed his toothbrush and was gone.

The following Friday, I went to The Madhorn. I knew Graham would be playing. I had worked out everything I was going to say. I was going to make him sit there and have a proper conversation

while the sun is above us

with me. I was convinced at this point that it had to be drugs. I knew how rampant they were in the scene. I was going to tell him that I was there for him, and he could lean on me for support. We could go to therapy together, maybe he needed rehab. I was going to tell him that he needn't be ashamed. And that I would never leave him; he didn't need to worry about that.

When I walked in the door, I saw them both at once, their backs to me. They were talking to each other, inches apart. They were sitting near the stage at a small table with a lit candle between them which outlined the silhouettes of their faces in the soft glow. She was laughing at something he was saying, throwing her head back just slightly and showing her top teeth. They were holding hands. I watched him lean over and kiss her lightly on the lips.

They didn't see me; it was dark. But I recognized her right away, Peg, their new bass player. We had only met once, the month before. She had shaken my hand and smiled. I remember thinking how tiny and cold and white her hands were, and I had wondered at the time if it wasn't hard for her to play a guitar, because of the size of her hands.

As I watched them, with the nausea spreading up my throat, it struck me that she seemed too young and small for him somehow. She wouldn't be able to take care of him properly. Those small hands wouldn't be able to make him his favourite omelette, or rub his lower back the way he liked, digging in hard with the knuckles.

Two days later I noticed the necklace he had given me on the day of our wedding was missing. I placed my palm on the top of the chest of drawers where I always put it, felt the cool veneer. Then I searched the entire apartment. I couldn't find it anywhere. It took me a long time before I could accept that I had not lost or misplaced it, but that it was gone. The pendant was a blue cat's eye, in the shape of a teardrop.

I hear the barn door slide open; light footsteps pad on the floorboards. Is it the one-armed servant? Two brown eyes peer in at me through the hole near the bottom of the door. A child. I move from my corner to the space, reach through with my hand. Try to touch him. A squawk, and he shuffles back, falls down. Covers his mouth with his hand. Is it a girl or a boy? I push my head closer to the space and see the child with her cheek pressed against the dirty floor, staring at me. Big, beautiful eyes, long lashes. A girl. Very young. She smiles at me, then covers her mouth again, hiding her teeth. She keeps her hand over her mouth while she explores my face with her large eyes. I wonder if she's ever seen a white person before. And then, just like that, she gets up suddenly, runs away. Bare feet pattering on the wooden floorboards.

The barn door shuts with a small thud.

∞∞∞∞∞∞∞∞∞∞∞∞∞∞∞∞∞∞∞∞∞∞∞∞∞∞∞∞∞∞∞∞

I get up slowly, and shift Rith closer to Adhar so that he will not be frightened if he wakens and I am not there. He is still suckling, and so for much of the day I carry him against me in a sling made from one of Father's robes. I have fashioned a smaller one for Adhar so she may carry him when I leave to go into the centre of town to fetch water from the well or buy food in the market. He does not like being without me, and his cries are more frequent than Adhar's or Khajami's were. I move to the window and suck the cool air into my body. There is a small bit of light rising up over the low huts now. I look back at my children. Their skin glows as the rising sun touches his rays onto them. They come alive in their own bodies as the sun comes alive on this day. In this light, Rith's face could be Khajami's, and even after all this time, it puts a strong pain through my heart.

On the day you came to me, I knew the terrible truth before my father spoke a word. I saw it in his eyes, in those same moments I first saw you. They were no longer my father's eyes, for they shook and darted, as though he was not certain which world he was in. This new part of him has travelled with him from the day of the raid to this day, and now it stays with him in his illness. Some days I must remind him more than once where it is we are living, or what part of the day we are in, though the sun is above us to see for himself.

For all the time of my imprisonment, I had prayed that Khajami was alive and well. That somehow he had escaped, that he had managed to live through it all and was now becoming a man. I continued to believe while up north that I would be there to see those things done to him to prove that a boy has become a man: as the spear pierces the skin to make the markings on the forehead, and as the chisel goes into the mouth to remove the front bottom teeth, a man must not cry. A man must show his strength. These things would mark Khajami as a strong Dinka man, like his father. I had to hold onto this hope that I would be there to witness this important time for my son, as weak or as false as this hope was, for these thoughts of Khajami carried me through the night and into the morning of the next day. They are what helped me to rise in the mornings in my cell and begin my many chores.

It may sound like madness to you, but, even now, the only way I can get through these days sometimes is by believing that Khajami's heart beats inside my own, as it once beat inside of my own body. Someone chose a different life for us than what we had planned to live. Is this not true, *khawaja?* These thoughts of Khajami are the only way I know how to carry this grief upon my back, every day.

I will not lie to you: in the moment that should have been my happiest, seeing my father at last after so many long years, I felt something die deep inside of me. Before he said anything, I looked into my father's eyes and felt the truth of Khajami's death land upon my back like the heaviest burden, and I crumpled to the ground. I believed in this moment that God could not exist. The connection that had held me to *Nhialic* through my prayers in my time up north, despite everything, was cut in that moment. I could not believe this very same God to whom I had prayed for all these years could dis-appoint me so completely. I believe now that he felt my lack of faith and cut Himself from me, and this was why I fell to the earth.

You were the one who helped me to my feet. You touched your fingers to the scar on my wrist, with a kind of wonder in your light eyes. I remember that the softness of your skin shocked me. This was the first time a white person had come so close to me, had looked at me in this way. As if you could see into my heart through my own eyes.

Father told me that Khajami, Tobias, and Mama had not survived the raid, but he would not tell me the details until we had arrived in Turalei, after our long journey. Here he told me Mama and some of the other women had been locked inside a hut, which the raid-ers set on fire. Tobias was killed because he resisted. He was shot with a gun just after he had struck one of the raiders in the shoulder with a spear.

Then he told me of Khajami — that he had seen with his own eyes Khajami's lifeless body by the side of the road, soon after we were taken. I never asked how he was buried. I could not bear to think of young Khajami sharing the ground with his ancestors. Not yet.

Father told me that the *murahaleen* would not have spared him. They killed all the little boys too young to take as slaves for fear they would grow up and carry guns, would grow up to become their enemies. The only ones they left alive in these villages were the elders, because they could not find a use for them. They left them to live out the rest of their lives with what they had seen on that day running endlessly behind their own eyes. Many of these elders died soon after from grief. Some left to try to find what remained of their families. But my father stayed, and waited. For you.

At least they did not take Khajami, Father told me. At least they did not make him one of their own, so that he might grow up and fight against his own people. At these words Father came to me and pressed down on my shoulders with his hands, squeezing into my bones. Was he trying to press me into believing that what he was saying was true? That it was better for my Khajami to be dead than alive and in the hands of the enemy? His trembling eyes were angry. I wanted to believe him, but God forgive me, I could not. I would rather that Khajami be alive and in the same world as I.

I did not cry at hearing Father's news. Instead it was as though my heart closed up and was changed into a shrivelled thing. It seemed that when my hope died away, it took along with it my tears.

Do you have a child yet, *khawaja?* If you do, you will know — there is a kind of darkness that comes in when the young and unformed are taken. It is something unnatural, as though it cannot be of this world. But I do not pretend to understand this world. I leave these things to God. I cannot end this madness. The war still goes on, despite what the leaders say, despite the suffering and this darkness that falls down over us.

To accept all that has happened is not as difficult in my waking hours as it is in the nights, when the dreams arrive. And then I think of Khajami, as I do right now, while I watch Adhar's and Rith's small chests rise and fall. I look out the window at the rising sun, which holds no promise of relief from these thoughts.

I heap the pile of clothes in the corner into the large blue basin Auntie Nyakiir bought in the market. I try to be quiet; Auntie and her daughters are still asleep on their cots. I slip on Father's sweater and walk to the nearby courtyard, balancing the basin on my head. Because it is so early there is no one at the well yet. The water falls into the basin, loud and clear and cold, soaking the clothing. My insides shudder as the water splashes over my hands in the chill of the morning. As I twist the heavy, wet cloth in my fingers I think of Saleh's house. It puts a fear into my heart, and I start to think he may come around the corner anytime, even though the other part of me, the part that is real, knows this is not possible. The sun reaches its tender arms of morning light down to the squares of concrete, revealing the dirt in all the uneven cracks. Soon the men will come to drink their tea. I will go now to boil the water.

"The water is cold this morning." Abuk has come to fill her own small basin. Abuk lives across the road from us. All four of her sons died in the war. Some people here say Abuk is mad. She only speaks of one of her sons — Salvador, her favourite. She speaks as though he is still alive, tells me stories about his life up north as a successful tradesman. She tells me he is coming back soon with all of his money to take care of her until she is old and dying. I stay quiet when she speaks of these things, as we squat side by side in the courtyard, bent over our basins, washing the worn clothes of our families. No one dares tell her the truth.

Then again, Khajami lives inside me still. A monster more terrible than the ones I have encountered could not drag my eldest son out of me. He planted himself within my heart the moment he was born. In my youthful ignorance, I was frightened of his squirming, wrinkled face when I first looked upon him. But while I secretly let myself believe Khajami's heart beats inside my own, I do not pretend my child is still alive somewhere, as Abuk does. Most of the other women ignore her. I listen to her sometimes. But other times I do not want to hear her nonsense, and so I pick up my heavy basin and sit elsewhere in the courtyard, away from her.

"The cold water will wake you up when you put your hands in it," is what I tell her. I pull the clothes through my slippery fingers. She stretches her back, long and straight, and looks down at me with her heavy-lidded eyes for a moment, then laughs out loud in the morning stillness. The noise breaks the air like the caw of a bird overhead, making its awful sound to wake the dead. She is still shaking her head and laughing as she walks away from me and back toward her hut, the soapy water swishing over the sides of her basin and onto the dusty earth making small, thick puddles.

I pour the grey water onto the ground beside the tap. It soaks the broken cement and dusty ground in a darkening river. Because I am the only one at the well now, I pump more water onto the clothes so they may be rinsed, a luxury these clothes do not usually receive, for the line in the mornings is often long, with the women sometimes pushing and arguing with each other. It is a gift to be here this early, with the others still in their sleeping worlds.

I stretch up and lean back with my hands on my hips, curve my head up to face the lightening sky. My back has been hurting me terribly lately; these days it is difficult to carry the wet laundry. I believe it is because all my worries sit upon my back, and the less I sleep, the more the worries pile upon me. There is nothing I can do but wait until sleep claims me in the nights once again. Until then, there are clothes to wash and people to feed. After I hang these clothes on the line, I will go wake Adhar to help me bring to the men their tea. I will give her the smaller bucket to fetch the water. I noticed on my way to the well that a couple of the old men have already begun to take their seats in the circle.

A terrible feeling settles into my stomach at this thought of all the men sitting in their courtyard circle. Ringo, Tobias's brother, has been coming to join this circle of men in the mornings. I had never met Ringo before he came to introduce himself to us several months ago. Tobias used to speak fondly of him — his much younger brother, a brother from his father's fifth wife. Ringo had defied his father's wishes and left their homestead to go and live in the east. There he had built up a strong head of cattle. He had accrued many wives and children over the years.

Ringo made his way to Turalei from his home in the east, many years ago. He and his wives and children came in the midst of all the fighting. I know this because a messenger came to tell Tobias one hot day, in the season before the raid, that Ringo was in Tura-lei, and that we would be welcome to come there to live with them, where it was safer. Tobias shook his head and told the messenger to go back and tell Ringo that nowhere was safe in Sudan. "But these rivers," he said, sweeping his long arm in the direction of the waters to the north of us, "guard us here. Tell my brother thank you. But we will not move."

Ringo came to see us when he heard my father and I had survived the attack on Akoch, and had arrived here in Turalei alive. Just recently, he began joining the men in their courtyard circle in the mornings. When I serve Ringo his tea, I will not look in his eyes. Nor do I smile at him, even though I feel him stare at me when I pour the hot tea into his cup. Father scolds me for this in the evenings. Last night, after a rare dinner of okra and chicken, I dared to tell Father I would never look at or speak to Ringo. Father yelled at me, "Adut, this is not your place! He means to be nice to you, so show him you are a proper Dinka woman!"

I know I must respect him, but I will only do so as the wife of his brother, never as anything more than this. For I do not want Ringo to think highly of me, even though I know this is wrong, and it is making Father angry, who only wants us to be taken care of. I do not want to leave Auntie Nyakiir's place, as overcrowded as it is, as poor as we are. I reach for the bar of soap in my pocket and begin to scrub. There is a tea stain on Father's white robe that will not leave.

I must set the water to boil for breakfast soon, so Auntie Nyakiir and her daughters can have a bit to eat before going to the market with their pots of *marissa* to sell. It never ends, *khawaja*.

When I think of Tobias it is not with the same feeling as when I think of Khajami. How could it be the same, when a child and a husband demand a different kind of love altogether from your heart? It does not feel as though Tobias is still inside of me. He was my husband, my protector, and I respected him. I miss Tobias, and I am proud that I was his wife. A kind of emptiness and happiness are woven together inside my voice when the other washing women ask me about what my husband was like, and I answer with words that lift up to the sky.

After we were first married, I had often watched Tobias during the day, secretly. It was difficult to believe that this serious, gruff man, who could wrestle the largest bull to its stake, could also make his strong, solid fingers soft enough for my body to sink at his touch. When our people would go on the long night walks into the bush, the men would lead the line and the women would follow with the food and children. I would look ahead, searching for Father and Tobias at the front of the group. It always struck me when I saw them walking together how alike they were, my husband and my father. Before I was married, I did not see that Tobias possessed the same quiet authority as my father. It was only after I was married that I began to see this in his calm eyes and the way he stood — as though he was pushing the crown of his head to the sun, and so it was up to him to pass the secrets of the sky on to the rest of us. People in our village often came to my father with their problems or concerns, about cattle bridewealth or an argument with neighbours. As Tobias grew older, people began to approach him as well to listen to his wisdom.

The last time Tobias and I were together in that way was the night before the *murahaleen* found us; the following morning we returned to the village where we saw too late the *murahaleen* waiting for us. I had hoped, afterwards, that I was with child from this time with Tobias, and that this unborn child would somehow protect me from Saleh when I first arrived up north. I see now how ridiculous this small hope was, but at that time it was all I had to keep me moving forward. I wanted so badly for Saleh to sense Tobias's strong spirit in my body, and to leave me alone when he saw my belly growing with the child of a brave Dinka man. A grave sadness filled my body when I felt the blood from my moon time come one morning as I scrubbed the silverware in my tiny cell, just a few weeks after I arrived.

That last night with Tobias is clear in my mind still. The sun had only just fallen down past the distant low hills. A group from our clan had settled into a small patch of bush and were sitting around a small fire, eating hard *durra* that we women had brought along with us, wrapped up in the pots we carried on our heads. Strangely, we had left the village in the early dawn, and so we had to reach the bush before the sun broke far free of the ground that morning to keep from being seen. We had not had time to pound the *durra* into meal before we left. Even though it would be hard on our children's stomachs, we had no choice — we had to eat to keep up our strength.

I remember that Khajami was sleeping in Auntie Nyakiir's huge lap, his head flopped over onto her plump arm. I remember staring into the fire. I did not think much then of the fires we built, assuming they would always be there, a part of my life forever. There is a magic in the shapes made by the sparks that fly up from the fire into the black night sky, as though the fire has its own world. If you look closely enough, you can meet some of the people or animals who live there: the grizzled face of an old man, a skinny horse with curved haunches, a huge tree with exploding branches. We were so very silent that night, everyone trapped under their own weight of weariness. I watched the flames lick at the wood, eating up the dry, thin branches, keeping our skin warm that cold night.

The elders looked so pitiful — sometimes I had to force myself to hold my tears inside when I saw them in these unguarded moments. Their skin was rough with lines made deep from years of worry, years of running. This was their time for resting, for bringing to us their wisdom in our gathering circles. Instead, they were spending their remaining years hiding and fleeing from the ones who would take it all away from them.

Tobias took my hand and led me far away from the others, behind a family of bushes. Auntie Nyakiir had taken Khajami with her to sleep under her thin blanket. Khajami loved Auntie Nyakiir, just the way I had loved her when I was a little girl. He loved her generous body, so comfortable and welcoming, her dancing eyes, and her loud laugh. No matter what you did, she would never scold you; everything you did, even if you were being mischievous, was wonderful and hilarious to Auntie Nyakiir.

Now Auntie's eyes have lost most of the light that lived within them. There is still a trace that remains, and in this small flicker you can sometimes see who she used to be. But most of the spark has been burned out by her own years as a slave, years she never speaks of. Now she often comes back from selling *marissa* in the market tired and cranky, commanding her daughters to rub her feet and bring her tea.

"My love," Tobias breathed softly in my ear. I forced my breath to slow down. I shivered from both the cold and my own fear. My entire body desired him, desired to feel his strong protection around me and within me. I wanted to escape this terror surrounding us that would not leave, no matter how far we travelled. And I could not help but fear that the *murahaleen* would find us here together, and kill us both. Just that morning I had heard Mama talking to the other women about how Deng Dit was becoming mad, how his talks with the earth spirits and the sky powers were no longer to be trusted. Mama said we were all in danger if we continued to put our faith in him telling us when and where we needed to move. This was in my mind as I looked into Tobias's eyes, though I said nothing.

Tobias held my face tightly in his large hands. I felt an urgency pressing upon my cheeks through his fingers. It was said that of all Tobias's four wives, I was his favourite: the last one. On our wedding night he had promised me he would not take another, and I believed him, for I saw how he had waited for me since I was a girl. I knew from an early age that I would become Tobias's wife; he had made a bridewealth promise to my father of a good number of cattle when I was still a child. Growing up, I would complain to Mama that he was too old for me, too gruff and ugly, and then I would hear Mama's constant scoldings for saying such things. It took me some time after marriage to truly see Tobias. And now I could see by the light of that night's full moon that his eyes held tears — of fear or sadness, I will never know. His hands, calloused and rough from years of working with the cattle, quickly found their way underneath my skirt. His heart beat against my own as he gently laid me down on the ground. We held fast to each other against this dark tide that loomed, that crept closer and closer no matter how far we ran or how well we tucked ourselves away in the wild. Coming together in this way made some kind of dire sense in that moment.

He slid his hands between my legs and I tensed up, scared that his strong fear would make his movements rough and painful. But Tobias made his movements slow; as though he knew, somehow, that this would be the last we would feel of each other's skin. He kept his face close to mine that night, so that it was as though we were breathing each other's breath. I clutched at his back and pulled him closer into me. I felt his fear and his strength together as one, and I felt protected by him. And also I felt that I wanted to protect him, though I could never admit such a thing as that to him.

After we were together, I could not sleep. I felt as though I needed to keep my ears awake, to listen for any strange movement. The rocks under my back felt very sharp, and the fires in the sky burned brighter than usual that night. I knew some boys from our village were hidden in some trees Deng Dit had led them to, armed with their spears, but Tobias and I had gone further away from the rest. As I lay there awake, I touched the tip of my tongue behind my teeth, slid it along the ridge where my teeth meet my gums. I tried to wriggle the very tip of my tongue into the space between my two front teeth, willing the gap to widen. Before she died, my grandmother told me that *Nhialic* had put a space there as a favour to me, so that wisdom could slip out in my words. After she told me this, I would often push at the backs of my new front teeth with my tongue, trying to make the gap widen even further.

I noticed then that Tobias had lifted his head and was smiling as he looked at me sideways, his eyebrows lifted. Then he laid his head back down on the ground, patted the top of my head tenderly with his large hand, letting his fingers rest there. He thought my grand-mother's words were just funny things women said to each other, words that did not make any sense. Yet I believe he knew they made sense to me, and that he even knew why I wanted this gap between my teeth to grow. I too wanted to speak wise words to the others, like my husband and my father.

"Always the little girl, even now as a mother."

He let out a small laugh then. Tobias was always serious and quiet; he rarely laughed. In the months before the raid, he did not laugh at all — there was no joy in him. I had caught him looking at Khajami and me often, with a sharp kind of fear in his eyes. There were new lines in his face and new grey in his hair. So this uncommon laugh was a gift to me on that night.

I reached over and touched his cheek. Even though it is not proper for a woman to tell her husband she loves him, I whispered in his ear that night that I did. I felt shy after I had done this, and I turned away from him as we both lay there quietly. But I am glad now that I did this one thing. For it was the first time I told my husband I loved him, and it was also the last.

Tobias fell asleep beside me, with his head touching mine and his hand resting on my stomach. While I was up north, I would imagine his hand on my stomach still. I pretended later that an imprint of it had been made there by the bright stars on that night. After, I would put my own hand on my stomach at nights, touching the imprint of his, as I lay alone on the dirt floor under the basin in my cell.

I tell you these things of my husband so that you may understand, *khawaja.* I have died so very many times in this one life of mine, and yet here I am still, walking along this thread, which weaves through others'. And it was along this thread we came to the place where you unknowingly bought my freedom.

III

Sandra

APRIL 24, 2003, EL-MUGLAD, NORTH SUDAN

Neither my best friend Geri nor I saw the pickup truck speed down the off-ramp and lurch out in front of us until it was too late. Geri had picked me up to take me out for dinner, her feeble attempt at trying to put a smile on my face, as she put it, a few weeks after Graham left. Within seconds, we found ourselves flying toward the truck's tail gate. The chipped paint on its back fender was framed by the tail lights: two red, angry eyes. Geri slammed on the brakes, pulled the wheel sharply to the right, and her little Honda went screeching toward the wall of the underpass.

I don't remember my forehead hitting the dash. But I do remember holding my hand up in front of my face. Underneath the dancing pattern of light there were smears of blood on my palms. I must have put my hand to my bleeding forehead, but I don't remember doing that. Everything felt slow and silent and heavy for a short time, as though I were underwater. Alternating red and blue lights played a silent melody on my skin — I thought it was supposed to sound like something, I thought it should be the beat to some kind of music, but I couldn't for the life of me think of the song.

The next thing I remember I was standing on the side of the road. The drizzle felt good on my head, tiny shocks of cold wet. Voices around me were loud, excited. The evening traffic grumbled as a steady line of cars idled and swerved slowly around us. I was holding a towel to my forehead: who had given me that? Geri held my elbow, muttering something about a fucking seatbelt not working, about a bullshit little car. Her other hand pressed gently on my lower back, while two ambulance attendants helped me into the back of their vehicle. A policeman was talking to Geri, nodding his head solemnly. The light played on his skin too, his face alternately spot-lit by different colours, music-less.

Did I scream? I still don't know. I can see this image of myself, my whole body an angry wire, lit up in the rain. My face is turned to the sky, my fists stuck against my sides, and I am screaming and screaming, mouth open wide, as if to catch raindrops. It feels good to hear myself, to feel the noise from my throat reverberate into the oppressive, wet air. I see that picture in my head, but did I do that? I can't remember now.

When Geri and I got into the accident, I still hadn't told Dad about Graham. He had called a couple of times in the weeks after Graham left, just to say hello, nothing urgent. I hadn't changed the message on the machine yet, a chirpy "Hi, you've reached Sandy and Graham — you know what to do!" I could picture him on the other end of the phone, sitting in his worn, green easy chair in the tiny living room, smoking his home-rolled cigarette, eyes squinted, listening for the beep.

When I called him from the guest phone in the hospital, he just coughed a little to assure me he'd heard all the information, about the hospital, about the possibility of a concussion, about the CT scan, about the gash on my forehead. About how they wanted to keep me in there for a few days to "observe" me. About Graham. I could see his eyes squinting up much more than usual then, his bright green eyes underlined by permanent dark shadows. He asked me if I was okay, if I needed any money. Should he fly down to Toronto from Halifax? He didn't raise his voice; Dad never showed fear or surprise or anger, even when we both knew he felt all of that, and more.

He's never told me that I disappointed him. He expected me to go to university, to get an education, maybe even become a teacher. He was always proud, and a little mystified, I think, that I graduated from high school with a 90% average. My old-fashioned father never mentioned anything about my waitressing wage sustaining Graham and me throughout our whole marriage. He never asked about my lack of savings. While Graham pursued his dream of making it as a musician, and I served beer to drunk and obnoxious university students, the country's next eminent lawyers and doctors, my quiet, hardworking father sat at home in our small, square house, alone. Still alone, all these years after Mom had left. I'm sure he worried I was wasting my time, but he never said it, not directly. Perhaps he never said anything because he actually liked Graham. Even though Graham's a musician and Dad's a miner, they hit it off. The son he never had.

I pressed my palm to the bandage on my forehead, took a huge breath before replying, my voice quavering just a little. No, I don't need money. And you don't have to come out here. I squeezed my eyes against the tears that were threatening to break loose, the cascade of emotion that I knew neither Dad nor I could cope with.

In the hospital, I shared a room with Delores, who was twenty-nine years old and a very heavy smoker. Her hair was long, blond and stringy, with a cap of dark roots. Her eyes were a translucent blue, set in a hard, pockmarked face. Delores looked much older than twenty-nine, but I didn't tell her this. She would walk over to my bed to visit me often, though she was clearly in greater discomfort than I was. I would watch her struggle to get out of her narrow bed, pain routing across her pinched and contorted face. She would clutch the metal pole on wheels that attached her scrawny arm to her IV machine and make her way over to me, stooped like an old lady, several times a day. The outline of her with her pole always made me think of a wounded crane. I could never tell if she was wincing in pain or trying to smile as she shuffled over. A shrill beep came out of the metal scarecrow every fifteen minutes; this was the signal that she was receiving a dose of morphine from the bag. She would often turn her head away from me toward the door and complain loudly to the nurse, who was supposedly out in the hall, that she needed more goddamned morphine, she was in a hell of a lot of pain, what the hell was this joint supposed to be, why were they only giving her bits of freedom every once in a while? Why not knock her right out, let her get some sleep, for Christ's sake?

The nurse — Chiefie, as Delores called her — would come into our room with angry clicking heels, sighing loudly and blinking her eyes. Firmly she would explain to Delores that more morphine was *not* what the doctor had ordered, that what Delores was experiencing was expected for women in her state.

When they wheeled me into the room that first morning after the CT scan, Delores came over to my bed, sat down slowly, and, craning her neck over her hunched shoulder, looked back to see if anyone was coming. Then she turned to me and slowly opened her fingers to reveal three long cigarettes lying in her palm. "Gotta go take a piss," she said, and with a sideways wink at me she dropped the cigarettes in her gown pocket and hobbled up to standing, her knuckles white as she clutched the metal pole with both hands. A minute or two later, the unmistakable smell of cigarette smoke breathed out from behind the bathroom door.

Chiefie strode into our room, rapped on the bathroom door. "Delores! We have told you, smoking is not allowed in this hospital.

I must ask you to please go outside!"

"Women in her state," I thought to myself. I was scared to ask, but curious.

Delores was sitting on the edge of my bed again, making my hard, narrow mattress slant to one side and my drugged, soft body roll toward her. My knees were resting against her rump. My head was really hurting. I kept hoping Chiefie would come back soon with her magic cup of pills.

"Bits of freedom," she whispered, laughed softly. "I'd like a whole lot of freedom right now. I could really go for a big, fat joint." She held on tightly to her IV pole so it wouldn't roll away. "So, what are you here for, kid? You didn't say."

"Car accident. Concussion. And this." I touched the bandage on my forehead with my fingertips. I didn't tell her then that I was worried about the gash in my head becoming a scar. For some stupid reason, I wanted to look tough in front of Delores.

"Shitty, man. Anybody get seriously hurt?"

"No, only me. The guy who pulled out in front of us is fine." Though he did come back to see what had happened after he heard Geri's little car smash against the underpass wall. He even sent flowers to my room. Orange daisy gerberas. Great. They arrived when Geri was here, and through stony-faced tears, she held the bouquet up to the ceiling with one hand, a chubby Statue of Liberty raising cheap flowers to the sky, and said he could shove his gerberas up his ass; she might even do it for him.

Delores pursed her lips. "I'm here 'cause of a tubal pregnancy."

"Oh. Sorry."

"Yeah. Sucks. My boyfriend and I have been trying to have a kid for a while now. They had to take out the whole damn tube." Her eyes began to water, her brows furrowed. "But then some shit like this has to happen." She pushed out a short laugh. "Fuck."

"I'm sorry," I whispered. I realized I still had my hand on my forehead. I laid it on my chest.

"Yeah, well, shit happens. What about you, you got a boyfriend?

A husband?" Her blue eyes smiled into mine, then stopped.

"Uh, no. I mean, I was ... I am married, but ... we just recently separated."

"Oh shit, honey, that sucks ass. What happened?"

The last thing in the world I wanted to do was confide in Delores, but I think I felt cornered. Or maybe it was the hazy world of painkillers dulling the edges of my life that I usually held in check. And for some reason, I didn't want to piss her off. I wanted her on *my side*. Besides, she just told me she'd had a tubal pregnancy, for God's sake.

"My husband left me for another woman." As I said this, I realized how common it sounded, how pedestrian. Ridiculous, almost. I had never actually said those words before. Not even to Geri. But there they were. Like a headline from *Cosmopolitan* magazine.

Delores squeezed my arm with her rough hand. "You poor thing. You know what, honey, that is total bullshit. My boyfriend has friends, you know ... If you ever need anything taken care of, you just let me know." She looked straight at me. Her smiling mouth didn't match her serious eyes.

I squinted at her in my confusion. She held my gaze while I tried to figure out what she meant. Then I got it, and I laughed out loud to the ceiling, looked at her again, and saw that her expression remained serious. I stopped laughing.

"Oh God no. I mean, that's all right. Thanks." It was all I could think to say.

She smiled and patted my arm again. "Okay, sweetie, but if you ever need something, you just let me know." Then Delores stepped carefully to the floor, wrapped her blue gown around herself and shuffled over to her bed, a fragile bent crane who would apparently not think twice about knocking off her hospital roommate's philandering ex-husband.

When Delores was asleep, I crawled out of my bed and shuffled to the bathroom. I noticed the magazine Delores had been reading, lying beside the sink. She'd said she was going to give it to me when she was through with it. While I had been trying to sleep my intense headache away the night before, I'd heard her flipping pages in her bed and muttering about all the horrible things happening in Africa: "all these poor goddamned blackie women getting raped, for fuck's sakes."

"You gotta read this," she'd practically yelled across her bed to me.

I didn't tell her I couldn't think of anything that depressing just now. My own life was in shit. Thanks, Delores, but no thanks.

I brought the magazine back to my bed. The article that Delores had been reading was about a group of Christians who had raised money in their hometown, then travelled to Sudan and redeemed captured slaves. Amidst several photos of slaves who were just freed, there was one photograph of a woman with her daughter, sitting in the dust. The little girl had nothing on but a string of beads. She was leaning against her mother, looking at the camera as though it were a monster. I stared at this woman's red-rimmed eyes, trying to get inside them, inside her. And then, something in me opened; a desire so strong rushed up that I immediately knew trying to push it down would be futile. I wanted to find her because I knew she had something to tell me. I knew there was something in her words that I needed to hear.

And there was also this — upon looking at her, I felt a deep love for her. Her face, her pain, crossed over and into my broken heart. I took the article with her photograph when I left the hospital, and this was the photo I took with me — and that took me to — Sudan.

◇◇◇◇◇◇◇◇◇◇◇◇◇◇◇◇◇◇◇◇◇◇◇◇◇◇◇◇◇◇◇◇◇◇◇◇◇

I spent the first few days working in the stables during the day and sleeping outside at night. Then the Head Wife of Saleh brought me to a tiny room. It was attached to the main house by a long, low tunnel. She told me I would be washing the dishes. She told me I must obey, or there would be trouble. I had no choice now, she said, this would be a new life for me, and I would have to do as I was told. She told me this was God's will. Then she walked away and left me alone in the cold, dark room.

The four close walls were made of dried mud. The room held only a tall metal washbasin on four long legs, and another smaller, metal tub, which sat in the corner. The floor was hard-packed dirt, and there was a small window with a thick slab of blurry glass above the basin, the only light with which I had to see the outside world with. Very soon the Head Wife added other duties — washing clothes, pounding the millet, fetching water for the cooking. I was busy with chores from the time I woke up until the time I went to sleep, exhausted and curled up in the dark, under the tall square basin set into the wall under the window.

Head Wife told me when she showed me to my room that the only time I would be allowed to go outside would be to fetch water from the well, to hang the clothes on the line, or to relieve myself. I soon learned I had to find my own place outside to squat, for I was not allowed to use the servants' latrine. When I first went to the latrine behind the house I found it locked. Head Wife came to me later and asked what I was doing there. I told her I needed to use it and at this she shook her head and *tsked* at me with her tongue. "That is not for your use, *abida*. You must use the ground." It was not easy to relieve myself outside unnoticed in this flat desert terrain, with so very few bushes to hide behind. Often I would have to wait for the mealtimes when the men who worked outside or the children playing would go inside to eat, so I could squat down in the narrow alleyway behind my cell wall. And I could not go out in the nights; the one door that I was allowed to use during the day was locked at night by the man with the gun who watched the yard.

In the nights, I lay under the big washbasin, trying to will the chill away by curling up hard and tight into myself. I did not even have a blanket, at first. I was not given one until Adhar came along, when Tazket, the old servant, took pity on me.

The first time I saw Nyikoc was the first day Head Wife showed me to my tiny cell. Not long after she left, a tall, thin Dinka boy walked into the room with a bucket filled with dishes. I was surprised to see him, someone from my people. Stupidly, my heart jumped up in a flash of hope. I leaped up from the floor where I was sitting with my back against the wall. I greeted him in Dinka and held out my hand to shake his. He did not smile at me or greet me. His face was sour and angry, and his cheekbones jutted out from his skin, drawing sharp lines on his face. He glared at me as though I had done him a grave injustice by speaking to him.

I would learn soon enough that Nyikoc had forgotten his own language and could only speak Arabic; he had not understood my greeting.

In those first weeks, he would not look at or speak to me. He simply walked into the tiny room, dumped the dishes into the washbasin or threw the dirty clothes on the floor in a heap, and walked out again, several times a day. I imagined him spending all day long walking through that huge house, going to every single corner in every single room, scouring both the men's and the women's sections for dirty dishes and dirty clothes to come and deposit in my cell. He did this until the late afternoon when he went to tend to the cattle in the stables. Every day, those dishes lay in the basin for me to scrape and clean, and the dirty clothes lay in their metal tub for me to wash, and more empty buckets sat against the wall, waiting to be filled with water and brought to the servants in the main kitchen for their cooking.

There was always so much food on these dirty plates, food that had gone uneaten. I wondered at how this Saleh and his guests could eat so much food, all day long. Dried meat, injera pancakes, dried okra, goat cheese. Sometimes, if I was very hungry, I took the food left on the plate and gobbled it down with my fingers, swallowed it in big gulps as I stood over the basin and looked out the thick window, watching the figures of the children playing and of the working men in their long jellabas. Other times, I would hold the food in my cheeks, keeping its taste in my mouth for as long as I could.

One such time Nyikoc crept up on me without my noticing him. I had not yet grown accustomed to the sounds of his light footsteps coming down the narrow passageway. I jumped at the sound of dishes clattering behind me. I stayed facing the window as he practically pushed me aside to dump the dishes in the basin. I held a large chunk of cheese in my cheek, not having had the time to swallow it down.

He turned to me and asked gruffly, "And so where did you come from then?"

It had been many weeks that I had been there, and so I was very surprised to hear him speak. He spoke in an Arabic that was different from the Arabic of the traders who had always come to the market near our village. My Arabic was not so strong. I had only spoken it when Mama sent me to barter for goods with these traders. He looked scared to be speaking to me, and I wondered if he had been given orders not to talk to me, as we were both Dinka. But in his fear ran also a strong current of curiosity, this I could see.

"I come from a village called Akoch, in the Bhar-El-Ghazal area." I spoke slowly, keeping the food lodged between my cheek and gums. I hoped he understood what I said.

He only grunted at my answer.

"Do you know where this place is?" I asked.

Again his face was like the grey clouds taking over the sun. He did not answer.

I tried again. "Where are you from?"

I thought he might become angry at this, since he was obviously a slave like me. Perhaps he did not want to talk about his home. But again he did not answer me. He grunted and stared down at the buckets against the wall for a long time.

I turned away and quickly chewed and swallowed the cheese in my mouth. I wondered if he was thinking of what to say next, or if he simply did not understand me.

Finally he said, "I do not know for certain the place where I came from, but I believe it was a village called Paguir, in the east. There was a large river near us, this I remember. I was taken away by Master Saleh when I was very young." Here he held his hand palm down to the floor, at the level of his thigh. "I had been walking in the forest, gathering leaves and roots for dinner. Master Saleh told me that after they took me away they went back. My whole family was killed and my village was burned. There is nothing left."

I wondered if this were indeed true. I suspected Saleh only told him this to keep Nyikoc from trying to escape. If there is nothing left, there is nothing to try to find.

When he spoke of Paguir, I could see a glimpse of his past life burning behind his eyes. But his eyes mostly stayed covered over with something hard and dark. I came to believe that his real eyes were hiding behind years of beatings and hard work and little food, years of being treated as less important than an animal. His body was ropy with muscle, his waist so thin I could have fit both my hands around it easily. I could see the flame of who he used to be when he stood tall beside me. The light from the window spilled onto his face. This flame had almost gone out, and yet I saw it, a tiny part flickering there still.

Nyikoc looked to be just a bit younger than me. The thought of him here this whole time, working for Saleh, made something cold and sharp pierce through my stomach.

I asked him if he had ever tried to escape.

He looked at me as though asking this sort of question was forbidden. And then to my shock, he laughed. This was the first time I heard Nyikoc laugh. It was short and mean, like a snort. "Where would I go? My family is gone. And if I tried to leave Master Saleh would kill me. Slash my throat." Here he drew his fingers across his throat in a slow, slicing motion.

It was after I had been at Saleh's for a season that Nyikoc began talking to me about his visits to the market. There was a market in the town a good two-hours walk from Saleh's farm. I was never allowed to go to it, of course, as I was only allowed outside to fetch water or hang the clothing on the line. But Saleh trusted Nyikoc, and so he would send him out every two weeks for goods such as sugar and tea, sometimes special spices the cook needed, or even for the expensive tobacco Saleh enjoyed. Saleh knew he could trust Nyikoc, who had learned how to barter well with these traders.

One Saturday as I washed the dishes, Nyikoc came into my cell with a red anger in his small eyes and his lips tightened against each other in a thin line. I was still a bit fearful of him, as I had learned by this time that he was strangely loyal to his Master, and had stopped looking for any kind of escape long ago; he had accepted his life here. And he had accepted Allah as his God and, along with the other servants, he stopped to kneel and pray five times a day. I dared to ask this quiet, angry boy what the matter was.

"What has gotten you, Nyikoc?"

To my surprise, he did not ignore me.

"There are vendors at the *souk* in the town who travel from the south with their clothing and trinkets to trade and sell. Today one of them, an Arab, tried to talk to me in Dinka. He asked me my family name."

"And so ... did you tell him?"

"Yes." He was shaking his head back and forth slowly, looking down at the ground. "I still remember it. It is Mabior." This last word fell softly down, a small drop of water landing on the dirt floor with a quiet thud. Nyikoc had almost completely forgotten who he was. Even when he said his old last name — for he was given Saleh's name when he arrived — it sounded dusty and ancient coming off his tongue.

"I told them the name of my village. I told them it was destroyed long ago. But they tell me my uncles are still alive and living in Paguir." He lifted his head and looked at me directly for the first time since I had arrived there. Here his eyes blinked rapidly, as if to hold back an entire storm. "This is not true," he insisted to me. "Master Saleh has told me that everyone in my village was killed on that day. I was the only one kept alive. I was meant to be here, I was chosen to learn the proper ways of Allah and to be with Saleh's family. I was spared because I am special."

Anger coiled in my stomach at his words. I did not want to tell him that I believed these vendors knew of his family, and that indeed his uncles were probably still alive, his village still alive. And that Saleh had turned his mind in order to use him and keep him as his prisoner for his own uses. After all, what would these vendors have to gain by telling lies to a poor slave boy like Nyikoc?

And then, something new became born in me. A sudden hope arose. I found myself forcing the words to stay in the back of my throat, stuck and quivering. I wanted so terribly in that very moment to ask Nyikoc if these vendors knew of my family, if they could find out where they were, if they knew if they were still alive. If they could send them a message and tell them where I was. If they could send for help.

With a very great effort, I stopped these words from coming out into the air between us. I knew I must wait. I needed to gain Nyikoc's trust. After this day, it was as though something hard and old had broken open in him, and his words became like water rushing out at me. He could barely contain his stories, his small, ancient memories, his complaints of the other servants, even his fears of his master Saleh. I had nothing to give him, except my attention and my silence. And in return, I desperately hoped he would help me find my way home.

IV

Sandra

APRIL 24, 2003, EL-MUGLAD, NORTH SUDAN

I found the pebble. It was underneath the article. Perhaps Mr. Cobra came in here and moved it. Clutched the stone in his fangs, slid it beneath the paper, stealthy and cunning. Then perhaps he slithered back down into his home beneath the earth. Some kind of subterranean jokester, this Mr. Cobra. Maybe he is watching me even now. Feeling his beady eyes on me, I close my own eyes, and hold the smooth, small stone in my palm. Throw it, lightly. Look down. Again it lands on the returned slave boy's head, covering one side of his face. One eye stares up at me, squinting, angry. Damaged.

The sores on my legs don't seem to be healing very quickly. They still hurt when I press down on them, and even though I've lost weight, my legs look swollen. Perhaps more so than when I was first locked in here. The thorns cut deep as we tried to run through the brush in the night, cutting a mesh of red zigzags into my shins and feet. They will probably scar. But not one of these cuts is in the shape of a half-moon, the shape of the scar on your wrist.

"This is not like you," Geri said to me six months ago, bewildered and watery-eyed, moments before I walked through the security gate to board my plane. Geri thinks I came to Africa on a whim to escape the whole mess of Graham and me. I didn't tell her the real reason I came here, what it was that had impelled me to quit my job, hastily sell my furniture and books at a sidewalk sale in front of my apartment building, and leave the rest of my few belongings in Geri's parents' spare room before jetting off to Africa, just weeks after being released from the hospital. I knew she would think I was crazy to go to a third-world country in the middle of a civil war, to look for a girl in a photograph.

I carried the article with me every day, folded into quarters in my pocket. I've shown her picture to so many Dinka people that the magazine clipping is now faded and worn at the creases, like an old map. Every time I travelled to neighbouring villages in Twic County, taking inventory of schools, I would take out the article, unfold it, and point to her picture on the lower right corner of the page, using mostly sign language to ask where I might find her. A group of women, men and children always immediately surrounded me, clamouring to see what I was showing them. Invariably, an elder man would tell Riak, the translator for the NGO I was stationed with, where he thought she might be, and Riak would translate for me, always with a smile on his face. He never showed any impatience at my seemingly fruitless quest. Thankfully, Riak never told any of the others about my search. Had Jim, the head of security, or any of the other expats I was working with found out, I'm sure they would have laughed at my naïveté. This secret between Riak and me became an unspoken agreement that forged our friendship.

Many had said the girl probably lived much farther north. Perhaps she retreated into hiding so she wouldn't be captured again, they said, or fled back to her home after the journalist had taken her photo. Perhaps she had returned to her family, to her hut in the hills. Perhaps she had died of any one of a thousand diseases. Riak told me just days before our journey to Pakor how the enemy brings disease: "They fly their airplanes over our land every day, spraying invisible poisons in the air. Forty years ago, this place was full of greenery and lions and birds. Now it is a desert." He turned his head, spat on the ground. His dark eyes were bloodshot, sad, and dry. "They are infecting us, making this place a desert, just like their own home. They would make us just like them."

I've left the pebble on the slave boy's head. I won't remove it until the one-armed servant boy comes with my food. This way, I will be keeping in line with the patterns, all the obvious patterns that are aligning themselves to free me from this place. The faint line in the dust Mr. Cobra leaves every time he comes to visit, for example, is telling me something, I'm sure of it. I don't know what it is yet. I think the trail might be the shape of a coastline, pulling me to a watery place, beyond this vast dry land. Perhaps I'll find my freedom on the coast of Kenya, near Mombasa. I haven't been there, but Solomon told me many times that I should go. He described it to me once as "white sand and blue water that goes and goes for miles." He extended his arm out when he said this, his short, fat fingers splayed toward the horizon. Solomon himself had only been to Mombasa's beaches once in his life, even though he was a Kenyan. It was all he had ever been able to afford.

I know they know I'm here. I know they are thinking about what to do with me. They have to come in here for me at some point. They have to release me. They can't just keep ignoring me like this. I won't say anything to anyone about them locking me up. They can just let me go. It can be easy. We don't have to make it hard.

On my second day in here, the large man who beat the servant boy came into my stall carrying a tall, empty pail. He had rough burlap-sack skin and wore a black kufi on his head. He reminded me of a bear when I first saw him, and not a friendly one. The pail he brought looked like it had once held rice in bulk, or some kind of grain bought from the market, with curlicued Arabic script written across it. He lifted it up to the level of his chest and then dropped it in the middle of the floor, where it landed on its rim and thudded over onto its side. Then he took a step toward me, bent down, put his face in front of mine. He yelled something in Arabic, the same thing, over and over, louder each time. He pointed to the pail and then to his butt, swinging his body around so I could see his rump, fully covered by his white jellaba. He pointed to the pail, then his butt, again and again, in a cartoonish manner. I understood, but I didn't let on. I didn't nod my head or say anything. I kept my expression mute. I might have blinked. Then he stopped gesturing and smiled. His teeth were brown and crooked. He blew air through his nose in a short burst, and stood up tall again. I kept my eyes locked on his, even though I was sitting in the corner with my legs pushed up against my chest. He frowned and walked out, wrapped the heavy chain through the door handle and the post beside it, then latched it closed with the enormous iron padlock, which, quite frankly, seemed unnecessary. I probably weigh just a bit over a hundred pounds right now. He shook the door once, and the chain heaved and clanked. He smirked at me through the slats again. I could just see his teeth and muddy brown eyes.

After he left, I turned the pail upright and set it against the back wall. The truth is I was grateful he had brought the pail — something was feeling very wrong with my stomach. I pulled my shorts down and hovered over the pail, my hands gripping the rim. It hurt. My hands hurt, my arms hurt, my guts hurt. Everything hurt. I was terrified kufi-man would come back while I had my pants down. I couldn't go. Something down there wasn't right. I pulled my shorts up and sat down in the corner again, cradling my stomach, which was beginning to spasm in small, sharp waves.

I've gotten a bit more used to the pain, but it hasn't gone away. Every time I finish using the pail, I tip my waste through a space between the boards into the next stall. I have diarrhea pretty bad. Sometimes I sit on that pail for a long time with my ears trained for any noise, and I usually go several times a day. I can feel myself getting weaker. It's getting harder to tip the pail over into the other stall. I think I've gotten used to the reek, miraculously. I can no longer tell the horse manure from my own waste. At first I had to breathe through my mouth, and cover my nose with my vest. Now I don't notice it as much.

I reach my hand up to my forehead, caress the smooth, jagged scar. On the day they discharged me from the hospital, the nurse came into the room to do one last cleaning on it before applying a fresh dressing. Delores and Geri hovered over Chiefie's shoulder as she peeled the bandage away from my forehead. I saw Geri flinch, and then keep her eyes still, as though trying to hide her shock.

Delores held nothing back. "Girl, that is one fuckin' mess you got on your head now." Geri shot Delores a dirty look. I asked Chiefie for a mirror. The wound resembled the blade of a serrated knife held together by a row of black stitches, sharp, thin teeth.

After Chiefie finished taping the bandage to my forehead, Geri left to bring the car around to the front entrance. Delores was propped up on her pillows and looked like she was absorbed in a *People* magazine. I stood at the foot of her bed.

"Hey, it was great rooming with you."

She looked up from her magazine with flat eyes. "They told me this morning that I can't have kids."

For some reason my chest deflated, as though someone had socked the air out of my lungs. I don't know why. I barely knew this woman.

"I'm sorry."

She looked back down at her magazine. I hoped that the tears I saw in her eyes weren't going to spill over. I didn't think I could handle the intimacy of tough Delores weeping.

A full minute passed, with her staring at and not reading the magazine, and me standing at the foot of her bed, trying to figure out how to get out of there with some semblance of grace.

Finally her hand slapped at the air beside her. "Fuck it." Her chortle stung the space between us. With a sudden jerk, she pushed her body forward on her bed and jabbed with her index finger into the end of the folded magazine I held tightly under my arm. Her IV machine bumped alongside her bed on its wheels. I took a step backwards, clutching the magazine even more tightly to my body. "I'm going there," she said.

"Where?"

Her face was close to mine. Her eyes were open really wide. She looked scared. "Africa. I'm goin'. Gettin' out of here."

I wanted to ask about her boyfriend, but I didn't. "How will you get there?"

"I know there are a lotta organizations, always wanting volunteers. But I want to make my own organization. Learn their language. Help the women there. All those women. Fuck." She swung her head back and forth, once, then stopped. "Nothin' for me here, now." Her brilliant blue eyes were now oceans threatening to flood. "I'm goin'."

My heart was beating very fast. I don't know why I felt I needed to hide my own desire. My desperation. The fact that I knew the organizations she was talking about.

At the end of the article, beside the picture of the woman and her child, was a list of websites looking for volunteers to work in Sudan for short stints. I had circled the Canadian ones with a pen I had found in the drawer of my bedside table.

She told me she had worked it all out in her head over the past week while she was lying in her hospital bed, unable to sleep. She had just enough money saved for a plane ticket and a few months to live in Africa. She was going to talk to a couple of these organizations about her idea and put together a proposal, with her sister's help, she said.

After she finished filling me in on her plan, we said goodbye, and I wished her luck. I looked back at her once as I stepped into the hall. Her eyes held mine with steely purpose.

I walked through the hospital's main doors and out into the sunshine. Geri sat in her parents' shiny new car waiting for me. She waved and smiled from behind the steering wheel. A hopeful smile. A smile that promised a new beginning.

I look down at the article laid out in front of me. The pebble is still exactly where it landed, right on the ex-slave boy's head. Sun is filtering through the barn and the light is turning orange; we are getting closer to sundown. If I had an English-Arabic dictionary with me right now, I could learn a few words, a few phrases. I would tell kufi-man to quit looking at me like he wants to eat me. I could tell the one-armed servant, "Please help me. If you get me out of here, I swear on everything holy to me that I will send you all the money I have when I get somewhere safe. I swear to God. To Allah."

Adut

◇◇◇◇◇◇◇◇◇◇◇◇◇◇◇◇◇◇◇◇◇◇◇◇◇◇◇◇◇◇◇◇◇◇◇◇◇◇◇

I have sent Adhar with the bucket to fetch water for the morning tea. When I bend down to light the kindling, the flame leaps up easily to greet me this morning. Auntie and her daughters are still asleep, so I quietly open the basket in the corner of the hut and see there are only two teabags left, and no money in the tin. We will wait to see what Auntie Nyakiir brings home today. There is still some sugar left for the tea but a line of ants is carrying pieces away to their home through a small hole in the side of the basket, one tiny grain at a time.

I saw Ringo out there already this morning, talking to Father. I felt both of them looking at me as I hung the wet clothing on the line. I do not want to see Ringo. I understand what is expected of me, and the weight of his eyes bears down on me heavily. "This is what must be done. We are Dinka people," Father tells me. But I cannot have this. I feel full enough with what I must live with inside of myself already.

Yesterday, when I was pouring Ringo his tea, he looked into my face the whole time I did so. Then he said to me, "You are looking lovely today, Adut." I wanted to throw the hot tea on him, forgive me. I do not want him to see me in this way. I said nothing, set the flask down on the rickety plastic table in the middle of their circle, and walked away without pouring the tea for the other men. I knew I would have to withstand angry words from Father later for this. But I do not want Ringo to believe I could be a good wife to him. The elders tell us we widows are to be married to our dead husbands' brothers, so we may continue to have children in their name. But how can I permit this? These men look at me with hard eyes because of my behaviour, and Father tells me he hears whispers that I am a bad Dinka girl, not offering to do my duty.

A long cough issues from Father's hut; I hear it tormenting his throat. He calls my name in his new voice, small and harsh. I go to his door, open it. He lies on his tiny cot underneath his goatskin blanket, shrivelled, the size of a young girl. How can I explain to you how difficult it is to see my father in this way? You probably did not realize, *khawaja,* on your long walk to the north with him, that my father was once a great man. He was our chief, well-respected by all the villagers, wealthy with a strong head of cattle. He wore a necklace of shells and beads and a feather in his hair to show to any visitors coming from the outside that he was an important man.

I could see the shame in my father's eyes when Rith, Adhar, and I were made to jump over the goat on our return ceremony; he knew we were meant to be given the strongest bull for this rite, not a mere goat. But all of his cattle were taken in the raid, and he has had nothing left to live upon since, nothing to trade or buy food with, nothing with which to perform proper ceremonies, nothing to show himself as a Dinka man.

Auntie Nyakiir tells me that when she and her daughters arrived from up north to the safer village of Turalei, she tried many times to get Father to leave his empty place in Akoch and join them. But he would not. More than once she sent their nephew Abraham on the long walk to urge him to join them. Always he refused, saying he would not leave until I returned. She believes he began to go mad, as he lived in his empty hut all alone, waiting for us to come back to him. He told Abraham that he was safer there; he said the Arabs were dropping bombs on all the places that held people, and that so long as he was left in his village alone, they could not detect him. But I know different. My father believes what he was taught to believe and what he taught others to believe: that to be forced to leave your home is the lowest thing that can happen to a person. Almost everything had been taken from him: his family, his cattle, and his people. All he had left was his place on the earth, where he had been born and where he had lived his whole life.

I often wonder how he spent his days there. Walking through the place that was once my home on the return from up north, I could not believe he had lived there all alone for so many years. The wind and the sun blasting at him all the day, the wild animals creeping outside of his hut at night — would all this not have driven him mad? And the absent voices of the people, voices meant to remind him that he himself was a person?

I tell him, "Father, Adhar is just coming now with the water for tea."

Father turns his head slowly to look at me from the bed, his eyes grey sunken pockets. He is barely able to lift his head, and I can see he means to hide this from me. It takes him much time in the mornings to gain enough strength to join the other men in their circle. I know in my heart that he would not get up at all, were it not for his insistence on having me betrothed to Ringo before he dies.

"This morning Achol will stay back from the market, and her and I will go to hear the *khawajas* talk in the town."

At this he turns his head back, looks up toward the skeletal wooden beams. "And how will these foreigners help you?" he asks. Father makes no secret of his feelings for these foreigners, who come to us in their large, shiny vehicles that roar around the dirt paths of the town, wearing their new clothes, their sunglasses, their hats, with their pink, sweating skin and their full bellies. Their too-loud presence here is yet another assault upon us — this is what my father believes. For what can they truly know of this war? Or of us as a people? Yet he knows that it is because they are here that we are here also; their presence is what keeps us safe from the bombs of the Arabs, for now. And their gifts of food help to sustain us. And so the elders do not speak so loudly against their arrival in our small town.

"They will have free food there, and clothing. I will come back with sorghum to boil for you today, Father. Perhaps Auntie will be able to buy some okra in the market after she sells some *marissa*."

He lies there, still as a bone. Finally he says, "Get me some tea when it is ready. And be sure to come out to the courtyard to greet all of us." He continues to look toward the rafters, away from me. If he were stronger, as he was before the *murahaleen* came, his anger would have come at me in a roar, unrelenting. But I know that he cannot manage this now, for the life in him has grown weak. I believe much of it was used up on his journey to retrieve us. He sacrificed too much for us, yet I still cannot come to agree to what he would have me do. I understand Father only wants us to be taken care of after he is gone; Auntie's wages barely fill the children's bellies, let alone ours. But the betrayal in my heart toward my dead husband would be too great. For Ringo is not Tobias, nor is he anything like him. I mean to go through this life with Tobias as my only husband, though I do not tell Father this, of course.

I leave the hut and see Adhar wandering down the path, an over-full bucket of water heavy in her small hands. I take it from her and pour it into the kettle on the grill.

"Mama, can I go wake Rith now?" Adhar looks at me with eyes lit like copper suns. She is a beautiful child, and Father has said more than once that she will get a good bride price someday. It would be unheard of for me, her mother, to take the cattle wealth. Father has worried too much about this dilemma of who will receive her bridewealth when she is ready to marry. I do not tell him that I think he need not worry. The days of bride price in Dinka-land are almost over now, even though Father does not want to see this. He does not want to believe that those days are no longer, the days when his mother the storyteller was bought as the eldest wife to his Father for several hundred cattle. So many of our cattle have been raided, and so many of our men have fled to other countries; now many of them deal in the ways of the white man's paper money.

"Be sure to wrap him in your sling, and do not wake him if he is still sleeping." As Adhar enters the hut, Achol is leaving; she almost topples her over on her way out.

"Aay, child, watch it."

Achol is built like Auntie Nyakiir used to be before the raid, heavy bones enrobed in a smooth layer of roundness. She is tall as well as strong, which has brought many men to Father asking for her bride price. Sometimes men without any cattle at all also come, hoping

Father will understand — that he himself, a great chief now without cattle, might be sympathetic to them. After they leave, Auntie asks Father why he did not send them away as soon as they arrived. "Do not waste their time, brother. Do these boys think we will continue to starve because they believe they are in love? Too many nights I have felt hunger in my belly. I do not need to entertain these ones who roam without cattle."

"And so are you ready to leave, Sister?" Achol asks in a rare sing-song voice. She is crouched down beside me and moves the kettle into the centre of the fire with her thick bare hand. She does not use a stick as I do, to save my hands from the heat. Her skin, like her character, is tough and unyielding. I can see Achol is trying to be bright, for we both know there is no food for the breakfast this morning, though we do not mention it. Usually I would put the sorghum on the fire now, so that Auntie and the others can eat before heading off to the market. On the good mornings we enjoy millet with milk from the goat. The bit of milk from our one thin goat tethered to the garden stake I will feed to Adhar this morning, but the rest of us will have only tea. This goat has not been producing enough milk, and we do not have the means to purchase another.

Lately the men have not been paying their accounts to Auntie. I was so very surprised upon returning from up north to learn of Auntie's new business. Never would she had been involved in this before the raid, this selling of the *marissa,* which causes men to fall down in the streets and sometimes go home to beat their wives. This selling of the *marissa* was always a job for the ones who held very few head of cattle, who could not receive a high bride price for their daughters. It was not something the sister of a chief would engage in. But war, *khawaja,* it can turn you toward these things that in your before-life you believed you could never be a part of. In war, you are safe from nothing, especially not from the one you think you could never become.

In these recent days Auntie has come back to us with a large white T-shirt bearing a picture of a man, with a necklace of black and white beads, and even with a large, shiny poster of the Christian Jesus Christ. But no payment of *dinars,* nor even food, has she been receiving lately from the men who take their drink. Their accounts are piling up, and Auntie sits at nights on her cot counting the money owed to us. Achai sits with her and writes it down on a small pad of paper with a stubby pencil. Achai learned writing and reading when she was up north as a slave with Auntie. She was the only one they forced to do this, leaving Auntie and Achol to their unlearned ways. Auntie believes that the son of the man who owned them took a liking to Achai, that he wanted his concubine to be educated, and so demanded from his father these lessons for her. Achai, tall, thin, and quiet, with her pretty eyes and fine teeth, would have caught the eye of these sorts of men, who would not have wanted Achol's heavy strength in their bed.

We have already fermented the last of the harvested sorghum from our garden and now we must wait for the next crop to grow. Usually there are four or five covered pots sitting against the hut wall waiting to be taken to the market, but these now sit empty. The stalks around our hut are still too green to till, and the stubborn rainless heat has not been pushing the sorghum to grow. These seasons are not what they once were. We can no longer depend on this weather to feed us, for her moods are always changing. And so we must wait. Achol and I will save much of the sorghum we receive from the *khawajas* today for fermenting new batches of *marissa.* Auntie is insistent we go to these *khawajas;* listen to their silly talk, she says, and take what food from them we can.

Auntie comes out of the hut just now and looks down at us crouched by the fire. She narrows her tired eyes. "Hurry with the tea now, so you can go listen to these *khawajas.* Do not be late!"

"But Auntie, Father would have me go to the courtyard to greet the men first."

"Ach!" She waves her hand at this, as though swiping through the air to hit at a mosquito. "Do you not want to eat? There will be a queue there, surely, and you will not receive anything. Now hurry!"

I retrieve the flask, tea bags, and sugar from the basket in the hut and set to steeping the tea. I deposit the last of our sugar into the cracked ceramic bowl. I am happy Auntie is insistent we leave this morning, for truly I do not want to go to the courtyard where Ringo's eyes press down upon me. Achol gives to Adhar a bit of milk from the gourd while Rith suckles, and then we set off toward the centre of town, leaving Auntie to deliver Father's tea to him and explain my absence. Adhar clings tightly to Achol's hand with her dainty fingers as she tries to keep up with Achol's long strides. Rith looks over my shoulder, his neck strong and his eyes alert, taking in with interest all the women in front of their huts pounding *durra* and the people on the road on their business this morning.

We arrive at the big blue building enclosed in an iron fence. The front door to the gate is open and the guard motions us onwards, where we join a crowd of other women sitting and standing under a large acacia tree. I do not see any white women in the crowd. Achol asks one of the others where the *khawajas* are, and she tells her that they have not yet arrived. We go to sit against the trunk under the deepest shade. I do not see the plump bags of sorghum I was hoping for, and I dearly hope they will not be forgotten. Last week Achai came to our hut and told us she had heard in the market that these white women who worked in the big blue building would give food and clothing to those who came to listen to them speak about help-ing women set up their own businesses. I did not say it to Achai, nor to Auntie, but this confuses me. I wonder who is paying them to make it so that we women are able to have a business of our own. And why would they leave the safety of their own country to come here to our land, where the fighting continues on? Do they not have their own families to take care of back home? I must admit to you that these questions in my mind made me very curious to look upon these white women *khawajas*. And I cannot help hoping, and per-haps it is nothing more than a fool's hope, that one of these women might be you. That you got out safely, somehow, and made it back down here to the south.

But soon these women appear, and you are not one of them. They come out of the big blue building and begin walking toward us, with several young Dinka men behind them carrying bags of sorghum tied up in brown string, along with big white plastic bags overflowing with clothing, and boxes of tinned vegetables. The boys set the bags and boxes on the ground in a large pile and the *khawaja* women stand in front of it, smiling widely at all of us assembled under the shade of the acacia tree. There is a woman with dark hair, and another woman with short, very light hair. Her hair is like yours, *khawaja,* the colour of grown sorghum. But strangely, she is not the one that makes me think so much of you, but the other one, the dark-haired leader addressing us. Why would she bring you to my mind so strongly? You are both white, but she is different than you. Her skin looks very rough, as though wounds in her past have healed over to become scars. And the colour of her eyes surprises me — the colour of the sky when the sun is at its highest reach. I cannot stop looking at her eyes. I do not remember your eyes being so very blue, *khawaja,* not like this, but perhaps my shock at seeing such eyes sets into me the same feeling I had upon seeing you on that day, unprepared as I was to behold such a thing as a white woman with my father.

All of us keep silent as the blue-eyed one greets us in a loud voice in both Arabic and Dinka. There are twitterings in the crowd at this woman's accent. She is very thin, as though she needs to take some of these bags of sorghum and tinned cans of food for herself. And yet she speaks with such confidence, as if she were a man. One of the Dinka boys, well-dressed, tall and without markings on his forehead, comes to stand beside her. After she greets us she begins speaking in English. My heart drops, for neither Achol nor I will understand what she is saying now. What if she is telling us how many bags we will be allowed to take? But soon, the boy beside her begins speaking to us in Dinka, telling us what it is she said.

"Miss Dee greets you all here on this morning. She comes from Canada and she can tell you the weather here is very different." Miss

Dee is still smiling. The boy continues, "These women have come a long way to help you. They have heard from their country of this war and have received money from their own government. They want to use this money to help you start your own businesses."

Here Rith begins to cry. Always this child is hungry. I put him to my breast and look over at Achol, whose head rests against the bark of the tree, her eyes closed. She is likely tired this morning from the lack of breakfast. The lack of food these past few weeks has made all of us tired and cranky. Achol and I both know we do not need to listen to this speech, for I am needed at home, and Achol is needed to help Auntie in the market. There will be no businesses begun by us, helped by these women. Besides, Father would frown on me working with these foreigners, this I know. I am keeping my ears open for mention of the food and clothing as Rith suckles and I look around me. There are some women here I recognize from the market. Adhar lies against Achol's chest, sucking her thumb. I swipe at her hand, pulling it from her mouth. She slaps her palms to her face, hiding her eyes. I turn to try to listen to what the boy is saying, but I too am tired. I rest my head against the tree as well.

The women in front of us are laughing, covering their mouths with their hands. What is this? One of the boys who had helped to carry the boxes is walking among the crowd of women with a small cardboard box, holding it out to each one. Each woman picks something from inside of it. Many of the women are giggling as the boy moves through the crowd with it. He brings it to us and I look inside. At first, I think it is many pieces of wrapped candy. Then I see that they are clear square packages with moistened rubber circles inside. I have heard of these. Now I understand why the women are laughing. The woman in front of us teases the boy with the box, who cannot be more than thirteen years. "You will use these too, child?" He scowls and his face grows a deeper red. He is unhappy with his job, and I wonder how the other boys made him be the one to do this.

The Dinka boy at the front is still talking. "Miss Dee and Miss

Grace want you to take as many of these as you want. Please feel free. The AIDS has not yet done its destruction in our land as it has in other African countries, and it is important to prevent this. Be sure your men will be wearing these."

I almost laugh out loud at this, for this boy is being paid by these *khawajas* to say something for which he knows another truth. Clearly he did not tell these women that our men would never use these. For how would they continue their own line of children by blocking their seed?

Miss Dee begins speaking again for some time, and the Dinka boy again translates. "Miss Dee would like you to know that there is a centre down the road that will help you if any of you have suffered from the forced entry by a man." I am thankful Achol sleeps, for I know she would not have stayed quiet as I do. She would have insulted these *khawajas* with her loud laughter at this. Again, this Dinka boy is not being honest with this Miss Dee by not telling her that many of us here are returned slaves, and have surely been forced already. And might be again, by our own men. Some of these men who have taken the *marissa* Auntie sells in the market hide in the bush and wait for us as we walk the roads to the outskirts of town for the dry firewood. Our clan rules are falling away in these times. Before the war, the elders would have made certain to have the attacker pay the family many cows for this injustice, for the spoiling of their daughter before marriage. But most of our cattle are gone now, and many of these men are no longer in their right minds from too many years of this war.

And these white women also do not know that some women go with their desperation and their hunger to this centre and lie about this forced entry in the hopes of receiving free food, medicine, or clothing from the *khawajas* for their families.

And yet, all of us women here have survived so far. We are the lucky ones. How could we tell these *khawajas* this, who stand under the too-strong sun, who look uncomfortable and hot in their long brown pants and pretty blouses and speak to us with their strong words as though they understand? I am grateful to them for what they offer us, but they have not lived what we have lived. And yet this blue-eyed one speaks as if all we have been through she has gone through as well.

"Please feel free to take two bags of grain each, one box of tinned vegetables, and only one piece of clothing from these bags." The Dinka boy barely gestures to the pile behind him before a throng of women fall upon it. Achol had awakened the moment the boy said this and elbows her way through the crowd with her large body to be one of the first there. I push behind her with Rith in one arm and Adhar clinging to my skirt. The Dinka boy yells for us to form a queue, but no one takes heed of this. Even with Achol's forceful pushes, we manage to get only one skirt, too small for me and much too large for Adhar, and no tinned vegetables at all. However, we do leave this morning with one bag of grain each balanced upon our heads. Eagerly we walk back to the hut with new life in our steps, as we know we can now eat what is left of the goat's milk mixed with porridge, which will feed us all for this evening's dinner.

V

After getting home from the hospital, I checked out all the websites I had circled at the end of the article, emailing every single one my resumé along with a cover letter. After one week, Aid For Sudan responded.

I met the director for coffee at a Starbucks on Bloor Street. She was a university student named Amanda. She made it clear that this was a new organization, and very small. It was trying to respond to the need for education in the midst of the Sudanese civil war. She was in the last year of her Master's program in International Studies at the University of Toronto, and she had received grant money for Aid For Sudan through a government-funded university program.

She wanted to get out there herself as soon as she could, she told me, but she wanted to finish her degree first. One of the requisites for the funding was that AFS had to have someone out in the field representing it. AFS had very limited funds, and had to keep costs as low as possible; I would be staying in a compound it shared with another agency. Necessities were flown in every two weeks.

"Please remember we have no money to pay you."

"I understand." I hoped Amanda didn't notice that I was trying to hide my desperation behind fast swallows of my too-hot coffee. I slid my slightly burnt tongue around the insides of my teeth, trying to cool it. We were sitting at a tiny table directly beside the long line of people being handed their lattes by the barista.

Her cellphone beeped, signalling a message, the fifth time since we sat down. She picked it up, read it, set it back down, took a sip from her cup. "Why do you want to go?" She almost shouted, to be heard over the espresso machine.

Stupidly, her question threw me. How could I answer her? Admit to her that I was looking for a woman in a photograph because I felt like she had something to tell me? "I really want to experience that part of the world. I want to help. And I've always wanted to be a teacher. I have a lot of experience tutoring, and I have a couple of years of teachers' college under my belt, but I had to quit because of finances. I've always planned on going back." She nodded her head as I finished my cup of steaming hot coffee in quick gulps, burning my lying tongue in shame.

Amanda's mouth formed an appreciative smile. "We just want to make sure that AFS is properly represented. We sure don't want any wingnuts in there. We've had a few of those ..." She paused, and looked me over. Her red curls hung in her eyes. She had to be at least five years younger than me. "But you seem nice." She giggled, and her cheeks turned a bright red.

Amanda said I would be stationed in the village of Wun Rok, acting as Aid For Sudan's Education Coordinator for Twic County. It would be my job to try to find out what kinds of education were already happening in the area: where were classes being held? How many? Formal or informal? And I would write up funding proposals for building schools and training teachers. I would also provide teacher training. All a part of AFS's effort to provide education in the midst of a never-ending war.

She picked up her cellphone, deposited it in her bag. "Have to fly. I'll email you tonight with more details. I'll need monthly reports from you via email once you're there. We should be able to get you off in the next few weeks. You'll have to get your passport, all your immunizations. Will you be ready?" Her eyes searched mine.

I swallowed and stood up. "Definitely."

"Great! I wish I could go too." She laughed and turned red again. "But I have to stay here, finish my degree ..." Then she threw her tan bag over her shoulder, which was bulging with books. She stepped in to give me an awkward hug. "We don't have money to train you ... right now ... but I trust everything will be fine."

I nodded vigorously, my attempt to convince both of us that it would be fine.

"Well, good luck!" She turned around and almost bumped into someone on her way out the door. That was the last I saw of Amanda, the director of Aid For Sudan.

My plane landed on a hot, rainy night at Nairobi airport a month later. It was another three weeks before I would set foot in Sudan. It felt like an eternity. It took me a while to understand that in Africa, everything happens in its own time. The sooner you let go of the notion that there is a plan you have control over, the less stressed out you will be.

Nila, originally from North Sudan, was an office manager in Nairobi and her husband was an Irish ex-priest who ran a small newspaper in South Sudan. His newspaper was partnered with Aid For Sudan, and they put me up while I waited for the paperwork that would allow me to fly into a small rural community in the middle of Twic County, South Sudan, where I would be stationed at the AFS compound. I was almost jumping out of my skin during those first few weeks as I sat around Malachy and Nila's place, going through all the books on their bookshelves, huge picture books of East Africa filled with rolling, iron-red savannahs and lions languishing under tremendous baobab trees. But there were no pictures of suffering, no pictures of war, of snot-nosed, skinny children peering into the camera, their wide eyes pleading for help.

Every so often I ventured gingerly out into the congested traffic that fills the dirty streets of Nairobi. I went to the markets and bought little wooden statues carved in the shapes of giraffes and elephants for Geri and Dad. And I complained in my emails to Geri that day after day went by and nothing seemed to be happening. Geri would respond with suggestions to go out and take in the city. When would I have another chance to do this? Maybe never, she said. But I told her I was uninterested in Nairobi, with its pollution and throngs of people. I wanted to get to the red earth of Sudan, the flat plains, the helpless people, all those babies, naked and hungry. It was there I was needed, I wrote to her. Not here.

Every day I went to the reception desk in the Minister's office off Ngong Road at the Sudanese People's Liberation Army Headquarters. Every day the secretary would promise that the Minister, the one and only man in the whole department who could sign my papers allowing me into the country, was away on business and would be back "tomorrow." One day I had talked Nila into accompanying me on her lunch break. The receptionist ushered me quickly into the office and offered me a seat on the ratty sofa. I swear I would have stayed on that couch all day had Nila not interrupted and saved both the Minister and myself from the silent game between us that I didn't, at the time, understand.

The paperwork consisted of one piece of sky blue, five-by-seven inch cardboard paper with my passport-sized photo stapled to it, my name in typed capitals (SANDRA BILINSKY), my physical description typed in smaller font (height: five feet, seven inches. Eyes: green. Hair: blonde. Discerning physical marks: scar on forehead), the country I was from (Canada), the organization I was with (Aid

For Sudan), my occupation (Education Coordinator — volunteer), and how long I would be there (3 months maximum). Three months is all you're allowed if it's only your first time in the country. But Malachy told me that even heads of NGOs usually take a leave after three months. "And besides," he grunted, as he took a drink from his tumbler of JB Scotch, neat, "you're going to need a break by then, Sandy. Trust me. South Sudan is no holiday."

I had been sitting in the Minister's office for almost an hour while he busily wrote on a large yellow notepad, the noisy scrawling of his pen sometimes interrupted by phone calls. He would speak in short bursts of rapid Dinka or Arabic, then hang up the phone and immediately go back to his writing. The shaky ceiling fan rotated overhead in a clunky, uneven rhythm. The air was dense and warm. I wiped the sweat off my forehead with the back of my hand, cleared my throat loudly in a futile attempt to get him to notice me. Had he forgotten I was there? This was ridiculous. It was a tiny office. I found out later from Nila that the reason he had made me sit there for all that time without once acknowledging my presence was that he was waiting for some kind of bribe. Something beyond the ten thousand Sudanese *dinars,* or fifty Canadian dollars, that I had already paid the secretary downstairs as the fee for the identity card.

Then I heard Nila teetering up the tiny spiralling staircase on her high heels. She knocked twice on the door before peeking her head in, smiled widely as she crossed the small space with her long legs, holding out her well-manicured hand to the Minister to be shaken. The Minister suddenly morphed into someone who could smile just as widely, be just as friendly and effusive. In moments, the tiny space transformed from dense silence into an overwhelming clatter of rapid Arabic spoken loudly between two gregarious, toothy people who seemed to have known each other for years.

It took half a minute. He scribbled his signature at the bottom of my identity card and shoved the blue paper across the desk to me while continuing to rattle off to Nila with an insane grin plastered across the lower portion of his face. I took the firm blue paper in my hand and stood beside Nila. We both slowly backed out of the small office, with Nila holding my arm. Nila clicked the door softly closed, putting an end to the loud, lively noises. The only sounds left in the immediate silence were the muffled, uneven beats of the fan behind the door.

As we turned to leave, Nila leaned her head down to mine and whispered in her strong, accented English, "See, my dear. That is how you do things in Africa. You do not wait. You simply take what is yours and you go."

When I finally landed in Twic County in South Sudan, hordes of people rushed at our plane on the blood red soil of the tiny airstrip. The woman in the photograph could be any one of them, I realized, peering out the thick, circular window. I wondered for a moment if the drugs in the hospital had fogged my rational thought and steered me here. I briefly wondered, upon landing, if I wasn't completely out of my mind.

Jim, the security man for RESCUE, an Irish organization that AFS shared the tiny compound with, gave me an orientation upon my arrival. He showed me to my tiny hut (called a "tukal"), warned me about poisonous snakes, malaria, and heatstroke (the three killers here, he said), and introduced me to Solomon, the driver, who would be chauffeuring me around to the nearby villages where I would be doing most of my work.

"Don't go anywhere alone. God only knows what could happen to you out there." He motioned with his head to the compound's entrance. His bushy red eyebrows hung in wisps over his eyes. I could tell he was trying to scare me, but I liked him anyway.

On my third day there he gave me the mandatory "safety orientation," where he showed me the bomb shelter and how to lie down in it, what to do in case of a raid (hide or run), where the safety packs filled with survival necessities were hidden in case we needed to run into the bush and hide, and ended the hour by telling me again that I was to keep inside the compound walls, unless I was going out to do my work, and then I must be with at least two other people.

About six months before I arrived, there had been a bombing just outside the compound. Both the Dinka people and the other workers in the compound told me the bomb landing so near had been no accident. Someone had been trying to send us a message, they said. Maybe, maybe not, said Jim. But the shrapnel had blasted into a nearby hut, and a mother of five had died and a two-year-old boy had lost both his legs.

After my first week there, Jim asked me to go see the boy, to shoot some pictures for head office in Nairobi, "because we need some kind of proof."

"For something we could never prove," I said, but I did what he asked. I wanted to make a good impression. And I had a feeling that no one else wanted to do it.

"War needs paperwork," he said as he handed me his camera. He didn't mention that I should take someone along, and neither did I. It was just down the road. So I went alone.

A long-limbed Dinka woman sat on the ground, head bowed, her dirty green skirt reaching to her ankles, politely showing her deference to me by not standing, while her baby cried and dragged his torso across the dirt with his hands, keeping his arms rod-straight, using them like stilts. His trunk was just a stump wrapped in a dirty shirt, the sleeves tied around his belly in a thick bow. I felt sick in the bottom of my stomach, and guilty that I was taking pictures of the tragedy that was his life. The one time I caught the woman's eye, she looked at me and smiled shyly. After taking only a couple of photos, I thanked her in Dinka and then walked the red, dusty trail back to the compound.

I peer down at the well-worn paper, at the boy with the rock near his mouth. He looks back at me. Will the one-armed servant come back with food today? Will he talk to me? Can I somehow convince him to get me out of here?

Adut

∞∞∞∞∞∞∞∞∞∞∞∞∞∞∞∞∞∞∞∞∞∞∞∞∞∞∞∞∞∞∞∞∞

The sun looked much different up north. I watched it through my tiny window every single day of my imprisonment, in the mornings as it rose from the ground and in the evenings as it fell from the sky. It seemed to rise and set the same way every day, so that it looked as though nothing could ever change. I had not known the sun's rising could make one's heart sink, again and again. Before, I had always thought of the sun with joy, had borne its heat on my body like I would the memory of my grandmother, with a kind of pain that is strong and alive. I remember the sun in the evenings, as I watched it through the small thick square of glass. With its soft blurred edges it looked like oil melting into the sandy hills. Then the earth would slowly swallow that yellow ball, drop it down into its belly.

Every single day since I had arrived at Saleh's house, I washed those dishes, so many of them, thick, cream-coloured dishes patterned in blue with tiny pictures of landscapes and windmills and white children dressed in overalls and caps. So many dishes, so many children, cattle, horses. So many beautiful, decorated things. The riches Saleh must possess, to be able to have all this. He even has big pieces of land elsewhere that he claims as his own, Nyikoc told me. I felt such a heavy weight press down on this house. I could see it collapsing onto the shoulders of the ones who lived here, the servants as well as Saleh and his family. I felt sorry for these people from the north, unhappy and bound under their great roofs with their many things. They were blind to the outside world, breathing in locked-up air, deaf to the voices of the sky spirits.

I no longer winced as the soap seeped into the raw cracks of my skin, etched there from all the hours and days and months and years of scrubbing and scrubbing, the endless task of wiping those dishes clean. Once I asked Head Wife for salve for my hands — one time only, in all the eight years I lived there. She beat me terribly with a whip for speaking to her without being spoken to. I never asked her for anything again after that.

The gash in my wrist still throbbed painfully sometimes. The skin had closed over it like a zippered tent. Even now, every once in a while, I will feel a pain where my scar is, as though something underneath still tries to break free from the thick skin and come back to life. This deep scar is now a part of me, a permanent marker of the memory I cannot forget.

On that horrible day in my village, the morning after my last time with Tobias, the *murahaleen* tied us to each other with rope, several women and children in a line, and then tied the rope to their horses, so that we were forced to walk behind them. Khajami was tied to one side of me by a rope attached to my wrist. Another rope tied me to a woman in front and another rope to a woman behind. One of the leaders cut the rope that tied me to Khajami, so I could walk faster. Right before he came at me with the knife, I heard him say, "Hurry, hurry, lose the boy!" Then the knife went down. He lifted it high up into the air and plunged it, swiping it through my flesh as though he were slashing a branch off a tree in his path. I could feel the earth slowly falling toward me as the blood gushed out. I knew I would crumple to the ground soon unless it stopped.

This man did not care that he had wounded me. After he had cut Khajami from me, he simply ran back to the front with the others and hopped onto the back of one of the horses. I looked down at my wrist, open and bleeding. The woman beside me took this very rope that had been attached to my son and tied it around my wrist to stop the flow of the blood. It took every single bit of strength I had not to fall to the ground and be dragged along behind the others like a dead animal. The only reason I managed to stay standing after I was cut was that I could still see my small son running beside me.

I screamed at him, over and over, "Khajami, go home! Go back home to Baba!" Though I knew most of the huts were burning and

I did not know where Tobias or my father were, I wanted desperately for him to go back: I did not want him to stay along beside me for fear one of the *murahaleen* would come and kill him on the spot with his machete. But Khajami, terrified and with tears running down his cheeks in wild rivers, continued to run alongside us for a long time. He ran and he ran before exhaustion finally overtook him and he fell behind me and left my eyes altogether. For a while I could only hear his cracked voice screaming for me to come back to him. When I could no longer see him or hear him I prayed out loud to the powers in the sky, to those greater than myself, so my tongue ached with the words, and everything inside of my body burned with the longing for him to live, for him to be safe.

For a long time afterward, I am ashamed to tell you, there were many days when I cursed this unknown woman beside me who tied that rope around my wrist. I secretly cursed her for saving my life. To this very day I have not been able to recall her face. She must have been from my village, as all of us caught and taken away on that day were neighbours, friends, and family. So many miles I walked beside her, so many hours in the dust and the heat, dragging our heavy, blistered feet over rough ground toward the north on a journey that seemed to last forever. So why is it that to this day her face is as a ghost to me?

We arrived at a compound after a day and night of walking. It was early morning — I remember looking at the sun coming up over the earth in this strange place. It was a cold yellow, the eye of a giant snake. They untied us from each other and shoved us all into a large, damp, windowless hut. We huddled together with the others we knew, like shivering animals. Some of us had been stripped naked by the *murahaleen* soldiers. Many of us were beaten and bleeding upon our arrival.

I remember seeing Aluel there. In the moment my eyes adjusted to the darkness, I spotted her in the corner, shaking and naked, her knees pulled up to her chest in a poor effort to cover herself. Upon looking at her there I remember thinking immediately of a cow I had once seen, dying by the side of the road. His eyes were rolled back into his head, his ribs straining to poke out of his skin with each rattled breath. There was a plain terror in those eyes; he knew his fate. Aluel lifted her head from where she had it resting on her knees and saw me. I was too frightened to go to her. We stared at each other for some time across the crowded space, our eyes locked in desperation across the sea of broken people.

A thin column of bitter yellow light bled through a crack in the wooden door. These were not only the people from my village; there were women I recognized from neighbouring villages as well, women I would pass on the road to the market, daughters of my cousins, wives of my uncles. We all huddled together in groups while whispers and cries pierced small holes into the heavy air.

Only when we reached the hut did I remember about my wrist. Perhaps that was because they had untied all of us once we arrived. Before shoving me into the hut the soldier ripped away the rope that had kept me bound to my life on the journey, and then the blood began falling from my wrist, like a careless, slow-moving river, unmindful of my own life coming out with it. Auntie Nyakiir had not been far from me in the line of tied women and children; she saw my bleeding, quickly tore off a piece of her skirt, and wrapped it tightly around my wrist and hand.

We were there for perhaps only a few hours before some men began coming to claim us. I was one of the first to be taken away. It was Khalid who took me from the big hut, pinning my arm behind my back as he handed one thousand *dinars* to the man who had sliced my wrist with his knife. I remember sitting by the door shivering against Auntie Nyakiir as I watched their tall figures in the doorway, dark and featureless against the sunlight, listening to them negotiate in their strangely accented Arabic. Khalid wanted to pay a lesser fee, as he could see I was wounded. "But I must receive a discount, sir," Khalid said to the soldier, smiling with his crooked teeth and pointing to my makeshift bandage. "She has been damaged on the way." They laughed and the soldier finally relented.

After their bartering Khalid walked into the hut. Before my eyes could completely adjust to the light, he grabbed me by the forearm. Auntie Nyakiir gripped me around the waist with her arms, her face unmoving, like a stone. Khalid had a time tearing me from Auntie's strong grip. He finally pushed her large body down to the ground, and after she fell back he gave her a kick in the ribs before pulling me with him and out the door. Behind me I heard Auntie's sharp cry, a crack of pain that travelled deep inside me. Even then, I did not cry. It was as though the sky had opened up already and swallowed me, *khawaja*.

Khalid tied my wrists together. The rope cut into Auntie's bandage and it slowly blossomed a deep red. He tied the ends of this rope around his waist. When we finally came to Saleh's compound, after a day of riding, it was nightfall. He lifted me off the horse, untied me, grabbed me by my arm and threw me to the ground. He walked away and into a big building. I heard him speaking to another man. This other man came out of the building. A large gun was strapped to his body, which he patted with his hand while he looked at me lying where Khalid had thrown me. Then he turned around and walked back inside. His jellaba fluttered behind him; I thought of the wings of a bird falling to the ground after it has been shot.

For the first days, I slept outside on the ground behind this building. It was actually two buildings side by side, and inside of them were many stalls where the horses and cattle were kept. A cold wind came up in the nights. I would press my body against the outer wall to try to get out of that wind. I wanted so badly to escape, but the man with the gun never forgot to lock the wide gate that closed off the compound. I was afraid of the wild lions that I knew waited just beyond the low hills, but Khalid was even more frightening than the lions. His murky brown eyes told me he would just as well kill me as let me live. And I knew if I tried to escape he would find me.

The ground was hard and there was no shelter from the dust and the sand that whirled at me in the nights. It was not only my skin that was cold as I crouched against this building, but my heart and insides as well. I shook so hard that I could not sleep. I wrapped my thin clothes tighter around me but it did not help.

After Head Wife put me in the small room attached to the main house, I pleaded with the other women servants who worked in the kitchen, just down the passageway from me. I asked them, "Can you help me to find a fresh cloth to wrap my wrist with?" The wound had not yet stanched and the blood kept coming out in slow, small blooms. The pain was spreading and I could not move my hand. I kept trying to wash all the dishes with one hand only, but it was impossible to keep up as Nyikoc kept piling them into the basin. When I did not think Head Wife was near, I would go into the kitchen and tell the servants how hard it was to scrub those dishes with this wrist the way it was. I would lift up my right hand to show them the deep wound. It leaked a whitish colour from its jagged edges, and the blood still weakly rose to the surface of the gash.

It is not allowed to heal with all this water, I told them in my simple Arabic, there is too much water, the air it is allowed to feel is too little. Over and over I said this while they gaped at me with dumb eyes. I thought it would soon become very infected. I was afraid I would lose my hand to this injury. I told them this. I spoke to them, certain they could understand my Arabic; I knew the traders at our market near Akoch understood me when I bartered with them. But they made no sign to show they understood anything. I told them if I lost my hand someone else would have to wash those dishes. I spoke loudly and pointed to my wrist, again and again. I must have looked mad. After awhile, I re-tied Auntie Nyakiir's piece of skirt around the wound, now stiff with a thick layer of dried blood.

I knew they must be pretending not to understand me; I saw the open fear in their eyes. I did not want to see this, but I did. I understood that if they were caught speaking to me, they would get trouble from Head Wife, who did not like anyone talking to me, Saleh's newest one. They knew Head Wife would punish them for helping me. She would not want me to find a new piece of cloth to wrap around my wound; she would not want me to protect this deep gash from the soap that bit. She wanted to provide me with as little as possible, she wanted me to have just enough strength for my heart to beat, only enough strength to breathe in air, to merely live and do this work, with nothing else from life.

Whenever I went outside, I felt as though the ground under my feet was all I had left to myself. I would try to move as slowly as I could. I would try to memorize the feel of this earth under my feet. I would pick up the dry, fine dirt with my toes. I would breathe in this strange outside world deeply, look all around me long and slow. I tried to carve the horizon, the hot, dusty smell, the yawning sky, inside of myself, so I could call these things up again in my mind when I was back in my cell, when my hands were in the dishwater, with only the world in its smeared bright shadows to look at through my window. I even pretended sometimes that I was back home in the south, where the sun did not hide from me behind whirls of dust and the darkness in my mind. My feet craved movement, escape. They felt swollen and hungry for the touch of the earth back home. They were lost; they did not know this ground.

I wondered at this, why Head Wife chose to not rebuke or beat me, call me names such as lazy and *sharmuta,* when she saw me walking slowly outside and avoiding my work. When she saw me outside my cell, rocking my heels into the dirt, taking my time to go to the well or the line to hang the clothing, she would set her lips in a thin line and turn away from me. Perhaps, having had other slaves before me, she understood about this border, the place where madness lives on just the other side. Perhaps somewhere inside herself she understood that she must give me this one thing. I had not been taken at a young age, and she knew I remembered a better life; perhaps she thought I would be more difficult to handle, because I had known freedom for so long. I believe this is also why Head Wife watched me more carefully than the others. She knew about this edge.

I heard stories about other slaves from Nyikoc. The ones who tried to escape were killed. Those who did not behave were beaten severely, or sometimes lost a hand or even a whole arm to the machete.

Sometimes they were given away to other families as gifts, families worse than this one, Nyikoc assured me. These servants who had bloodied the ground of this cell before me hung their absence in the air around the tiny room, murky and thick. Sometimes at night, when I would wake to the dark, just before I remembered where I was, I could feel these slaves who were here before me. I could smell their wounds; the stench of the loss of who they once were filled the dark gloom. One time, I reached my hand out to touch what I thought was the ghost of a slave who had stayed in this cell before me. Half-awake, almost choking on her fear, I thought I felt her there. But my hand touched nothing, only inky black air.

More than one time, I stowed away the dirty knives brought to me by Nyikoc. I put them under a bucket against the wall. But I could never create enough courage in myself to do what I truly wanted with them, in all those long eight years. I only washed those knives and, later, chopped vegetables with them for the kitchen servants. Never did I use them for the purpose that I dreamed of so often.

I believe Head Wife knew that her husband came to visit me at nights. She saw I was more tired than the others. And I believe it was exactly for this reason that she was very hard on me. Would she rather have him in her bed? Why ever would she want his rough hands, his grunting noises, his coarse, hairy skin, his horrible horse smell? I stopped struggling not too long after I arrived. I am ashamed to say this. I am ashamed that I did not struggle every time he came to me. I am ashamed, God forgive me, that I did not use my hidden knives to kill him.

That first night, I had been sleeping outside on the ground behind one of the stables when I woke up to see him walking toward me where I lay, walking very quickly, as though he had something important to tell me. I thought this was just another man here, like Khalid, who was going to command me to do more work, even though night had fallen long ago and the moon was up above us, burning down its pale light into the yard. I had already worked from the time I arrived until late into the night. After Khalid had thrown me off his horse onto the ground, he had ordered me to sweep the floors of the stables and feed the horses big pails of oats. At first, I had tried to resist what Khalid demanded. I was so exhausted after everything I truly did not think I could do it. But then the man with the gun had come; he had lifted the gun up and pointed it directly at me. Then Khalid had pushed me toward the pails and the horses, pointing roughly at them, and told me in his strange Arabic to feed them, and I had done what he said. I had not been around horses before, and their bulk and their whinnying sounds terrified me.

So it was that when I saw this man walking quickly toward me that night, to where I lay against the outer stable wall, all I could think was that I would not be able to do any more work. I was scared that if I refused, he would beat me, or bring back the man with the gun. I learned soon enough that this man was not like Khalid; he was the owner of this compound. Everything here was his. He was the father to all the children who played in the yard, the husband to Head Wife and the other three minor wives. He gave the orders to Khalid, and to the man with the gun, and to the others. But when he came to me that first night, I did not know this.

I struggled and scratched him with my good hand until his arms and face bled. But he did not give up. I was so very tired from the journey. I had already lost so much blood from the wound. I do not know how long I fought before giving up. It seemed like a very long time. But I could not match his strength, his weight. I could not get out from under him, no matter how hard I tried.

But that is not what I remember most. What I remember most about that first time is that my lips were very dry, and caked with tiny grains of sand and dirt from the lack of water. I remember that I ran my tongue over my lips, barely feeling the grit dissolve. I did this one small thing, just after I stopped struggling. Then I focused on my own breathing; I tried as hard as I could to inhale short gasps of air into my body from the night and the stars and the pale light above me so I could live and not die while this thing was happening to me. The pain of him pushing so hard inside me was just another pain. It did not hurt more or less than getting whipped, or having my wrist cut so deeply, or being dragged behind horses for so very long that I preferred death. It was just that it was inside of me, the private place I shared with my husband only, the place from where my son had first come to me. That he was doing this thing to me after my family and my home had been taken, and my son, made me feel that as my breath left my body it took with it any reason for staying alive, the last smoking wisp of a dying fire absorbed into the dark night. I did not know as he grunted his rough way into me what life would be left inside me after this.

This was when I heard their voices. Women's voices, a deep chorus, their sound floating down and into me. Where were they? I looked from left to right but could not see anyone. At the movement of my head, Saleh grabbed my jaw with his hand and held my face still. But I continued to hear this chorus, beyond me. What were the words? For a brief moment, I thought I had truly gone mad.

And then I saw the faces to match the voices, as Saleh kept his hand on my jaw to still me and I was forced to look over his shoulder and up to the sky. When I saw the faces among the stars, I remembered sleeping outside our hut with my mother's arm under my neck, the night after my first moon blood came to me. These Women were now witnessing the horrible thing Saleh was doing to me. I prayed in my mind to these Women to make him stop, and to reach down inside of me and mend me, for I feared my insides would shatter completely.

Their eyes were large and sad, their faces smooth and shining against the night sky. They sat around a large fire, all in their circle. Every one of them — I counted thirteen — was staring down at me. Who were they? And why were they coming to me now? When I was a little girl, Mama told me that everyone has angels, and most of them are our very own ancestors. Were these Women in the sky my great-grandmothers, my great-aunts?

When he finished, he stood up and walked away. I stayed on the ground, turned my head to the side, and watched his heavy boots thump in the dirt with each step he took away from me. His boots had hard steel points on the ends of them; they were unlike the soft sandals the other Arabs wore. I reached down and pulled my skirt tight around me, just in case he came back. I wanted to sit up, but there was a weight in my lower belly that would not let me move. I rolled over to a new place on the ground, away from the wall. This new ground was cool under my back and legs. I closed my eyes and willed the air that I sucked into my lungs to make the shaking stop.

I looked up at the cold night sky again, and saw that the Women were gone. I was terrified in that moment that they were gone forever. But they came back to me, again and again, all the time I stayed at Saleh's house. And so it was that every time Saleh came to me, I began to search out the Women in the sky. Even when he came to me in my cell, where there was a roof over us, I could close my eyes and see them in my mind. In the spaces between his violent thrusts, I could feel their presence, and the strength of the light from the huge fire they sat around, and I could hear every one of their voices singing down to me.

So you see, it was the Women who saved me in the end. They helped me remember who I was while I was living this new, strange, terrible life. They gave me hope that I might survive and might someday leave this place. They gave me hope that I might see Khajami again. They did not tell me these things. But they kept something small in my heart burning, like the tiny flame you could still see in Nyikoc's eyes if you looked very closely.

A few mornings after Saleh first came to me, I heard footsteps coming down the passage toward my tiny room. I was all alone; Saleh had ordered Nyikoc out to the stables earlier that morning to tend to the cattle. I knew right away these footsteps were not Nyikoc's — his were quick and light. These new footsteps shuffled along slowly on the dirt-packed floor.

I took my hands out of the water and dried them quickly on my skirt. My right hand was numb from the pain where the open wound lay. Auntie Nyakiir's cloth from her skirt lay on the floor in the corner, stiff and shrunken, like a small, dead bird. My heart was beating so fast I thought it would fly out of my chest. I looked around wildly for a knife. There was only one small, dull knife lying in the dishwater. I picked it up and held it in the grip of my good hand.

Surely Saleh would not come to me in the morning, with everyone awake and Head Wife and the children near? The bottom of my stomach rose up in a wave, and stopped up the breath in my throat.

The shuffling footsteps stopped just outside the door. I stood, my hand holding the knife behind me, facing the empty doorway. There was one loud knock on the wall beside the entrance. Then an old woman's raspy voice spoke a word I did not understand. I let out my breath in a slow stream of air, but I stayed where I was. I called out for her to enter. I said it in Arabic, not knowing if she understood my words, but hoping that she understood what I meant.

She came around the corner, her head and torso bent almost to her waist. She looked very, very old, like my grandmother right before she died. Her grey hair was tied back tight in a small knot, and her face was drawn with a hard life's worth of deep lines. She was wearing the house servant's clothing, the long grey skirt and apron and the white, high-necked blouse. She craned her neck upward, painfully it seemed, so she could look me in the eyes. I recognized her then; she was the woman I had seen in the sewing room. I had gone to her asking for a cloth to wrap my wrist with — before Head Wife told me that the only rooms I was allowed in inside of the house were my cell and the main kitchen. But this old woman had only stared at me blankly, shaking her head.

Now she held out her hands to me, palms upturned in an offering. She took another few shuffles toward me, and I saw the gifts that lay in her small, bent fingers. There was a clear bottle of red liquid, some cotton swabs, and a roll of white tape. These looked like a doctor's things. There was also a thick, white cloth. And one side of it was wrapped in thin, waterproof plastic.

VI

Sandra

On the day that changed everything I asked Riak if I could join him
on their trip to the village of Pakor. I wanted to try to get some
sense of whether a school could be built in the area. Solomon and
Riak were headed to Pakor to check out progress on another compound they were building for RESCUE, and they told me I could
come along. The building of the compound had been going on for
a few years. The local people were making bricks manually, using
the clay from the riverbed and laying the blocks in the sun to dry.
Every time Solomon returned from Pakor, he would report to head
office that construction was going very slowly. Upon his return he
would often procrastinate, drink a Tusker, shuffle some paperwork,

before finally making the call. Head office seemed to not understand that things happened in their own time here.

I was filling up my water bottle from the cooler in the mess hall when I heard Solomon starting the truck outside the fence, and I didn't think about changing into my skirt until we were on the road. My skirt, the only one I'd brought, stupidly, was lying on my cot back at the compound. Jim had let me know very clearly in his Irish brogue that he thought it was bad form to wear shorts in front of the Dinka workers, even while inside the compound.

"You're a woman and you need to be more careful," he had said. "This isn't the U.S. of A."

"I'm Canadian," I'd told him.

But he ignored this and told me that for my own good, I needed to wear skirts whenever I left the compound. Long ones. To my ankles.

I didn't want to tell Solomon to turn back, because I knew they were already in a hurry. It was late morning and it was a good two-hour drive. Possibly longer, depending on the road. Another of Jim's constant phrases rang in my head as we drove away: "No movement outside the compound after dark." We had to be sure to leave in time to get home before sundown.

I sat between Solomon and Riak in the tiny cab of the truck. My knees were pressed together, hands in my lap, acutely aware of my bare legs. Maybe it would be all right this time. Maybe everything would be all right. Though Jim had said there'd been a lot of "activity" lately.

"What kind of activity?" I had asked.

Jim's eyes were squeezed shut against my question, but I already knew the answer: "There are no details provided about any activities." Jim couldn't get answers from any of the Dinka people we were working with. They didn't want us to leave — our organization brought them food, clothes, medicine, and books. So many valuable necessities, after being shut out from the rest of the world for decades. I had a feeling that even if Riak wanted to tell us what was really happening, his elders would have advised him to keep quiet.

All of us in the compound secretly wondered if the promises of ceasefires in this area had been bullshit, if the government in the north was only saying so on the radio to keep the world's nose out of what it said was its own business — and what a lot of the rest of us called genocide. What the government said came to us in heavily accented English from a radio high on a dusty shelf in the mess hall. If reporters wanted to live, they told stories in a way that would make it look as if everyone was getting along just fine. Except, of course, for "warring tribes." Nobody could control them, the voice would often emphasize. The voice from the radio never mentioned the government outfitting the northern tribes with guns and horses to do the killing for them.

And yet, I didn't see the ghost outline of an encroaching rebel tribe on the horizon, headed our way to annihilate us all, as Jim did. When I stepped outside the compound, I only saw teenage boys reinforcing a wall of their hut by slapping mud onto it with their long fingers, making tracks like butterfly wings compressed into the hardening muck.

We arrived in the early afternoon. I didn't find any kind of schooling happening in the tiny village, not even the usual classes taught by volunteers under trees. So, with Riak's help, I talked to a couple of the male clan elders about the educational needs and desires of their community, scribbling their answers in my notepad so I could later type up some kind of report in an email to Amanda. I spent the rest of the day waiting for Solomon to finish conferring with the workers on the building. I even showed the picture of the woman in the article to a few people. Of course, no one knew her; they all pointed north. I was beginning to think the Dinka pointing north was code for, "You will never find her, *khawaja,* what are you, insane?"

An elderly woman was talking to some Dinka workers just outside the compound fence. She was large-boned and her skin was dark and shiny. Wherever she went, children, women, and even men would cut a path for her. She sat down on a small wooden chair in front of one of the *tukals,* set her large backpack at her feet, and began talking to an old man who wore a red and white T-shirt and a fisherman's hat.

Suddenly she looked over to where I was sitting against the compound fence with my notebook. Shielding her eyes with her hand, she waved me over. I walked to her and stood in front of her, offering what I hoped was a respectful smile. The sun was behind me. I moved so she could see me better. She wore a long flowered skirt and a matching floral blouse. Her legs were spread wide apart, and one elbow rested on her knee. I had never seen a Dinka woman sit like this before.

She motioned toward the chair across from her that the old man occupied. The elderly man she was talking to quickly got off it.

"Please, sit."

"No, no, I couldn't ..."

But the man said, "I will be going," in perfect English, and with a nod he sauntered off to join a group of several other men sitting under a large tree, who were talking loudly and drinking tea.

"Men like to talk with men," she said, and laughed. She turned to me. "Why are you here?"

I sat down. "I'm interested in helping your people."

"Mmm." She narrowed her eyes; I could see she didn't believe me. I pulled the article out of my pocket, unfolded it, showed her the picture of the woman.

"I'm looking for her." She took the article from me, brought the paper to her face and peered at it closely. Then she folded it before handing it back to me.

"Why are you doing such a thing?"

I paused, speechless. "I ... I don't know." None of the other Dinka had asked me this before. How to answer? I looked down at my bare toes. They were dirty. Dust was caked under my toenails. The old woman was wearing sneakers so white and new it almost hurt to look at them.

"There are too many slaves up north. Not many have returned. All of us here have relatives who are now slaves up north. Every single person you will talk to here would tell you this."

She swept her long arm through the air toward the smattering of nearby *tukals*. In front of their huts, a few women were pounding grain with heavy pestles, slamming them up and down into deep wooden bowls. Some children were teasing a tied goat, pulling its tail and then running away and laughing while it brayed at them threateningly. The group of men sitting in the circle were arguing loudly in Dinka, most likely about politics, or cattle.

"But you must know this." She paused. "Why worry about one who is now free? What of the others, who still must be freed?"

I didn't know what to say. By this time I had been in the country for close to six months. My ID card had expired months before, and I was now in the country unofficially. I didn't want to tell Jim this; I knew he would send me back to Nairobi. But I wasn't ready to leave. I still hadn't found her.

This woman looked at me hard, waiting for my response. Who was I kidding? And what if I did miraculously find her? What would I even say to her? In the hospital I had been somehow strangely convinced that if I met her, she could help me. She could tell me something I needed to hear. She could mend something that was broken; *she* could help *me*. I leaned back in the chair, wiped the sweat from my forehead with the palm of my hand. The shame I felt burrowed its way down into my bones, into my heart.

After a while she spoke again. "I was educated by the British." I looked up at her small grey eyes. Her hair lay in tight cornrows against her scalp. "Ever since the Brits left, the Arabs have been trying to get rid of us. It was 1950 that the British left. I am in the last generation of women in my country who were properly educated. Now, I'm in my sixties." She reached down into her bag, pulled out a thermos, and drank from it. "This is why I can speak English so well. Women and girls younger than me have been too busy running from the Arabs to become educated. This idea of yours, for the schools, it is a good idea. But the war is still happening. The schools you build will be open only for a short while. They will come and burn them to the ground. We know this. Perhaps this is why my people have not been excited about your schools. Not as excited as you think they should be." So she knew. The old woman held out her arm and offered me a drink from her thermos. I took a couple of sips, wetting my tongue and throat. I wiped the rim with my hand and gave it back to her.

Then she stood up and heaved her backpack over her shoulder. Her wide frame blocked the circle of arguing men behind her. Behind her, I could see Riak coming for me. It was time to go.

"Hey, hey. Why frown? You will leave here one day. Back to your home and your life once again." She raised her index finger and bent her head down to me. Her voice was a rough whisper. "But I think, perhaps, you will remember us." The sun behind her touched the horizon.

We were going to be late getting back. The dust flew up behind the truck, leaving a wake so thick you couldn't see the village we were driving away from. The conical mud huts and skinny children and dogs playing on the road were blurred behind mounds of red, powdered earth. The sun bled through the wispy clouds, making its descent past the horizon, back to the underworld, its sinking light a brilliant orange and pink.

Solomon was laughing at something Riak was saying. I was squeezed between them, and I didn't understand what they were talking about. Solomon understood much more Dinka than I did. He told me that his native language, Swahili, was similar to Dinka. I had been picking up Dinka and Arabic words here and there, and I was getting better at it, sometimes surprising Riak with what I knew. "*A pad a pay,*" I said to Riak once, and waved my hand like I was brushing something aside, when he apologized for showing up late to interpret for me with one of the teachers: *Never mind, it's okay.* And then Riak laughed so hard he bent down and put his hands on his knees, his long fingers wrapping around the knobby bones.

Solomon had told me a few days before that his wife was expecting their fifth child. She stayed at their farm in upcountry Kenya with their children and his mother. I imagined all his kids looking like him — incessantly happy, squat-bodied, chocolate-skinned little boys and girls with boundless energy and an unrelenting desire to please. He had seemed very excited about the news. I think he had thought there would be no more children for him; both he and his wife were in their early forties. "But it is God's will," he had told me. When I had told him I was childless at twenty-eight, he had looked at me with a big frown and sad eyes. I had laughed out loud at this, but his facial expression had made me feel empty inside. Here they say children are like riches: they exhibit your fertility, your abundance, and your strength. And your future: so that when you die, you don't really die. You don't vanish off the face of the earth.

As we drove along the dirt road, Solomon and Riak's words and laughter became a comforting background din. I took pictures inside my head of the skeletal trees against the sinking sun, the skinny cattle on the side of the road, and the young boys: proud, angry, and dusty, carrying their long sticks and singing to the cows.

We stopped four times on the way back to pick up people who needed a lift. By the time we were halfway back to Wun Rok, there must have been seven or eight people on the flatbed of the truck, hanging on tight as we bounced along. Solomon pressed his foot down on the pedal; he shouldn't have stopped, he said, since we would already be missing curfew. Just then one of the people we had picked up on the way, a young boy, leaned through the open window from the flatbed of the truck, and yelled something to Riak. Then I heard it, that sickening thump, the one that can still be heard in my dreams.

Auntie Nyakiir insists we rub our bodies with dirt and ashes before the ceremony.

"These are the old mourning ways of our people, we cannot forget them now."

"But where will we get the ashes?" I wonder this because there are not cattle around us, and so we cannot take the ashes from their burnt dung. She clucks her tongue and looks at me, as though I have forgotten how to be a Dinka, like some of the girls in the town who bleach their skin in their desire to look like the white foreign aid workers who drive around in their big, shiny vehicles.

"We will burn a fire in front of the hut, use the ashes from the cooled sticks. And we can use this dirt here." She rubs at the dirt in front of our *tukal* with her bare foot.

I do not want to ask her where Father will be buried, for I fear that I already know. He will not be buried in front of the cattle byre in our ancestral home of Akoch, as he would have been if the raiders had not come. I feel bumps rise on my arms at the memory of walking through my old village with Father on our way back from Saleh's in the north. The dust swirled in the wind, as though our ancestors in their loneliness were calling us back. I hang my head in shame at the thought of burying him in the gravesite outside of Turalei, already overflowing with the vast dead of this war. He had been our chief; how would my father's grave be marked from the others?

"Adut, why do you shiver when it is too hot? Come inside. I will fetch for you some water."

Something has come alive in Auntie Nyakiir upon Father's death. She no longer seems too tired, her eyes are not heavy-lidded. Instead they are now set with a grim purpose; as the elder woman of our *tukal,* she has taken seriously her role to make certain Father has a proper burial. She grows stronger with this task, yet she is still not the person she had been before the raid. When Father first brought us to Auntie Nyakiir's place after our days-long trek from up north, I saw immediately that she had left the old Auntie Nyakiir behind in our old village of Akoch, with the other ghosts. Where her body was once plump and generous, now her skin hangs in loose folds from her bones. Her eyes are dull and heavy with a thick sadness, and they no longer look at you in that laughing way she had.

There were times since my arrival in her home that Auntie Nyakiir has looked at me and the shame is so alive in her that it hurts my eyes to see it. For we both know I saw what happened to her on the day of the raid. It is one thing to be soiled by a dirty *murahaleen,* another thing altogether for your beloved niece to see it. In the midst of the burning *tukals* and the gunfire, everyone was running like mad for their lives. I was running too, running with Khajami in my arms. I ran behind my father's *tukal,* and there I saw: Auntie Nyakiir lay with her skirt pulled up and a *murahaleen* raider on top of her. His gun was strapped over his shoulder, and it banged against his back as he forced himself inside of her. He was thrusting so violently I thought he might break her. I started forward — I did not know what I was thinking. But she lifted her head and with one arm waved me away wildly.

Auntie was taken with Achol and Achai together from the crowded hut to a farm further north. All three of them worked there for several years before being traded to another family. But Auntie had been clever; she had managed to steal some money from the first owner in small amounts over the years. On their way to the other family's home she gave most of this money to the trader, buying their freedom. From there they fled here to Turalei.

Now Auntie Nyakiir dips a ladle into the pot and hands it to me, full of water. I sip from it and with my back against the wall I slide down to sit on the floor. Achol is teaching Adhar how to separate grain; Rith crawls toward me and grabs at my breast with his small, eager hands.

The guilt eats at me now. Father wanted me to go with Ringo

while the sun is above us

not only so he could take care of us, but also so that I could bear children in Tobias's name; Ringo would be duty-bound to give his brother's name to children he sired by his dead brother's wife. Father loved Tobias like a son, and he had watched him die while trying to fight the *murahaleen*. Upon his deathbed I saw in Father's sunken eyes how it hurt him that I remained resistant to marrying Ringo, that I would not promise him this one thing before he left this earth altogether.

The week before he died I shamed him again; I raised my voice to the circle of men who drink tea in the mornings in the courtyard. They were talking about the peace agreement, what many people believe to be our one chance for salvation from this war. Abraham, my cousin and one of the younger men in the group, was telling the others that he did not agree with this pact, that it would mean we were giving in to the Arabs. I felt my face flush with a deep heat. How could he possibly expect us to go on like this? How could he expect us to win against the northerners?

He spoke to the elder men in the circle with his index finger pointing upward to the leaves on the tree that shaded him. "God is on our side. We are Dinka men. We can win this war." Abraham had the deep ritual scars across his forehead, six fresh horizontal ridges, and all six of his lower front teeth were gone. As he spoke he would raise his fingers to his lower lip, pushing it against his new toothless bottom gums. Father told me that Abraham was taken as a slave as a young boy and so never received these manhood rites. His father finally bought him back a few years ago, after building up a strong head of cattle through his daughter's bridewealth. Upon Abraham's return as an adult, he insisted they put him through these rites that he missed, to show himself as a true Dinka.

I waited at the edge of the group, the flask of hot tea slipping in my sweaty grasp. Would the men say nothing to him? They took sips of tea from their cracked cups and nodded, "Ay." How could they agree to this madness? Did they fear they would be disrespecting the ancestors by challenging a proud, traditional Dinka?

I stepped forward. Abraham glanced at me. He waved me away with his hand, assuming I was about to fill his already full cup.

"This is madness," I said. My voice did not sound like my own. "How can you expect us to continue? The northerners have more guns and more money, and the support of all the other Arab countries whose lands are rich with oil. We do not even have horses. Too many of us, millions of us, have died or have fled from our land altogether. How can you expect us to go on? Finally there is a chance for peace and you resist this?"

My father stood up then. It took him some time. One of the men sitting beside him cradled Father's elbow as he struggled to a standing position, leaning heavily on his walking stick. His eyes were not angry, but I could see they were weighted down with his illness and with my new shaming of him. He shook his head in a small manner before saying quietly, "Adut, go now."

I looked around the group. Some of the older men were shaking their heads, making shushing noises, shooing me away with flicks of their hands. Abraham was staring at me in disbelief. Surely he had never before been spoken to this way by a woman. Truly, my hands were shaking, and the flask felt as though it would slip away from me at any moment. I glimpsed Ringo, who was sitting with his back straight, and with small eyes seemed to be considering me. I set the flask down on the plastic table in the centre of the men. The legs of the table wobbled unsteadily. I turned around and walked back to the *tukal*.

This was the last day Father joined the group of men for tea. He spent the rest of his days lying on his small cot while we tended to him. Every time I entered his hut, I felt in the thick air his desire for me to apologize. And more than that: his desire for me to make a promise to him that I would go with Ringo. Forgive me, but I could not. I could not do this, even in the moments before he died, when his breath was laboured, and we all hovered over him. The guilt, *khawaja,* I tell you; it feels as though it eats away at my heart now.

Auntie Nyakiir reaches up behind one of the rafters and pulls a thin wad of *dinars* out of the straw. She plucks a bill from it and hands it to Achai, tells her to go into the market to buy a chicken. Auntie kneels in front of me, places her hand on Rith's warm head. He suckles loudly, as though he can never get enough.

"We will kill this chicken by cutting off its head. In this way, *Nhialic* will take away your father's illness from this place." She points to this *tukal,* and then to Father's, across the small yard from ours. I think of Father's body in his *tukal,* lying on his cot with a sheet draped over him, stiff and finally freed from his breath. That morning, Auntie, Achai, Achol and I washed his body and slathered it in oil bought from the market before covering it with the sheet. His thin, wrinkled limbs and face shine in death now.

"We will do this thing after they bury your father. Come now, Rith," she coos in his ear, rustling his fine curls with her fingers. "Finish eating so Mama can prepare for Baba's burial." She stands up slowly, looks down at me, a rare smile on her face. "You are your father's daughter, Adut. He will live on in you." She reaches down and cups my chin in her hand. I try to smile. I cannot tell Auntie Nyakiir of my guilt for fear she will scold me for my sins. She leaves the hut and I hear her outside chopping some wood for the fire to make the ashes with which to cover our skin, to show our proper mourning for Father.

Adhar walks slowly toward me, carrying Father's gourd that he used to drink from before he fell ill. She hands it to me, a question on her face. "Baba is gone?" I bring her close to my side, kiss her cheek.

"Baba is gone, love." I wish I knew what to say to Adhar, whose eyes look upon me, waiting for me to speak to her some kind of wisdom. Truly I do not know how to tell my daughter that I do not understand the afterlife and its frightening mysteries. Adhar loved her baba. He lavished much attention on her — and not just because he thought her light-skinned beauty would bring to our family a hefty brideprice of cattle someday. Father loved Adhar's sweet, gentle nature.

I hear the burial hymns begin. The men are walking past our *tukal* toward the gravesite, singing the death song. They will go now and begin to dig Father's grave. I peek out the doorway. They walk in a line with their shovels, Abraham in the lead, calling out the song, and the others behind him repeating his words. Ringo is among them. All of them are singing and stamping their feet:

> *Some people say, "Our Chief is no longer Chief."*
> *The man who has no Chief may leave the country,*
> *I am taking my Chief into the sun;*
> *He is taking himself to the spirits above,*
> *He remains our Chief.*
> *Father, son of our Chief,*
> *You are going to the spirits in the sky;*
> *You will sit in the centre of the spirits above.*

Auntie Nyakiir stands from her work at the fire and bows her head as the line of men pass. I wonder if this new life in her is due to what she knows to be true: that she will be free of us now, she will no longer need to feed four extra mouths from her small wages. With Father's death, her burden has been lifted. For she knows, as do I, that with Father gone I have no choice but to marry Ringo. There is no longer a man to care for us now, and when Ringo comes for me, I must go.

I look at Adhai who stares at me with her unblinking eyes, the colour of lightly steeped tea. She tugs at my sleeve, "Mama, do you think Baba is up in the sky? Can he see us from up there?" I look out the door and see the fire finally take to the kindling, and Auntie Nyakiir stand to watch the flames rise.

We rub the cooled sticks on our arms and faces, Auntie Nyakiir, Achai, Achol and I. I reach down and rub some ashes on Adhar's cheeks. Even though Adhar is not allowed to come to the gravesite because she is too young, she must mourn her baba too. We moisten our skin from the pot of water and use dirt from the ground to cover

while the sun is above us

the parts of our bodies not covered in ash. Then the men come. They lift Father's body from his cot, and carry his stiffening corpse upon their shoulders. Some of the women begin the call and response song of death. We start to leave for the gravesite in a queue — Achai stays back with Rith and Adhar, standing outside the hut watching us leave. Auntie holds onto my arm as we walk behind the men and my father's body. My own body feels clenched. I feel Father's spirit looking down at me, waiting for me to surrender even before Ringo comes for me. Why am I being this way, undutiful? Even after all Father went through to come for me up north? Auntie Nyakiir lets go of my arm to wail and pull at her hair. I know this is my cue to do the same, but God forgive me, I cannot; my grief is locked up too far within me to mourn my father properly on this day. Even in this, I fail him. I continue to stare down at the ground before us, dusty and littered with old plastic bags and refuse, so unlike the smooth, clean roads of Akoch.

We come to the edge of the town where the men dug Father's grave earlier that day. All of us step carefully around the other plots. It is hard not to step on the other dead as they are pressed so closely together. The men place Father's body in the fresh hole, and the sheet falls away from his face and leg. It has been only three days since his life left him and already his skin is pulled tight against his cheekbones, and his teeth are bared, like an animal's. My heart beats hard inside of me, like the wings of a wounded bird feebly trying to take flight. I watch as Auntie Nyakiir and the other women kneel on the ground and wail.

I feel eyes on me. I look up. Once more Ringo stares at me. Does he think me disobedient, unable to weep for my own father, even after shaming him so? How could I ever explain that the grief I feel for my father and all my lost family runs so deep that it has carved dry rivers into my bones?

Abraham steps forward and beseeches *Nhialic* to tell the spirit of my father that we thank him, that he was a good man and a strong leader, and we hope his spirit will continue to watch over us now, a chief and a most powerful ancestor we will not forget. The men begin to shovel the dirt onto my father's body. I see some clumps of dry earth begin to fill his open mouth. I turn my face away.

After they have filled in the hole, Abraham and Auntie go to the mound of dirt now lying on top of Father and pat it with their palms, muttering their own silent prayers. Auntie looks up at me from her crouched position, with her eyes imploring me as his daughter to do the same. I kneel down and touch the loose earth, cool under my fingers. I close my eyes, but no words come to my mind. Inside of me it is cluttered; I cannot find the room which contains the clear, true words to speak to my father. What can I say that would touch him and set his spirit free?

Everyone begins to disperse, and Auntie and I wander back to the *tukal.* Though the children are hungry, there will be no food or drink this night, in honour of Father's death. Auntie Nyakiir has become quiet as we walk solemnly in the dusk toward home. We are not paying attention as we should be, and we have already stepped onto the road to cross when I look up to see that a white foreign aid vehicle has stopped to let us pass. In the front seats are the two women who had spoken to us that day under the big tree. The one with the light blue eyes smiles at me through the dusty glass windshield.

Back at the *tukal,* Adhar runs to me and slips her small, warm hand in mine. I kiss the top of her head and whisper to her that she must join her brother in sleep now, there will be no dinner this night. I find myself going outside and wandering into Father's empty hut. Am I looking for forgiveness? What can I say to him when in my heart I do not want to do this thing that is asked of me?

I sit on his narrow cot and the old bedsprings croak loudly at me. Father's gnarled walking stick rolls toward me from where it lies, now lonely and useless. I pick it up and stroke its worn wood. Abraham had whittled it for him as a gift, to use in his final weeks.

The light in the tiny hut is fading fast, but the dying sun reaches to something on the floor against the opposite wall. I kneel down to it and see that it is Father's feather and his necklace of shells and beads. He was never without the feather tucked in his hair and the string of beads and shells around his neck so that any strangers he met would know he was a chief. He continued to wear these every day, even after Akoch fell. My heart sinks. These things should have gone into the earth with his body; Father was meant to take his beloved possessions with him into death. I remember now removing the feather and necklace before preparing his body for burial. How could we have forgotten? Yet another sin to weigh down my heart.

"Adut." I look up at the doorway and see the figure of Ringo standing there. In my crowded thoughts I did not hear him approach. How long has he been there? I stand up, put my fingers to my dry lips. Surely he does not expect me to leave with him now.

He enters the hut, carefully, and comes to me. He places a firm hand on my shoulder. "I am sorry for the loss of your father. He was a good man. We will all miss him. But he lives on in you, Adut — and your future sons."

I look into his eyes but I cannot see what they hold, for the sun has vanished now and the darkness has closed down upon us.

"I must leave next week, I can delay no longer. I must go back to my home in the east. My cousin's son has been taking care of my cattle which remain there. Some of my wives and children have already left to go back and begin rebuilding our homestead. I cannot hide here in this town any longer. The *murahaleen* are not so much a bother to us out east now." He drops his hand from my shoulder, walks toward the door, turns around. "I will come by here next week. Please prepare yourself for the journey. See you then, Adut."

He almost bumps into Auntie Nyakiir on his way out. She comes to me, peers closely at my face. For a moment I think she may rebuke me for being alone in a hut with a man, but then I can see through the new darkness that her eyes carry pity. It is then that I realize I am silently crying.

"Ah, child." She wraps me in her arms, and the memory comes to me strong of sitting in her lap in front of the fire as a small child with my ear against her bosom, listening to her laughter inside her chest. "He will be a good husband, you will see." I let her hold me for a few moments. "I came to tell you the children are sleeping ... ah, but what is this?" She picks up the feather and necklace and gasps. "Oh no, we have forgotten!" She sits on the creaky cot, holding them as though they were foreign things, not something she has seen my father wear every day. "Ay, we have disappointed him now."

I could not stand this thought. I could not stand more disappointment raining down on me from Father's spirit. "Could we not just lay them on his grave, Auntie?" I realize as I speak that I need to choke out the words.

"No, no. It is too late. Ach." She puts her hand to her forehead. "If we were still in our village, we could just bury these in front of his cattle byre, but here," she motions in the direction of the graveyard, "the dead lie almost one on top of the other. Birds or animals will take them, or even children will take these and sell them." I take the necklace and feather from Auntie's hands, carefully.

"Perhaps I could go to Akoch, bring them there to bury?" I see Auntie's face shoot upwards at me from where she sits on the bed.

"Alone? Do not be crazy, Adut. Who will take you there? Besides, you must leave soon, with Ringo. Did he not just tell you this? We must prepare for your departing. These things are yours now." She stands up and pushes my hands that hold Father's precious possessions to my heart. "At least you can pass them on to your children. Tell them your father was a great chief in our village and a leader of our clan, the Padiangbar clan." I imagine in that moment Rith wearing the necklace, too large for him, the shells rattling against his belly.

Auntie Nyakiir squeezes my shoulders in her hands. "Come, child. It is time for sleep."

The next morning I wake before everyone, and slip out the door. I do not tell Auntie or any of the others where I am going. I look down at Adhar and Rith, fast asleep on our mattress. I tucked Father's feather in Adhar's small fist when I came into the *tukal* last night. She still holds it in her hand loosely, the soft, worn spine rising and falling against her chest.

I stride at a rapid pace toward the big blue building in the centre of town where the white women are staying. Hardly anyone is awake. A few women are in front of their huts pounding *durra* or winnowing grain; there is no line at the well. I come to the gate, and through the iron poles I ask the guard's permission to enter. He allows me in and tells me I will have to sit down on the bench against this fence and wait until the women have awoken and finished their breakfast.

My insides squeeze and turn against themselves. I touch my father's necklace at my throat, and wonder if his spirit will rebuke me or bless me for what I am about to do, as I wait for the white woman with the blue eyes to appear.

Tazket, the old woman servant who had given me the bandage for my wrist, was there when I gave birth to Adhar. When I was heavy and slow with Adhar inside me, I could see her observing me closely. Whenever we were both in the kitchen at the same time, she would watch me, her eyes moving up to mine as she extended her neck slowly upward from her bent torso. Whenever I snuck into her small sewing room for a new cloth for the dishes, the creaking of her old machine would stop abruptly as she stared at me. She began to come into my cell sometimes for a glass of water, but never would she say a word. This was strange to me; never did the other servants come into my cell. Sometimes they would stop at the door only to give me an order, command for me to chop the vegetables for supper that night or pound the millet, as they were too busy with their other chores.

It was when my belly was growing larger with Adhar's life inside of it that one of Saleh's minor wives came to me to teach me the Islam. To this day I do not know if Head Wife had seen my belly and guessed at what her husband had done. Perhaps Saleh himself had ordered this wife to give me lessons. I wondered why Head Wife herself did not come to teach me. But I was glad that this minor wife, Halla, came instead, for she was far gentler than Head Wife, and she never threatened to beat me. She only took off the veil that covered her face when she came into my cell. When I would gather water from the well in the daytime, I would sometimes see her with the children in the yard, or leaving through the open gate with one of the servants to go to the market. Always she would have her face and hair covered completely, even in the harsh heat of the midday sun. I only knew it was Halla underneath her concealing dress by the slow and careful way in which she walked, as if the ground were a carpet of scattered thorns and her feet were bare. When she told me that she was Saleh's fourth and youngest wife I thought briefly

while the sun is above us

to say that I was also my husband's youngest wife. But then I could not; for to bring Tobias's name into her confidence would betray him, my brave husband, who had died at the hands of her people.

Besides Saleh's unwelcome visits in the nights it had been only Nyikoc and Tazket who had entered here in all the time since Head Wife had shown me to this room. When Halla came she had tucked under her arm a large book, covered in black leather. She did not say a word as she entered and took off her face veil. She went to the wall to overturn one of the buckets, on which she then sat. She motioned for me to sit before her. I did not understand at first, and I stayed standing in front of the basin, my hands dripping water onto the dirt floor. She flapped her hand vigorously, nodded her head toward the floor before her. Slowly I sat down before her, wiping my hands on my skirt.

She spoke very slowly and loudly, as if I would not be able to hear her, as if she were far away. "It is time to teach you the true word of Allah, child." I wondered at her calling me child when she looked younger than me. "Perhaps you think you are in a prison now, but trust me, you are in the right place. Even though you come to these teachings late, it is important that you come to know them. They will become a part of you. We are all servants of Allah and we must obey his word." She looked at me with her dark brown eyes, very seriously. It was difficult to think of her as a teacher. Her long eyelashes and soft voice were that of a teenage girl's.

I knew of northern traders in the market and even some of my father's friends who practiced this Islam, but never was it something I thought I would be forced to learn. I did not understand why it was so important. After Halla began coming to me with her big book I wondered, as I lay alone in my cell at nights, what I had done wrong for my entire life before this. Had I truly been living a wrong life up until then? Mama had taught me that my ancestors and the powers in the sky were there to protect me if I respected them. Never had she told me of this Allah. I did not want my mind to be turned the way they had succeeded in doing so with Nyikoc. When the sun came up full in the daytime, I would always remember who I was again, and that their need to force me to believe what they believed was only a strange thing, confusing.

There were many things to learn with this Islam. Halla began by showing me how to get down on my knees and bow my forehead to the ground, five times a day, no matter what I was doing. Even if I was gathering water from the well, even if I was washing the clothes, I had to stop what I was doing to do this thing, and I must always point my head in the same direction. And so even as my belly grew larger and it became more difficult to bend down, I did as Halla said, for I knew if I did not that the whip of Head Wife would be waiting to strike me.

On the night Adhar came into the world, I finally understood why Tazket had been watching me as she had. I was leaning over the basin, holding on to it tightly, my knuckles turning white each time Adhar bore down, the pain rushing through me. And so I barely noticed when Tazket came through my door, carrying a tin bucket of steaming water, holding the large handle in both of her frail hands. Many cloths from the sewing room were bundled under her arm.

She came to where I clutched the edge of the basin, stooped over in her way that she moved. I grabbed her thin arm and told her I did not think I would survive this. Khajami had been so much easier than this, I kept saying to her, over and over in my Dinka language, not thinking that she did not understand my words.

"Shh, shh." She dipped one of the cloths in the bucket and wiped my forehead, and then she guided me onto the floor. I lifted up my skirt, crouched down onto my knees with both of my palms flat on the ground. I pressed my forehead to the cool dirt, breathed, waited for the child's next thrust. Tazket knelt down beside me and squeezed my forearm. I was surprised to feel inside of her bony fingers a raw strength. I turned my head and saw the glint of a knife peeking out from her apron pocket. I knew this knife would not have to be for me. My people did not cut their little girls down there and then sew them up again like her people did so that their women had to be cut open again to give birth. She dipped the cloth into the bucket of water and pressed it to the back of my neck. After some time, I realized she was swaying forward and backward, murmuring soft words, like a chant. Was she singing a passage from her holy book? I did not understand her words; this did not sound like Arabic she was speaking, yet the rhythm seemed familiar, and in those long night hours I tried to move my mind into her song.

I only screamed once. Her old eyes flew open at the sound, the sudden opening flap of a bird's wings. She put a crooked finger to her thin lips, and pressed hard against them. For the rest of the night, I kept the screams inside myself. We did not want Head Wife to hear; if she came and saw this baby's brown skin, we did not know what she would do to the child.

Tazket continued to murmur softly in her strange language until the sun's red glow began to lighten the room through the tiny window. Adhar came out to us as the dusty light fell across the floor. Tazket had stayed the night, lulled me through the rushing passage of this other world where women must go for their babies to be born.

When Adhar was finally suckling at my breast, I looked up and saw that Nyikoc was there as well. Not in my cell, of course, as a man is not allowed to be near a woman who is bringing life into the world. But I saw his foot peeking past the doorframe, as he leaned against the other side of the wall. I saw then that he had been bringing the boiled water in buckets and setting them inside the door for Tazket to carry to me. He had sat outside the door of the kitchen cell all the night, keeping watch.

VII

Sandra

APRIL 28, 2003, EL-MUGLAD, NORTH SUDAN

Everything is blowing inside me. I can no longer hear the world clearly; everything is muffled. I am being blown away; heart, vessels, organs are beginning to tear apart.

Why haven't they come for me? Why is it taking so long? Is it because my ID card expired and my presence here is officially non-existent? Is it that simple — just some red tape? I wonder about Riak. Did they let him go, did he make it back, was he able to tell Jim? Would it be that hard to find me?

I wonder about the old man too, and about you. I pray that you told someone about me when you returned. That you sent some-one to come for me.

I hear the barn door slide open. *Please, dear God, don't let it be Kufi-man.* I hug my knees, hold my breath as footsteps thud toward my stall. I see those huge eyes, the whites a burnt red against black pupils. He looks at me through the slats, the one-armed servant. What are those eyes saying to me? Does he have food? What can we exchange? How can we help each other? I want to ask him this, but I don't know the words. He stares, unblinking. But I blink, and a tear falls down my cheek. He takes his eyes away, leaves. The barn door slides open, and closes.

Late last night, Kufi-man came in here. The noise of the heavy latch opening was like thunder rubbing up against my skull. There must have only been a small sliver of moon, for I could barely make out his enormous outline. I heard him kick the pail over with his foot. It clattered sideways, bumped against the floor, hard plastic on dirt. This morning, when the light seeped through, there looked to be bits of dark, splattered blood against the dusty floor. But it was just my own shit. I stood up, stepped in it, smeared it across the dirty wooden boards with the sole of my sandal.

Before, when Kufi-man brought me the pail, he searched my pockets. Did I already tell you that? He took my Ziploc bag; in it were my Swiss army knife, my panadol pills, my malaria pills, and my lip balm. What would I have given to have that bag last night? I could have numbed this hell with drugs, and I swear I would have stabbed Kufi-man through his fat throat with my knife. I would have had to dig in deep, push right to the knife's hilt, but I could have done it. I would have used all the strength in my body. It's amazing what you can do when everything is taken away from you, when all you want to do is die.

When Kufi-man entered the stall, Mr. Cobra stayed underneath us in his tunnel, listening. For all his kingly power, perhaps Mr. Cobra is terrified of Kufi-man's crooked smile, his noisy, smelly bulk.

I know why Kufi-man came in here. But I don't know what made him decide not to do it. He stuck his thick fingers under my armpits and scooped me up like I was a small child. Struggling against him was like a piece of straw struggling against a strong wind, ridiculous. He pushed me up against the wall, pinned me there with his wide chest, his breathing on my cheek ragged and rank. His eyes were black stones. After a few seconds he blew a short breath out of his nose and dropped me back to the floor. Like I was nothing to him, a small rodent he wanted to be rid of but couldn't bring himself to kill, or maim. I scrambled back to my position in the corner. Then he left.

I don't know why he let me keep the article when he took my Ziploc bag on that first day. And just now I have remembered to throw the pebble, though the light streams bright through the spaces between the slats in the wall, and the servant boy has not come with any food. I need to know what today will be. I close my eyes, toss it to the worn paper. Open my eyes, look down. It has landed on top of her. It rests on her cheekbone, almost covers her entire face. Half of one small eye peeks out, angry and unyielding.

Is it resentment I feel toward her now?

We'd been giving rides to the locals on the flatbed of the pickup truck ever since I'd arrived. There were always people walking on the roads, carrying heavy loads of food, water, babies. Giving them a lift was just a way of helping them out, making their day a little easier. I didn't think one of them would jump. Everyone knows you're not supposed to jump off the back of a quickly moving vehicle.

Solomon was driving faster than usual, trying to get us back to the compound before total dark. The red, dusty terrain was laid out in front of us, interrupted by blots of scraggly trees. When I heard the odd, sickening thump, my mind went blank, as if to make room for the ensuing horror. And the worry about being late that was sitting in my belly became an electric snake that travelled up my spine to the back of my head and coiled, hissing like mad.

We went back to retrieve the boy's body. His head had smashed on the ground first; his body was a crumpled mess of bones and blood, more or less held together by his skin. He couldn't have been older than twelve. I found out later that he had yelled to Riak "stop here" in Dinka. But before Riak could tell Solomon to stop and let him off, he had jumped.

Blood poured out of his head and onto Riak's hands and shirt as Riak dragged him over to the back of the truck. Riak was crying out loud like a child. I backed farther away, off the road, and stood in a clump of trees. The others we had picked up on the way had jumped off the flatbed and stood around the truck; no one spoke. Solomon and Riak heaved the dead boy onto the back of the truck. My body wanted to shut out what my eyes were seeing. A thick, metallic smell of fresh blood rose up from the boy's body and filled our nostrils. I watched the other people scatter away from the body. Silence stretched along the red dirt road. The only noise was the wind, high and whining in our ears.

Riak, Solomon, and I drove the boy's body back to Pakor and dropped it off at the medical clinic, a simple one-room concrete building. The blood from his head had spilled in thick rivers down the runnels of the flatbed floor. Solomon drove right up to the front door of the clinic, jerked the truck to a stop, and he and Riak jumped out and carried the broken, dead boy through the clinic's front door. I stayed in the truck. The nurse followed them out and looked at us with slitted, dark eyes. I turned back to see her shake her head slowly as we drove away.

There was much arguing between Solomon and Riak about what to do. It was Solomon, in the end, who decided to steer clear of the main road. Riak gripped the dash with his bloody hands. The smell was pungent. I tried to block it by turning my face away from him and concentrating on breathing through my mouth. They were both on the edges of their seats now, their faces close to the windshield. I sat rigid between them, listened to the hissing in my head. The sun had gone down and darkness fell over us like a heavy blanket. Solomon said something to the effect of "a hail of gunfire" to Riak.

"Who are we running from?" I asked Riak, aware of how ignorant

this must have sounded to him, but needing to know. I was still trying stupidly to piece together what was happening.

"His clan," he said. "They will be out for our blood now. A life
for a life is the rule here."

The way we were travelling there was no road at all, just lots
of bush. The small Toyota truck crept through the bush more and
more slowly; the gas gauge was almost empty.

I kept waiting to feel terror. This may sound strange, but besides the distant hissing, I only felt an uneasy calm. My heart was
a quiet lake.

"Will they kill all of us?"

"What?" Riak kept staring through the windshield into the small
expanse of forest we were driving the little Toyota through. The
skeletal trees ahead of us were lit up in a bright white wash by the head-
lights; their branches and trunks kept shifting into grotesque shapes.
A minute later he answered me, still looking through the windshield,
as though his brain needed all that time to formulate an answer.

"They won't care." He paused. "This is a bad, bad thing. This
is a terrible thing that has happened." He kept staring through the
window at the path we were cutting before us.

The truck sputtered to a stop. The roaring noise of the engine
eclipsed from a whine swirling down a funnel, to a dead quiet. Our
bodies hummed with adrenaline. The echo of buzzing felt loud in
my ears against the black night. Solomon put his head on the wheel.

Riak looked at my feet. "How are you going to walk through this
with those on, miss?" I looked down at my sandaled feet and my bare
shins. I knew the brush was covered in thorns. The Dinka always
made fun of us *khawajas,* telling us we had no idea how to "walk."
These are people who walk for an entire day for a bag of sorghum or
a five-gallon container of water, which they heave onto their head
or their back to return home with.

Solomon tried to radio Jim. Just static; we were out of range.

We all got out of the truck. We had to keep moving. Riak put
his hand between my shoulder blades, firmly. The lake of my heart

became unquiet, and now it was battering in waves against my throat. I looked down at the ground, searching out the thorns.

We began walking.

∞∞∞∞∞∞∞∞∞∞∞∞∞∞∞∞∞∞∞∞∞∞∞∞∞∞∞∞∞∞∞

It does not take long for her to appear. She wears a beige skirt that brushes against her shins as she walks toward me. Her thin, short-sleeved blouse clings to her small chest. As she comes nearer, I can see that already the morning heat has sprouted beads of moisture upon her brow.

"*Marhaba, Cheobak.*" She says hello in both Arabic and Dinka and then smiles at me as though she is very happy to see me, even though she does not know me. Her skin is so white, it is difficult to turn my eyes away from it, and those eyes are such a light blue, I wonder how she can see out of them properly.

Upon looking at her this closely, I find my feet feel light under me, for there is something in her that reminds me so strongly of you, *khawaja*. Something I cannot name, for she is thinner than you, and the details of her face are arranged differently. Her skin is rough, and she has dark hair where yours was light, but still it is you I think of as I stand so close to her.

Then, she does a strange thing: with her hands she pulls her damp hair back tight from her face, and quickly ties it with a band worn around her wrist. I wonder if she is so very busy as to not have found a moment to do this upon waking, before her breakfast. Then she grabs my hand and shakes it up and down. Her strength travels into me, and I realize my hand lies like a weak fish in hers.

"*Chinkarach?*" she asks, still pumping my hand up and down. *How are you?* I smile despite myself. She has already learned our custom of greeting one another in Dinka. This is the way some of our elders greet one another, grasping hands and repeating this word over and over until you think they will not stop, so happy are they to see one another. But this sounds funny coming from a white woman, with her eyes carving into mine, and with her aggressive and over-happy manner. I keep my laugh at the back of my mouth for I do not want to seem disrespectful.

She turns to the guard and speaks to him in English. He goes away. But I do not want this guard to leave, for now who will tell this *khawaja* what I have come here to say to her? I feel a sharp point of envy in my chest at their easy way of speaking. Many of our men are educated to learn English, and so now can work with the foreigners to make money to give to their families. I know that these white people have much money to give; if I could have learned to speak their language, I might have found a job with them too. I would have had a chance to afford medicine for Father, to keep him alive.

The guard returns with a tall Dinka boy; this is the same boy who spoke to us for this *khawaja* on the day we sat under the tree, waiting for the bags of sorghum. This boy is well-dressed. He wears a clean T-shirt with English words written on it, and blue jeans, neatly pressed. Achol told me, shortly after I arrived to Turalei, surprised as I was to see all these white people, that those who work for the *khawajas* are not only given much money but also free clothing from their countries. I do not let my eyes stare at this boy's fresh new clothes for long; I do not want him to see how I admire them.

He greets me in Dinka. "Hello, my name is Kwol. I am the translator for Miss Dee." He shakes my hand. "Have you come to register?" I do not want to seem stupid in front of this boy, younger and better educated than I am. Even though I do not understand what he means, I nod my head.

"Come then. Already there are several women inside waiting to register this morning." I follow Miss Dee and Kwol into the big blue building. The light-haired *khawaja* sits on one side of a table, and several women stand in a queue on the other side. I recognize some of them from going to the centre of town to gather water at the well. On the way to this table we pass another larger table with a stack of plates, some white napkins, and food such as I have never seen it. Two large bowls filled with porridge, several colourful boxes of cereals, cooked eggs on a plate, two packages of white bread, a large square of butter, and several jars of sweet things with which to spread on the bread. I recognize these jars from Saleh's; I was not allowed to eat from them, but I watched in the main kitchen one time as the cook spread a purple jelly from one of these jars onto a piece of bread for one of Saleh's small sons to eat. I notice a plate of sliced green melons sitting at the edge of the table. I so terribly want to reach for a slice as I pass; my mouth is dry from the heat and the walk. I can imagine it would feel sweet and cool on my tongue. But I know this is not possible, for I do not have a pocket in my skirt to store it in. And I do not want Miss Dee or Kwol to see this and think me a thief.

Two southern women are taking the dishes and plates away, still filled with food. They both wear the same dark blue T-shirt with English words written on it. I cannot help but wonder at how many *dinars* they are given for cooking and serving this food to the foreigners. Surely the *khawajas* let these women take the food that remains back home to their families? The knife of envy pushes itself even deeper into my chest, as I think of how many times I have made a simple dish of sorghum last for several days for all of us, during the times when the men were not paying Auntie for her *marissa,* allowing their accounts to build up.

Miss Dee sits in a chair beside the other white woman. Kwol motions for me to join the back of the line, and then he goes to stand behind Miss Dee. There are five women ahead of me. These women must have been waiting here in the building while Miss Dee finished her breakfast. Did they watch her eat? I wonder if she gave them some of this food. I wish in my heart I had departed even earlier from the *tukal.*

I look to the front of the queue and see a Dinka woman who carries her newborn against her breast. She speaks to Kwol, who then translates what she is saying to Miss Dee. She has told him her name and the village where she is from. Alek, from Maridi, in Western Equatoria. Miss Dee nods her head at what Kwol tells her and writes something onto a piece of paper with a pen. Then she smiles wide at the woman, as she did at me earlier. I listen for what else the woman says to Kwol, but the women in front of me are talking loudly, guarding the words I am trying to hear.

The young girl before me wears her hair short-cropped, and she speaks excitedly with the older woman in front of her. Then she turns to me. "Ay, so you are leaving this place also?"

I clutch the shells of Father's necklace in my fingers and take a step back, surprised at her words to me. How does she know I am to leave with Ringo for the east next week?

The girl laughs; it sounds like tinkling glass. "Ay, Sister, do not look so scared. You look as though I just told you we are going up north to Baggara-land where the *murahaleen* wait for us! These *khawajas* will take us to a village in the west. They say it is an old village, destroyed long ago by the *murahaleen*. With the money from their country they will help us to start our own businesses there. It is only the women they will help."

My village is west of us, I want to say. But it cannot be, so many villages in this area have been lost to the *murahaleen,* many each year since the war began. Father and I only walked through it not so long ago, when we felt the ghosts of our dead sit upon our backs, and we listened to the wind sing its lonely song through the empty, cracked *tukals.* I rock my bare feet on the ground, trying to feel them. They feel strange on this cold, hard floor.

When these *khawaja* women gave us free bags of sorghum and clothing, they told us about the Women's Cooperative they were starting. I remember as I sat under the tree with Achol they explained what this meant: they had received money from their country to help us start our own businesses. Achol and I knew we could not escape our duties at home to do this thing they were offering to us. And so I did not bother to listen so closely to what they were saying. I was only thinking of receiving bags of grain with which to go home, and then cook and feed to Father, who had not been eating. Had they told us on that day under the tree that if we joined them we would have to leave Turalei? What else had they said? I wish now that I had listened more closely to them.

I had come here this morning to speak to Miss Dee, to tell her that I also want to start my own business, so that I may make money and show Auntie Nyakiir that she can keep me and my children living with her after all, and I do not have to go with Ringo to the east. And now this news of leaving for the west, leaving Turalei altogether ... if this is true, surely Auntie will not permit me to go, especially without a husband or elder, and especially when plans are being made for me to leave with Ringo so soon.

"What are these questions?" I ask the girl, motioning with my chin to the table where Kwol stands behind Miss Dee. I strain my ears to hear the words as he asks the woman questions and then tells Miss Dee her replies.

"This is like an interview. They want to know your skills, and also your name, and the name of your village. They gather this information so they can keep track of us, and also to please the SPLA. My brother, who is a soldier, told me the SPLA have been making it difficult for them to begin this Cooperative of theirs. The soldiers want some of the money we will be making to pay them for protecting the *khawajas* while we are there."

Two of the women have left. Now there are four of us in line.

"Sister, what are your skills?" the young girl asks me.

"I can cook and clean, wash clothes, pound grain, build *tukals*." She and the older woman in front of her laugh at my answer.

"Ay, we can all do this! You must think of something better to tell them, or they will not take you, my friend."

"Will there be cattle?" I ask this even though I fear they may laugh at me once again.

The young girl shakes her head. "No cattle, though that would be good." She motions to herself and the older woman with a sway of her index finger. "Both of us here worked in the cattle camps after our moon ceremonies. We know what it is like to milk and care for the cows." The older woman in front of her clucks her tongue in agreement. I do not tell them that I also worked in the cattle camps before my marriage to Tobias. For a moment all three of us are silent. Perhaps we all are remembering in secret fondness our days of working in the cattle camps, sleeping and roaming with the cows, drinking the milk for our strength.

My feet feel strange, too light. Again I rock them back and forth against the floor, heel to toe, hoping no one might notice this. I think of Auntie Nyakiir and the others back at the *tukal,* waking up and wondering where I am. She will be angry with my absence, and one of her daughters will have to stay with the children until I return, which means she will receive less help at the market with making and selling the *marissa.*

It is now the young girl's turn. The other women have left through the big door. I step in close so I may listen. Kwol asks her, "Name and home village?"

"Abiong Majak. I was born in Wun Rok." My heart jumps. I want to tell her that is very near my village of Akoch, that we are neighbours, but I know I must keep quiet. It makes sense now — there is something in the girl's manner and the rapid way she speaks that had made her seem familiar to me.

"What are your skills?" Kwol asks her. Miss Dee continues to write on the piece of paper.

"I can sew, I learned as a child from my grandmother. Also, I can harvest; we had our own plot when I was very young. And, I can fish." Kwol speaks to Miss Dee, who replies to him while nodding her head at Abiong Majak, and smiling.

Kwol turns to Abiong. "Two of these skills will work; we will be growing crops on plots of land outside the village, and we will also have several sewing machines for making the school uniforms. Have you worked with one of these machines before?"

She stumbles on her reply. "I ... I have seen them, Brother, I have been near them."

"But have you worked with one?"

She looks to the floor. "No."

"No matter, you can still come for the harvesting. Miss Grace," he nods toward the other white woman sitting beside Miss Dee, "will be training those who will work with the sewing machines. Because the sewing machines that were donated from Canada are few, those who have already worked with one will be the first chosen for this task."

I think of Tazket, and how she must still, even now in this moment, be sitting in the tiny, dark sewing room at Saleh's house, stitching the clothing for all his many children. Many times after Adhar's birth I came to this room. Many times I sat on the floor with my back to the wall opposite her, Adhar nestled against my breast, lulled by the rhythm of the machine. I would watch her pump the creaky pedal with her foot, or thread the tiny hole of the needle with thin string, while both of us kept our ears open for Head Wife's steps. She was the only servant with whom I never spoke, though she is the one I went to when my mind threatened to drown my heart in sadness. I never understood Tazket; I did not know of her dialect or where in the north she came from. I assumed she still spoke the ancient tongue, and this was why I could not understand her while the other servants could. She never taught me how to sew. But if she had done this and had we been caught, one cannot know the cruel things Head Wife might have put upon us as punishment.

Kwol tells Abiong, "We will leave in two days. Be sure to bring with you your clothing and any necessary belongings. It is a one-day trek. We will stop to rest and eat along the way. The women here," he nods toward Miss Dee and Miss Grace, "will be driving their vehicle and will meet us there. There are men already there who have been restoring the village for some time. With the help of these businesses of yours, this village will come alive again." Kwol smiles at this. I can see he is proud of being a part of rebuilding the south in his small way, even as this war continues, and the men still fight in the north, and the raiders still threaten to strike us down in the nights.

"Which village is this we will be going to?" Abiong asks.

"It is called Akoch. It was destroyed years ago by the *murahaleen*. A rebel army group inhabited what was still left of it for some time, but now they have been defeated by the SPLA. It is free again, waiting for us."

I step forward without being asked and grasp the hard edge of the table with my fingers. My feet are now two birds, threatening to take flight out from under me completely. I touch Father's necklace to my throat and feel the cool shells in the hollow of my neck.

"Sister, are you all right?" Abiong's eyes set their concern into mine as she holds my elbow.

I nod my head. "Ay, it is only the heat." Miss Dee speaks quickly in English to Kwol, who departs and comes back with a glass of water. I take it from him and drink all of it before handing it back.

"Thank you." Miss Dee looks through me with her pale eyes as I stand straight again. I shuffle my feet forward in a small step so that I may feel them still holding me.

"I am okay, tell her," I say to Kwol. "And please, Brother, tell her I know how to use a sewing machine."

I could hear Nyikoc coming toward my cell; his familiar, quick steps echoed against the narrow stone walls of the tunnel. Today, those steps filled me with hope.

I lifted my hands from the hot, soapy water and dried them on my skirt before turning to face the door. Adhar was playing in the corner with the old cloth that Auntie Nyakiir had torn from her skirt so many years before. She had folded it so it looked somewhat like a small doll. She cradled it and spoke to it as if it were her own child. The cloth was no longer stiff with blood, for I had washed it many times in my attempt to release the memory of that day from the material. But the blue and white flowers had lost their original colours, now choked out with a faint wash of deep brown.

"Hello, Sister." Nyikoc flashed his large white smile at me.

When I first arrived to Saleh's, I had not known Nyikoc could smile. But in the past couple of years, Nyikoc had changed his expression much with me. I believe he had fallen in love with me, though he had not told me this. For why else would he risk his life to do this thing for me? Saleh he respected and feared, and I am certain he believed his Master when Saleh told Nyikoc that he was as a son to him. Nyikoc did not wish to anger Saleh, and he always tried to be a good servant by doing Saleh's bidding and following the ways of Islam. Nyikoc even believed he owned some of the cattle he cared for, which Saleh said he had "given" to him. This was non-sense — how could Nyikoc own these cattle which were Saleh's? I never tried to turn Nyikoc's mind to the truth of it, that Saleh only used him as his slave boy, and cared nothing for him. I knew Saleh would just as easily kill him or trade him off if Nyikoc were caught doing this thing for me. I had seen those flat brown eyes of Saleh's too closely, too many times. I found there was no guilt living there, only his belief that it was his right to do as he pleased.

Perhaps you think I was too selfish, *khawaja,* for putting Nyikoc in this danger, when I knew he was risking himself because of how his heart reached toward me. And perhaps I was selfish. But it was not for me only. The thought of staying here any longer, even the thought of going to sleep and waking up here again, one more day, in this cold, damp room, would sometimes make me pray for death. But then I would quickly force myself to stop these thoughts, for I had a child now who needed me. If I was using Nyikoc, it was for her as well as for me.

Adhar was a good girl. Sometimes she would help me wash the dishes, her small hands rubbing clumsily at the plates with the cloth. Then she would hold the still-dirty plates out to me, one by one, smiling proudly at her work, as I piled them up to be washed again. Sometimes she would help me hang the laundry on the line behind the house, holding the wet clothes high above her head so they would not touch the dirty ground, as the water dripped onto her face. This was her favourite thing to do; it meant she was out of the cell and able to feel the sun upon her skin. It pained me greatly to watch her play her made-up games in this tiny room, with no other children to play with. When I could see that Head Wife was not in the yard I would take Adhar with me when I went to fetch water from the well. We often had to pass Saleh's other children who were playing, and hear them mock us. Adhar looked at them with eyes big and curious, not yet understanding this dirty word they called her, *abida,* black slave. When we came back to the cell from hanging up the clothes or getting the water from the well, she would always cry, but not because of what the other children said. She would cry because she missed the feel of the sun on her face and of the earth under her feet.

I tried to never let her out of my sight, for I knew the danger was too great with the cold, watchful eye of Head Wife always near. She would surely steal Adhar away at any given chance, perhaps even give her to another family to be made into a young slave or a concubine. Head Wife did not like the looks of pretty Adhar, who wore Saleh's fine nose and lips. And so I kept her hidden away from Head Wife as much as I could. I knew that as Adhar became older, the danger would grow greater, and Head Wife would do whatever she could to hide this insult from neighbours and friends who came visiting.

Nyikoc continued to smile at me. I was trying to keep this rushing storm inside of me, but I was afraid I could not. I wrung the bottom of my skirt until my fingers ached. Adhar ran to him, lifting her arms up to him so he would hold her. She was quite attached to Nyikoc, as he was the most frequent visitor we received. We were the only two slaves at Saleh's, though I believe Nyikoc did not think of himself this way. The others were servants from the north who were paid a small sum of money every month for their work.

Nyikoc lifted Adhar up into the air and swung her around while she screamed and laughed. Her new skirt billowed in her flight. Every so often, Saleh would come by and bring old clothes for Adhar that his other children had outgrown. He called her "*Malaika*," which means "angel" in Arabic. I did not tell him my secret name for her, Adhar, after my beloved grandmother. I did not want him to have this name on his lips. And I did not like his affections for her, nor hers for him. But how could I resist these things he brought for her?

It was a great terror within me, this thought that Adhar would grow up to become a slave herself, never knowing freedom or her own people. I watched Adhar laugh as Nyikoc tickled her, and I turned away. Adhar was getting older, she would be three years soon. We needed to leave.

I leaned my back against the cool mud wall and stared at Nyikoc, willing him to say the words I needed to hear, wanting to grab him and shake him, force them from his smiling, laughing mouth. Why did he wait like this? Always I had to be so careful, to be certain my plan would work. I could never fully trust anyone, not even Nyikoc. I could not anger him, for I saw how his loyalty lay deep for his Master. I had to pretend this favour was not as important as life or death — but it was. My hands felt for the cracks in the wall.

I began pulling away chunks of dried mud, breaking them apart in between my fingers.

Nyikoc put Adhar back down. "This man at the market, he has just come back from the south. He has spoken to your father now."

I tried to swallow but could not. I forced myself to stay very still as my ears pounded with the sound of my heart, beating as though it wanted to escape my body altogether. Tears filled my eyes; I looked down so Nyikoc would not see.

He stepped closer. "This was his message to you: he said he is happy to know where you are now, and that you are alive. He cannot come for you just now as he has no *dinars*. He has been living off what he can harvest from the land and the kindnesses of neighbours all these years. He says sometimes the big steel birds drop bags of food on the ground near where he lives, and these can sometimes last him for a whole season. But, God willing, he will come to you someday soon. He is still in your village of Akoch. He has not left."

I tried to see in my mind Father harvesting a small plot of sorghum around our half-burned hut. How would he know how to do this woman's work? Was he there all alone, with no women to do this for him? It was difficult to imagine my father, a chief, sinking down to this for his survival. I tried to see him bent over the earth, his shoulder muscles straining with the work of the hoe, but the picture would not come. I knew of the planes that dropped the food Nyikoc spoke of, for they had dropped these bags near our village when I was a girl, one season when the rains did not come. At first, we were all frightened; we thought the steel birds held the bombs from the north. Once the roaring sound of the planes retired to the other side of the sky, we were very surprised to find grain inside the heavy bags scattered over the ground.

"And my son Khajami? And my mother? My husband Tobias? What of them?" I knew Nyikoc might not want to see me hunger for information of my husband, but I could hold back no longer. I searched Nyikoc's face as though it were a map that pointed the way toward freedom. But he looked down and away from me.

"There was no word of them in his message." My heart sank. How could Father have forgotten to tell me how they were? Would he not want to tell me that they were alive, or even let me know that they had died in the raid? But, all of them? Dead? It could not be. I kept hoping that Tobias, Father, and Khajami still lived in Akoch in our homestead, that they had rebuilt it after it had been burned. That they were still there, waiting for my return. Or planning to come for me, to take me back home.

Often I had thought back to that day when we arrived up north, all of us women and children thrown into the large hut, waiting to be bought. I could not find Mama amongst the others, no matter how hard I searched for her in the crowded space. And sometimes, the thought had crept into my mind late in the nights that if Tobias were alive, surely he would have come for me by now, after all this time. He was strong and powerful, and he understood things. Somehow, if he were still alive, he would have found me by now and brought me back home. I brushed these thoughts away. The crumbled mud fell from my hand onto the dirt floor.

Adhar was pulling on Nyikoc's pant leg; she wanted him to lift her up again. He did not seem to notice her. He still kept his eyes on the floor.

"Thank you," I said. Nyikoc met my eyes and smiled again.

"I will go to the market again in two weeks. Who knows, perhaps your father will have found money by then to pay Master Saleh so you may return to your home."

And so it was that every second Saturday I was unable to properly do my duties, I was even unable to eat, as I waited for Nyikoc to come back from the market. I found myself impatient with Adhar on these days, even punishing her for trying to leave the cell, as she tried to do more and more often. On these days I would not allow her to come outside with me to fetch water. For the brief time I was gone, I would tie her wrist to a hook on the wall with a piece of string so she could not follow me. She would cry the whole afternoon at this injustice, but it was as though I barely heard her as I waited for Nyikoc to arrive back with news. And every time, the moment he stepped into my cell with his serious look I knew there was not a message for me that day. In all my time at Saleh's, no message ever came telling me that Father was on his way for me.

I began to think that perhaps Nyikoc had lied to me, only telling me he had heard from Father to please me. Or, that he secretly did not want me to leave Saleh's and was not passing on the messages for this reason. Other days, the worst days, I would know in my heart that Father could never gather together enough *dinars* to free me, never enough to satisfy Saleh. Our cattle had been raided by the *murahaleen* on that day, and if what Nyikoc had said was true, now Father lived off what he grew on the land, and what was given to him. How could an old man like my father find work to make money now, as this war continued on? It was difficult to believe that a proud Dinka man such as my father would accept these survival gifts from anyone. But in a war, one's character changes much, *khawaja*. You change in ways that you yourself do not even notice. Often, you can only see these changes later, by looking at those around you. When your surprise at what they have become sinks down into your own body, you are then forced to realize how this war has also changed you.

It was as though this message from Father drove me closer to madness than ever I had been before. Sometimes I would not wash myself for many days. More than once, when I looked in the corner to check on Adhar, she was not there; she had wandered off without my noticing. In some of these times she had walked into the main kitchen where some of the other servants worked. It was understood by everyone whose child Adhar was — the servants did not look at or speak to her. I watched them as they pretended she was not there, even when she tried in her childish way to communicate with them. It was up to me to keep Adhar invisible, for if the servants were seen giving their attentions to her, they would get into trouble from Head Wife. These were the few times when I struck Adhar. She would cry terribly afterwards. How could I explain to her that I hurt her so she would not leave me?

After many months, when there was again no message from the man at the market, I became desperate. I could no longer stay like this, knowing Father was alive and not able to come for me. And not knowing what had happened to Khajami, Tobias, and Mama, whether or not they were still alive and on the same earth as I, was becoming too much to bear.

I began to plan my escape. I watched the two big stables that stood on the outside of the yard, where I had slept and worked in the first days after my arrival, before Head Wife brought me to my kitchen cell off the main house. One stable held the horses and the other the cattle. There were usually three or four guards with big guns strapped to their bodies surrounding the stables when they were filled with cattle and horses. When the cattle were taken out to graze, some of the horses and one guard remained behind. It was always the same man. I did not know his name, but I remembered too well how he smiled at me and patted his gun when I had first arrived four years earlier. He was tall with a thin face and his tendons stretched the skin of his long neck. He spat on the ground a lot. I never knew when or for how long the cattle would be taken out to graze, or when they would be coming back. I noticed that the others were gone, and that only this one guard remained, walking around the stables and the outer area of the yard slowly, watching everything with his small, mean eyes.

A high fence contained the yard. The only opening was near the stables. It was wide enough to let several cows pass through at one time. I saw that the guard no longer locked this gate in the nights as he had done when I first arrived. It was through here, near the stables, where I would have to leave.

Nyikoc was my only hope. But I had to be careful. I wondered sometimes at how he could not see my need to escape, rising so high within me I feared it might break me open, tumble out into words that would cause suspicion. Perhaps he did not see this because he did not want to.

"Ay, Nyikoc, that man who guards near the stables, what is his name?" I knew it was one of Nyikoc's duties to tend to the cattle and horses in the stables, so I knew he worked alóngside these men.

"Eh?" Nyikoc's eyes narrowed as he looked up at me from the floor where he sat playing tic tac toe with Adhar, using his finger to draw in the dust. I turned back toward the basin and tried to pour this desire to escape through my hands into the water, where it might drown so he could not see it.

"This man, his name. The one who guards the stables." Even now through my tiny window I could see him walking across the yard, his gun swaying against his back, laughing with one of the children running past him.

"This is Hassan." Nyikoc's voice was strange. I stayed with my back to him.

I heard Adhar telling him it was his turn to go. "You, now, you, you you."

"Why does he guard the place so?"

"He guards the yard from lions and other animals that may harm the cattle or horses. Also, he guards it from thieves. He is protecting us."

I continued to look out the tiny window above the basin. The glass was too thick and warped to see out of clearly. But I could see the guard's long shape, his slow walk, and that gun. And I did not need this window to know that beyond the stables and the edge of the yard were low rolling hills, without any bush for many miles. In the day, one could watch Adhar and me walking away for a long distance. It had to be done at night. This fear of lions had kept me a prisoner here too long. I knew I could not leave with Adhar as a newborn, walking through those hills, and later, through the bush, with the yellow-eyed ones looking upon us. Even now, her voice and young smell might attract them.

I was not allowed outside in the nights, but I could remember those first days after my arrival when I had been forced by Khalid to work in the stables among the cattle and the horses, and when I had slept outside on the ground. In the nights I would hear the men walking around talking to each other in their coarse language, taking turns keeping watch. How could I pass Hassan in the night without him noticing? Surely he slept, but when?

The walk back home would take at least a week or more with Adhar on my back. How could we survive without food and water, or shelter, for all this time?

I looked back at Adhar and Nyikoc, still playing. I could see he was letting her win. They were sitting on the edge of one of the blankets given to me by Tazket after Adhar was born. I could use this as a makeshift sling to wrap her in, and steal some food from the kitchen to wrap in it as well. I surprised myself with this easy thought of thievery; how far I had come from the girl I had been in my home village of Akoch.

"Adhar has won again!" Nyikoc clapped his hands and Adhar mimicked him, laughing, so very proud of her victory.

That night, Saleh came to my cell. It was late. I sat up quickly at the sound of his footsteps coming down the narrow tunnel toward me. Loud and heavy. After Adhar was born, Saleh left me alone for a long time, and I had hoped I was free of him. But just recently he had started coming to me in the nights again. The first time he returned to my cell was just one moon ago. I had asked him then, in my broken Arabic, "You mean to use me in front of the child?" He ignored this and took one of the blankets I was using as a pillow, unfolded it, and spread it out on the ground opposite where I had just been lying with Adhar. He pushed me onto the blanket and yanked up my skirt. I started to struggle at first, but soon knew it was useless. The bearing down of his bulk on to me was too much. He covered my mouth with his large hand, and his fingers practically blocked the breath from my nose. When Adhar cried out in her sleep, reaching for my body, he stopped his hard thrusting and, breathing heavily, waited for her to quiet down. She rolled over toward the wall and began to breathe steadily again, and then he finished.

Now the sound of those steps filled me with a fresh dread. I could not continue this. He would fill me with his seed again. How would I travel on my own to the south with two babies? Already one was nearly an impossible task. I scurried up to the basin and groped in the dark for a knife. I had washed one of the carving knives just that morning, and I knew it lay somewhere near the basin. I could not see, the moon was hidden this black night. My fingers touched the smooth edges of plates and cups as I searched for the feel of the sharp metal blade —

He was behind me. I felt his warm breath on my neck. The ends of my fingers rested on the cool blade of the knife. I did not breathe out and my heart worked against my ribs in its desire for air. He spun me around and pushed me onto the floor, not bothering with the blanket, not caring that his noise might wake his *Malaika*. I brought my knees up to block him and he punched me straight in the nose, hard. The pain was so great that for a few moments I did not know where I was. I felt the blood from my nose trickle down into the corners of my mouth as he began his hard moving inside of me, harder this time even than I remembered it being before. Did he know what I had been about to do? Could he read my mind, my actions at the basin? He pushed his anger into me with a great force.

I closed my eyes and called for the Women. I did not realize I had spoken my request for them out loud until he clamped his hand over my mouth to silence me. Did he understand my language? My fear at breaking this spell with the Women by having him hear and understand what I had said was too much. I called for them again in my mind, over and over, pleading for them to come to me.

They took too long, it seemed, but finally two of them appeared. Why only two? Where were the others? Always there had been thirteen of them sitting around a crackling fire, offering their solace with their clacking tongues and their songs, taking me away from the thing Saleh was doing to me. That very first time they came to me, when I was still a girl, I understood the words their song contained. It spoke of my future hardships, a difficult journey. But since they had been coming to me up north, I had not been able to understand the words in their songs. It was as if the language they used was an ancient one, beyond my ear's understanding. I had never questioned this, for their voices always lulled me to them, their chorus journeying me elsewhere.

But now I demanded words from them, words I could understand. These two Women stared at me, their eyes large with sorrow, but they did not speak, no matter how much I silently beseeched them to. I wanted them to tell me when I should leave. I asked them, again and again, but they did not answer. Their faces loomed. There was no fire burning between them, only the darkness behind them. Were they angry with me? Disappointed, perhaps, at my plans to leave, putting Adhar in danger in the wilds? This was the first time in all these years all of them had not come to me. No songs to warm me on this night, no presence of the entire circle to help me through. What did these two Women's faces in their sorrow foretell?

Saleh finished and pushed himself off me. I continued to lie there as his heavy steps echoed down the tunnel toward the main house. Adhar slept; I could hear her steady breath. Now the Women had left. How they came to me this time, wordless and without the circle, terrified and confused me. What did it mean? Was I losing them? I could not lose these Women. They were the reason I had continued on to this day.

I stood up and reached my hands toward the door in the dark. The house was too quiet. I stole down the narrow tunnel toward the main kitchen. I knew if I were caught I would be punished beyond measure. I had heard from Nyikoc of other slaves or servants caught stealing food in the night; they had their hands chopped off as punishment.

As I reached the door to the main kitchen, I stopped. The sound of a faint snoring floated toward me. How could I have forgotten? The cook slept off the kitchen, her room was just beside it. Her door was ajar. I continued past, sucking in my breath.

I could only see the outlines in the dark: the large table, the chopping block in the centre, the tall cooler near the door, the basin on its four skinny legs. This room was so much bigger than my cell, many times bigger. Nyikoc spent much of his days carting the dirty dishes from this room to my cell to be washed, and then carrying the cleaned ones back again in his large blue bucket. He also spent much of his time, when he was not out in the stables tending to the cattle and horses, or out being trained to graze the cattle, gathering the dirty clothes from around the house and bringing these to me in a large basket to be washed. And he was the one who picked the clothes off the line outside once they were dry, and brought them to me for ironing.

Nyikoc told me several times that I was to ask him when I needed to gather water from the well, or when the clothes were washed and needed hanging. He did not say why he wanted to take my outside time away from me, but he and I both knew that Head Wife liked me out of her sight. I never did ask him for these favours, for how could I give up this one comfort, of feeling the air and the sun?

In the centre of the chopping block sat a large bowl. I moved toward it, bent my face near it so I could see what it held. But before I saw it I smelled it: fruit. Oranges and papayas. I grabbed one of each and placed them in the cradle of my lifted skirt. Then I moved to the countertop beside the cooler. I opened the cupboard above it. Here, a loaf of bread. Beside it, cans of food which I could not open. Should I take the entire loaf? But this would make us very thirsty. And what about water? Adhar rarely suckled anymore, she had learned to drink water and milk out of a cup. I remembered then that we had crossed four rivers on our journey up north, and the men had stopped to drink from each of them, allowing their horses to drink as well. They did not allow us to drink, however, and tied together as we were, we could not run to the water easily. Some women had pushed forward toward the water anyway, pulling others with them. But they were pushed back by the men with slaps and punches. Some of us looked as if we would die of the heat before arriving.

I looked around in the dark to see if there was a container I could take and fill with water when we crossed the rivers. Then I remembered there were cups in my cell, washed just that morning. I placed the loaf of bread in my skirt. I could not see any other food on the countertop. I placed the rest of the papayas and oranges from the bowl in my skirt as well. The very smell of these fruits made my mouth water, for Adhar and I were only allowed leftovers from the kitchen at each day's end, usually just sorghum and bread, sometimes milk or cooked beans. I could not remember the last time I had eaten a piece of fruit. It had to have been many years ago now.

I began to move slowly and quietly back toward my cell, my gathered skirt heavy in my fists. I would try not to wake Adhar as I bundled her and the food in the blanket and tied it up around me. Luckily, she was light and small for her age.

Just then, a large papaya dropped out of my skirt and thumped onto the floor. The noise of it echoed in the narrow passageway. I stopped at the sound, just in front of the cook's door. I could not hear the snoring. The papaya rolled in its crooked path over to the corner of her door where it stopped. At this moment, she could open her eyes, turn her head, and look right at me, see me stealing away with my skirt held high, filled with food, showing my bare legs. If I moved now would she hear, would she wake up completely? Still I did not hear the snoring. I had to pick up this papaya, but I was afraid the other fruits would topple out as well. The thought came to me that I had become greedy and so would be caught before we even left the house, but I brushed that thought away as I might a spider's web. I had to think of leaving only.

I stood still. I did not even turn my head toward her door. The sweat from my scalp ran into my eyes and down my face, where it stung as it mixed with the blood from my nose, which I realized in that moment I had not even wiped away. Sweat and blood gathered together on my lips. I forced my breath to be so small that my head became a light thing on my neck. I tried to blink away the salt that crept into my eyes.

And then the sound of snoring, so faint. The bedsprings creaked. A pause. Then snoring again, this time deeper. I carefully gathered my skirt more tightly together and held it in one bunched fist as

I bent down to retrieve the papaya with the other hand. Quickly, I moved back to my cell.

In the entryway of my cell I almost hit Adhar with my knee. She stood there, swaying, as though she had been keeping a fatigued watch for me.

"Adhar? What are you doing awake?" I whispered.

She did not answer but continued to stare out the door. I realized then that she was sleepwalking, about to leave the cell and wander off down the tunnel on her own. She had begun sleepwalking soon after she had learned to walk. In the nights when I lay with her it was with my arms wrapped tightly around her small body. Each time thus far I had caught her as she tried to rise up.

I dropped the food into the basin and gently lifted her down onto the blanket, stroking her head back into the world of deep sleep.

I looked through the kitchen window. Darkness. I would never be able to see Hassan now, nor know if he was walking around the yard or sleeping outside the stables. I looked at Adhar, sunken down now into sleep, her face smooth and unmoving, her breaths steady. I did not know if this moonless night was a benefit for us or not.

I gathered up the thinner blanket and fashioned it into a large sling. As I tied it around me, I realized that it would become very hot during the days when we travelled. But I had no other choice; it was all I had. I hoped that we would come upon some kindly people on the road who might give us a lift on the back of their lorry. Once we reached a road. I did not know where to go, exactly. But I knew which way was south, and I was sure the town of El-Muglad was south of us as well, the town where Nyikoc went every second Saturday to see the market men. I would go there and look for this man who knew my father. He could help me. This thought strengthened me, pushed the fear a little bit back.

I stored the food in the sling, where I had fashioned a makeshift pouch, and also took one of the cups for the river water. Then I heaved Adhar gently up and carried her on my front, with her arms around my neck and her legs wrapped around my sides. She still slept. I would wait to wake her; when we were far from this place, I would put her properly on my back. It was very important that she did not wake now.

I walked quietly down the narrow passageway toward the kitchen, past the cook's bedroom and the sound of her snores. I would have to leave through the large metal door from the kitchen that led into the yard.

I reached the other side of the kitchen and stood before the door, put my hand on the cool metal, and pushed, lightly at first, fearful of the noise it would make. It did not budge. The few times I had come into the kitchen I noticed it was always open to the outside. The door that I was permitted to leave the house through in the daytime was on the other side of the passageway, closer to my cell, and I knew that it was locked every night; I had sometimes heard Hassan come and turn the key from the outside. What if they also locked this door from the outside every night? Stupidly, I had not even thought of this. I pushed on it again, hard. Nothing. I felt with my fingers for the latch and found a deadbolt. Slowly, slowly, I worked it across to the other side. It clunked and echoed in the dark. I stopped my breath; I did not hear the cook's snoring. But I could not stay motionless like this, Adhar was growing heavy in my one arm, and my heart was like a bird imprisoned for too long, flapping its wings against the bars of its cage in its desire for flight. The door creaked on its hinges as I pushed it open and stepped out into the cool night. Was the cook awake now? I did not close the door behind me but began walking straight across the yard toward the opening by the stables.

The moon's light fell across the well, the stables, the fence. She had come out from her hiding place behind the clouds now. To light my way? Or to shine on me and stop my escape? I did not see Hassan, I did not see anyone, and I did not turn my head to look behind me. The wide open passage and the world beyond it was all I could see, all I cared to know. I walked faster. My heart pounded at my throat.

As I walked past the stables, I glimpsed Hassan, sitting on the ground with his back against the nearest stable wall, his head rolled to the side, his gun cradled in his lap. Asleep.

I began to run.

The ground under my feet was fine dirt and sand. It was cool now, but I knew that with the heat of the day's sun upon it, the sand would cause my feet much pain. I did not own sandals, and Head Wife had given me none. On the trip up north, many of us with our bare feet had suffered from the hot sand that scorched our soles.

The walking was more difficult than I had imagined. As I had stared out at the low hills every day from my blurry window and from the well in the middle of the yard, I had seen myself and Adhar slowly becoming tiny insects on the horizon. But there was horizon after horizon; walking up these hills made me realize how heavy Adhar was becoming. But I could not stop, not now. I needed to reach bush to hide in, for Saleh's men would be out looking for us as day broke. Perhaps once I got to El-Muglad I could get some water and rest a bit before moving on. For now, I needed to get beyond these hills that reached forever. Hassan and the others must not wake up with the morning sun and look out to see us in the distance, escaping.

I walked for several hours, and finally the land levelled out. Small families of trees and low bushes began to gather. These would not be enough to hide behind, but they set my heart lighter all the same. As the sun's faint orange light began to bleed just above the edge of the world, the outline of a town glowed in the distance. I did not know for sure, but I thought it should be El-Muglad. I sat behind a few bushes to rest.

Adhar's head was slumped over my shoulder. Once we had made our way far enough past Hassan that I was sure he would not hear her, I had woken Adhar and placed her on my back, with the blanket tied to support her weight. She cried a bit, and asked many questions. She did not understand where we were or what we were doing. How could I tell her that someday she would understand that what Mama was doing was good for her? Her tears at leaving all she knew behind made my steps stronger, for I did not want Adhar to know only that life. Soon enough she fell back asleep.

I peeked at the food in my pouch. Should we eat some now? But it would be too long and we had no money. We must save our few things for the journey. We would eat the fruit first, since it would spoil. But the smell of the papaya in my nose was almost too much to bear. Without thinking further I bit down into the skin and peeled away a section of the fleshy inside with my teeth. The juice and the pulp in my mouth was a kind of pleasure I had forgotten. Sweet and yellow, it sang around my tongue and gums and I could feel in the free air of the morning sun the tears falling down my cheeks and I did not brush them away. I had forgotten what this happiness was like. I took three more bites, then forced myself to stow the rest of the papaya away with the other food, for I wanted Adhar to share in this taste with me, I wanted her to take her first bite of fruit and laugh at its sweetness in her mouth and in her belly.

I looked toward the town again. The small outlines of the buildings were becoming clearer against the waking morning. What if someone there knew Saleh, and recognized me as his slave? Someone who had perhaps seen me hanging clothes in the yard or fetching water from the well when they came on their visits? My skin was not so different from the skin of many of these Arabs I saw. But my clothing, this skirt and top I had worn for four years, ripped and stained, and my speech, my broken Arabic, all this would tell people I was not from this place. But I needed to ask directions, I needed to know which road to take. There were two roads to follow back home to Akoch, this I knew. The faster road, the road we had taken up north, had four rivers crossing it, and many people upon it. The other one, which took longer, also had four rivers in its path. But I did not think we would have the time to take the longer road, with our little food and no water, even if it meant fewer eyes upon us.

I thought again of the man in the market Nyikoc had spoken with, the one who had spoken with my father. I did not know his name, but I was certain if I could find him he would help me. He would tell me which way was home. Perhaps he would give me directions in exchange for a piece of fruit.

I shifted Adhar to my front and cradled her against my breast as I lay down on the ground beside the bush, not bothering to unwrap the blanket. I was so tired. I would just rest a bit before moving toward the town.

When I awoke, the sun was halfway to its fullest height above us. There was the sound of voices, men's voices. I stayed down where I had been lying for some time before finally leaning up to peek through the scraggly bush. Not too far away was a road that looked as though it could lead us into the town. Two men stood on the road, each holding a horse by the reins. They talked to each other in Arabic, too fast for me to understand. We had somehow walked near this road in the night. We must be on the path Nyikoc took every second Saturday. Perhaps we were unknowingly following his footsteps.

My mouth was dry; I needed water. I felt Adhar's head, still nestled against me. Her forehead was too warm. The sun had beat down on it all the morning. I grew worried that she still slept; I did not want her to become sick from the heat. I had not taken care to shelter her with the blanket before lying down.

The men continued on their way, in opposite directions. This blanket was too hot upon me and there was no shade to be found among these small bushes. I unwrapped it from my body and carefully laid Adhar on top of it. Then I set out our food before standing up to stretch. I could see some more people on the road coming this way, their bodies tiny against the town behind them. I shook Adhar.

"Adhar, wake up. It's time to move." She opened her eyes slowly. They were red and I could see the corners of her mouth were dry and white. She needed water soon. She was not accustomed to being outside in the heat for this long; she only knew of waking up in her cool cell in the mornings.

She began to cry, softly. I was worried the tears she shed would be stealing from her body the water she needed to continue on.

"Shush now. We are almost there. Climb on. There's a good

girl." I crouched down so Adhar could climb onto my back, and I fashioned the blanket again in a way that would support her and the food. I walked quickly to the road.

The people we passed greeted us in Arabic and I greeted them in return, hoping they would not hear any strangeness in my accent, but by their manner they seemed not to notice. The walk felt long; the road was flat and so had tricked me into thinking the town was nearer. By the time we reached the outskirts of El-Muglad, Adhar was again asleep, her head rolling upon my shoulder. I reached back and tried to shield her from the heat of the striking sun with a piece of the blanket.

As we entered the town there were people filling up the road. Was the market nearby? This must be the road leading into the centre of the town. It had been too long since I had been near this many people at one time. I walked more slowly than the others and looked around too much, showing myself as a foreigner to this place, I feared. I needed to take care not to be noticed. Several of the men who passed by sat high on their horses in their jellabas and turbans, and yet I was surprised at how many people I saw who looked like they came from the south. Dark skin like mine, and some had tribal scars on their cheeks and foreheads. But I did not see any Dinka markings. Certainly there would be someone here, another Dinka perhaps, who could help me.

The buildings along the side of the road were made of crumbling mud and cement, all in their many colours of grey and rust. Shopkeepers hung out of their doors, smoking *cigaras*. Some of the shops had words in Arabic written on them. I could tell by the smell of one shop we passed that it was a bakery, for the sweet scent of bread charged at my nose. The place beside it had shelves of glass bottles in its windows, and they looked to be filled with herbs and pills; this had to be a pharmacy. There were women wearing dark-coloured abayas that hid their faces and hair, carrying children and plastic bags of goods. Men gathered at the side of the road talking to one another, but not one of them looked at me. Where would we find water? I kept my eyes open for a well, but could not see one.

I felt that Adhar was awake now and looking around her. She did not make a sound; what a thing for her to see all these sights and different-looking people she did not know existed before this moment. On my back I could feel her fear at all the people around her.

As I was about to go toward one of the women to ask her if she could point me to the market, a tall young boy approached me. My heart leapt with joy at the sight of him, for he looked to be a Dinka, though he did not have the scars. Many of our young men were no longer practicing these rituals, however; usually the educated ones chose not to. He wore a white jellaba and skullcap, which is not our Dinka custom, but when he greeted me it was in both Arabic and Dinka. I guessed that he could see from the colour of my skin and the way my face lay that I was a Dinka.

"*Salam alaykom, Cheobak,* Sister. Would you like some fresh bread this morning?" He pointed toward the bakery. "You look to be hungry." I could not believe I was speaking to another Dinka in my own language after so many years, and so close to where I had been imprisoned. I did not know what to say to him at first. I had only spoken simple Dinka to Adhar these past few years.

Finally, I said, "Brother, could you help me? As you can see I have walked a long way, my daughter and I are tired, and we need some fresh water. Do you know where I can get some?" Speaking in my own language to another Dinka made my tongue feel dusty and sad.

"I can get you some water, Sister. Would you like to buy some bread, or a sweet for the girl? I help Mister Abbas bake the bread every morning." We had walked to the bakery while we were talking and were now standing before it. The smell of the bread was making Adhar cry.

"Mama, want some, want some!" She said this in Dinka. Her little fingers were pointing past me to the door. I shushed her, not wanting the men passing near us on their high horses in their turbans to hear her shouting in Dinka.

"Do you want to buy some bread for your girl?"

I was getting tired. "Brother, we do not have money. Please, if you could tell us where we can get water." I reached into the pouch of the blanket for the cup, which was under the food. The half-eaten papaya fell to the dusty ground. The boy picked it up and tried to dust it off before returning it to me, but bits of red earth clung to the flesh. The other fruits and the loaf of bread looked about to topple out of my pouch as well as I quickly tightened the blanket around me.

"Thank you."

"I will get you water Sister, no problem, *a pad a pay*. Wait here." He pushed the cup back toward me and went around to the side of the bakery. There was no shade anywhere. I leaned against the wall. It was warm; the sun struck at the paint that covered the cement. I moved away from it, put my hand to my head. I was sweating. Adhar still cried, but quietly.

The boy came back with two large cups full of water and handed them to us. Adhar grabbed hers greedily with both hands and drank, and I could feel the water from her cup spill on to my neck. I finished mine quickly and we handed them back.

"Thank you Brother, you are so kind."

"This is nothing, Sister. Where is it that you are travelling to?" His face was open; smooth, shining planes in the noonday sun. Here he reminded me of Nyikoc, of what Nyikoc would have been if he had not been captured in the forest that day, gathering food for his family's supper.

"Could you point me in the direction of the market?"

"My uncle is a vendor there! I can take you!" As we followed his quick steps around and past the many people on the dusty road, I could not believe my luck. Could his uncle be the man who knew my father? I had never imagined meeting another Dinka here. I wondered which clan he came from, as this is usually the first question we will ask one another upon meeting. But I did not know the ways of these Dinkas who had moved to the north. Perhaps their customs were different.

Soon we came to the market. It looked to be quite empty on this morning. There were only a few stalls set up, and not yet any buyers. Perhaps it was much busier on Saturdays, when Nyikoc came and there was certain to be more produce and goods to buy. Today was two days past Saturday, for it was only two days ago that Nyikoc had come to me with the look on his face that told me there was no message from the market man, again.

The boy turned to me. "Is there something you would like to trade?"

I was waiting for the boy to point me to his uncle, though of course I could not be certain this was the man who had spoken to my father. "I was looking for someone. A man." I realized then I did not even know what the man sold. I looked around at the stalls, at the few men sitting behind their wares. "Perhaps one of these men knows a boy, named Nyikoc. He is my friend, and he comes here on Saturdays sometimes. I have a message for this man from Nyikoc, but I do not know his name." The lie came easily to my lips. I did not want to tell this boy that I was escaping four years of slavery and needed to get home quickly, for what if he knew Saleh?

"I will ask my uncle. Wait here." I reminded myself to be careful. I watched this boy go over to a man sitting behind a wooden stall. I was surprised at his uncle's skin, so much lighter than this boy's. I stood in the middle of the empty market under the beating of the sun and watched the boy point at me. Again I was struck at how he resembled a happy, youthful Nyikoc. As they continued to talk I looked up at the sky. The sun had now reached its highest point. I walked over to one of the empty stalls and sat down against the boards, slipped Adhar from my back to my front and rocked her. She began to cry softly.

The boy returned to me. "My uncle knows who you speak of, but he tells me he is not here this day. He only comes on Saturdays. Perhaps you want to give the message to him?" He pointed at the light-skinned man who sat behind his stall. This man offered a small smile. I turned to the boy and shook my head. Already we were tired and thirsty. What would we do now?

"Perhaps you need a rest, before you continue on your way?"

The sun was too bright against the back of his head and I could not see the boy's face properly as he bent down over me. I shielded my eyes. "I need to know how to get to the village of Akoch in the south. Which way do I follow?"

He looked surprised. "Akoch? Ah, that is a long way." He seemed to think for a moment. Then, "I do not know myself. But I can get this information for you. Come to this place here," he motioned for me to follow him, "where you can rest and wait for me to return."

He led us to a spot behind the market. There was a large tree and a long wooden shack, and no people to be seen. Underneath the tree was a small piece of shade. He turned to me. "I will not be long." His bold, youthful smile set my heart a little bit at ease. But I was beginning to get anxious; we were keeping within the perimeters of this town too long. I feared too many eyes had already seen us.

I sat against the tree with Adhar in my lap and pulled out the half-eaten papaya. I put the fruit to her nose. She did not know what to think of it, as she had not come this close to a piece of fruit before. I tried to rub as much of the dirt away from the flesh as I could, and then lifted it to her mouth, encouraging her to take a bite. She took a small bite at first, then grabbed it from me with both hands and began eating the pulp and the skin together, sucking the juice from it noisily. I rested my head against the rough bark.

Too much time was passing. Where was the boy? Now that we were cured of our thirst and hunger, I wanted very badly to begin walking, to leave this place altogether. I knew Saleh's men would be out looking for us. Perhaps it would be better now to wait and leave in the dark of night? Maybe the boy would hear of a way we could go which would be hidden, a path beside the main road so we could travel unseen.

At one point I got up and walked to the shack. I thought perhaps we could hide in there until the boy returned, as the fear of Saleh's men looking for us was growing stronger within me. But the door to the shack was locked. It would not budge.

I did not think at this time to ask for the Women's help. I often thought afterwards of how this was my one mistake. Had I taken that time under the tree to ask for their help, I am certain they would have appeared and told me to leave, leave right then, and would have told me which way to go. Somehow, they would have sung to me my way toward freedom. But I stayed, I did not move away, trusting this boy whose name I did not even know, trusting him with our salvation. Even as my stomach twisted, urging me to leave, or hide, I stayed where I was. I wanted so badly to be certain I would be taking the proper road home. I knew our survival depended upon how quickly we travelled.

When the sun moved halfway between the top of the sky and the horizon, Adhar and I slept. I unfolded the blanket for us to lie upon, and I put the bread and fruit under it, by our feet. I did not dream, nor did the Women come to me in my sleep. Perhaps if I had a dream it might have foretold the horrible vision my eyes would be assaulted with upon my return to the waking world. For when I awoke, Khalid was there, sitting high on his horse, looking down upon me as though I were nothing better than a stray dog. The boy stood beside him. I watched as Khalid bent down to give the boy some coins. The boy looked at me once, then began counting his money as he walked away. To this day I do not know what that look meant; I did not see guilt or shame. Perhaps it was only survival that lay upon his calm face.

Khalid threw us onto the back of his horse roughly. Adhar began to cry loudly now, pointing at the blanket. She was upset that we were leaving the blanket behind, or perhaps it was the rest of the papayas that lay underneath that she cried for, having now tasted its sweetness. But I prayed he would not turn back. Were Khalid to find the fruit, there would be the proof of my thievery, and I would surely lose a hand to the machete for this crime. Already my future was uncertain; I knew my life lay under Head Wife's control now.

On the way back, the wind drew up red dust from the road to spray our faces and our bodies with, stinging our skin. I did not care. I sat like a dumb thing, Adhar limp in my arms, with the butt of Khalid's gun that was strapped onto his back jutting hard into my inner thigh. I knew I had made the most horrible mistake now, and I wondered if I would die. This would not be such a terrible thing, were it not for Adhar. But if my punishment meant taking her away, but keeping me alive, I truly did not know what I would do.

It took me some time to understand how it was Khalid had found me. My mind was too crowded with these other thoughts to understand it all on the short journey back to Saleh's, but later, I understood that the man in the market must have known Nyikoc was Saleh's slave, and one look at me would have told him I was also Saleh's slave, obviously escaped. With this information, the boy knew he could make some money, and so waited for Saleh's people to arrive to tell them where I was. In my desperation, I had blindly trusted someone who came from my people, and it cost me four more years of my life.

When we entered the yard, Khalid threw us down onto the ground from high on the horse, like a sack of *durra*. Luckily, Adhar held fast to me, even as I fell. Hassan wrapped his fist tightly around my upper arm and dragged us into the barn where he threw us into a horse stall, locking the door behind us with a heavy padlock. Now Adhar was really crying. What had I done to us?

We were perhaps locked in there for two days without any food or water. Perhaps it was longer. By the end of that time, Adhar's breaths had grown shallower and her cries had stopped completely. The sweat did not even come out of our skin anymore, our bodies were so badly in need of water. I lay there, slumped against the corner, knowing we would die; I only prayed that Adhar's death would be painless, that it would find her in her sleep.

Then there came the sound of the heavy lock opening, and Nyikoc stood before us with a cup and a tin pail filled with water. He set them down on the ground. I crawled to it, drinking greedily from the pail's edge. I dragged Adhar toward it from the corner where she was curled up, scooped the cup in to the pail, put it to her lips. She drank it slowly, as though her mouth and tongue had already forgotten how to guide the water down her throat. I think she was so close to death that if Nyikoc had not come, she would have been gone that night.

I looked up to where Nyikoc stood. His eyes were not the same eyes I had come to know, happy to see me, filled with something for me that perhaps lay beyond friendship. Now they were solemn, dead. He was angry with me, disappointed in what I had done. I had angered his Master. I knew Nyikoc falsely believed that if my father paid for me to go, Saleh would let me leave. He did not understand the truth of things; his mind had been turned by Saleh for all these years. He did not understand about freedom anymore, that we were slaves, that we were nothing better than animals here. Now I could see that Nyikoc had not seen my need for escape rushing out of my body, as I had feared. I had lost my one and only salvation in this place by angering Nyikoc.

"What will happen to us?" I did not know if Nyikoc would answer me, but I could not keep the words down.

He hardened his eyes. "Master Wife will come for you soon." Then he left the stall. The sound of the heavy lock echoing shut after him shuddered through my bones.

Head Wife came not long after Nyikoc left. It was dusk. She had a servant with her, one of the women from the kitchen. They opened the stall door and stood before us. She held a whip in her hand and the servant carried a machete. The sinking light of the sun crept in through the cracks in the wall and rested on the blade, burnishing it with a glowing orange. Head Wife stood before me where I sat in the centre of the stall, tall and covered head to toe in her black abaya. But her face, tightened in anger, was not covered; she let us see the wide flare of her pointy nose, her eyes black and alive with her fury. The faint hairs above her lip darkened as she drew her mouth into a straight, hard line. Her skin was the colour of sand.

I stayed sitting in the centre of the stall while she whipped me. I did not want the whip to go near Adhar, who crouched screaming in the corner as it bit down, lashing through my top, making long tears in the fabric. It did not seem like Head Wife would ever stop her whipping. Her anger came through her hands and travelled through the whip into my back, making bloody, deep welts that did not leave for months. Even now, the faint marks from these welts can still be seen on my skin. I yelped at each lash at first, and then bit down on my lip until it bled, thinking that if I was silent this might make her stop. But she did not stop. I knew that she was whipping me not only for escaping, but also for what her husband did to me in the nights. And also for this insult curled up in the corner of the stall, screaming.

By the time she finally finished it was hard for me to stay in this world. I made my mind hold on to Adhar's screams, a rope that could lead me back up to the surface.

Head Wife pulled my arm straight out from my body and pinned it to the ground with her foot. She grabbed the servant's machete.

"Did you steal the food from the kitchen, the fruit and the bread?" She was bent down now, her face close to mine. Her breath curled into my nostrils, her voice pierced the inside of my head. "Answer me! Did you?"

My words sounded thin and exhausted, clinging to life. "No, Master, no, upon Allah I did not do such a thing."

At this she lifted the machete high in the air and brought it down, hard, an inch from my curled fingers. The blade dug deep into the wooden floor. She pushed my chin up with the toe of her foot so I could look at her face.

"We will be taking your little girl then. Clearly you are not fit to be a proper mother, stealing her away in this heat without food and water." She nodded toward the servant who grabbed the screaming Adhar. I tried to move to grab Adhar but Head Wife fastened her foot on my neck and pressed down. She loosened the machete from the floor. She stared down at me, her eyes now hooded semi-moons.

"Did you not think that taking this ..." she pointed to Adhar, now trying desperately to break free of the servant's hold, *"child with you would not alert the others to your place, abida?"*

The truth of her words hit me, as I lay there struggling to find breath. Of course. And to think I had not considered this, in my narrow thoughts toward escape, in my desperation for freedom. Those who would have seen Adhar's light skin would have noticed she had been sired by a northerner. And then they would have seen me as nothing more than a concubine. To think that I had thought we were moving unseen — how great my need was that I did not consider these things. And that I had taken Adhar with me to the town to display in front of everyone's open eyes must have truly angered Head Wife, for I had shown to the others what her husband had done.

They left. The snap of the lock's jaws tore at my heart, and as my body found its breath again I crawled to the door and banged with my hands, scratched at the wood with my fingers, howled with whatever was left in me. Adhar's wails became quieter and quieter, until the sound of her voice left me altogether and I could hear nothing at all.

VIII

We walked for hours in the dark, Solomon and Riak and I. The air between us was thick with our fear. I became used to the sharp sears from the thorns, felt drops of blood on my shins and ankles, but my strides stayed long and urgent. Riak kept behind me, almost stepping on my heels.

We saw a clutch of huts as the light of the sun crept over the horizon. Perhaps they would have an NGO stationed there, with a radio, some food, ointment for my legs, perhaps even a vehicle to get us back to our compound. We needed water, too. Riak had been smart enough to remember to bring my Nalgene water bottle from the truck. He had zipped it into his backpack; by now it was only

169

about a quarter full. But we had made it; nobody had died. They hadn't caught us. I remember thinking this, especially.

I looked down at my legs and feet. There were zigzags of pink and red welts on my shins and ankles, drops of congealing blood on my sandals. I knew my legs needed medical attention right away; I remember thinking that I would need to book a flight to Nairobi as soon as we got back to the compound. It's almost funny now, that my main worry just then was that my legs would scar and look hideous whenever I wore shorts or a bikini.

We stood at the edge of the tiny village and looked around. There were several tents and two small huts. Several other structures looked to be crumbling. Decayed walls of huts without roofs, with brush grown up around. I was thirsty but I didn't dare take a drink from our bottle. I didn't want to waste any of our water until we knew for sure there was more.

I knew the Dinka woke up with the sun, especially the women, to begin their day-long chores. But I saw no women here. No single file line of women carrying *durra* on their heads, wrapped in tall, bulky sacks, perfectly balanced under their slow, swinging hips, singing their pretty songs under their breath. Only men; all of these people milling about at the break of dawn were men or boys. But no morning songs, no young boys singing about their cattle — I didn't even hear any birdsong. I wanted to ask Riak why all these tents were here, but I thought I should wait until he talked to someone and explained our situation. And then I realized that most of the men were wearing fatigues and carrying guns. Others wore ripped trousers and t-shirts that hung off their skinny chests. t-shirts that said "Coca Cola" or "I love California." Walking tall and proud in their flip-flops, with AK47s slung across their chests. Toes encased in dust, toenails like dirty scalloped seashells. One of the boys looked over at us and stared at me with his hard eyes.

Then some of the other soldiers saw us as well and shouted at each other, and at us. Their activity seemed to stop completely as they all stood and stared. Then a tall, husky man in fatigues with a shaggy beard began walking toward us. The dusty horizon behind him was birthing a bright circle of sun. His eyes were a brilliant white against his rough black skin. The AK47 slung over his shoulder banged softly against his hip as he ambled over to us. He was looking right at me, and at my bare legs, grinning.

Mr. Shaggy Beard and Riak started talking in Dinka. Mr. Shaggy Beard was acting cool — friendly, even — as he smiled and fingered the barrel of his gun. I didn't know what he and Riak were saying. I noticed Riak was gesturing with his hands less than usual. The boy's blood was still caked on his fingers and palms. Mr. Shaggy Beard was staring at Riak's hands while he talked, squinting.

I wondered then if they would think to ask me for my identity card. I instinctively reached into the side pocket of my shorts; I felt the dusty, rolled-up Ziploc bag full of panadols, malaria pills, my Swiss army knife, lip balm. The folded article with the photo. No identity card. And nothing to give for a bribe.

Mr. Shaggy Beard seemed to be watching me intently as I rooted around in my pocket. This was when it struck me that we were probably in trouble in an irreversible way. I had forgotten my identity card once when I left the compound soon after I first arrived, and Jim had gone nuts on me. Any SPLA soldiers could demand to know who you were and what you were doing in their country at any time, and you had to produce the card to prove your business there. I then whispered loudly to Riak, while Mr. Shaggy Beard stared at us, "Let's give them something for a bribe. Maybe they'll help us then."

That was when Riak made the painful, slow movement of turning his head to peer down at me through squinted, bloodshot eyes. His eyes were all at once a stranger's eyes, which told me, while blinking slowly, that I was stupid, that it was too late. I had never seen such a look on his face before — it was devoid of hope. His eyes made the white hot in the back of my head snake down to my belly. Then Mr. Shaggy Beard spoke up, his accented English strangely like the voice that came out of the radio in the mess hall, "We will take no bribes, Miss." His teeth gleamed in the sun's light as he laughed, chin tilted toward the morning sky.

They were holding all three of us prisoner in one of the huts with a roof, after much shouting from Mr. Shaggy Beard and pleading from Riak. Two young boys prodded us with the ends of their guns, corralling us into the hut.

Riak was shouting through the closed door in Dinka. He moved to the open window and leaned his torso out of it, began shouting again. The sinews in his back rippled through his T-shirt as he waved his long arms about.

I yelled at the back of his head, pulled on his sleeve. "What are they doing? What are they saying?" Riak continued to shout as he reached back with one hand and pushed me away. I felt Solomon's thick fingers around my forearm, gently pulling me back. He put his arm around my shoulder and tried to get me to sit down on the floor with him, but I pushed at him, frantic. "Solomon, what..."

"These are not our soldiers." Solomon spoke quietly but when I looked in his eyes they were full of animal fear. He took quick breaths and stared at Riak's back.

"What do you mean?"

"These are not the SPLA. They are rebels. They are against the SPLA. Against us." I turned back to Riak. He was still leaning out the open window. I had heard of one army rebel group quashed by the SPLA years ago. They weren't Dinka, but Nuer. They travelled on foot from town to town and forced the villagers to give them food and shelter before moving on. They wanted to lead the south, lead the war.

"So this abandoned village is their headquarters?"

"Yes, it looks to be like that. They may try to ransom us to the SPLA for demands for more weapons. The SPLA will not want this news of a westerner held hostage in their own territory to spread to the media." Jim had told me that the SPLA was outfitted with weapons and financial support from the West, that America had been keeping this war alive — keeping the south alive.

I took a breath, about to ask when he thought they might let us go, but Solomon put his hand up, shushing me. He leaned toward Riak, listening. His eyes searched Riak's back and the wall opposite, his ears pricked to the strange syllables I didn't understand. Then the conversation between Riak and whoever he was speaking to outside stopped. Riak drew his torso back into the hut and stood, unsteadily, in front of the open window.

I scrambled up to Riak and stood before him. Behind me there were noises. I turned to see a board being fitted across the lower part of the window with nimble, long fingers. Then the sound of pounding. They were closing off our only light.

Riak's face had lost what held it; his cheeks and eyes were slack. I wanted to shake him. "Riak, what?" My voice was louder than I intended. Almost a scream.

He didn't look at me, but stared past my shoulder at the boards being nailed over the window. "These men are from the boy's clan. The boy who died. Someone from his village has already come here to tell them what happened. They have been expecting two black men and a white woman. They must now do their duty, Sandra."

Riak didn't say all the words. He didn't say that they had to kill one of us.

We had probably been in the hut for about fifteen hours when I began to hear talking outside in low voices. If it hadn't been for the death of the boy, they could have just held us prisoner and waited for the international community to find out. That would have put pressure on the SPLA, which in turn would have met their demands for weapons. But now, who would live and who would die? Each of us stayed mute and alone against our own space of wall, with this question stuck in our throats.

I put my tongue to the roof of my mouth. It felt gluey. I looked over at Riak, at his bare hands. His bag had been confiscated by one of the young boys before they threw us in here. I needed water. I wanted to lick the wounds on my legs. The cuts were a mixture of caked dust and blood. I wanted to stop the stinging ache. But I didn't have enough moisture in my mouth.

The smell of blood bloated the damp, enclosed air. I focused in on Riak's hands again. The boy's blood had dried to a brownish colour, and it blended into the colour of Riak's skin. His white T-shirt was also streaked with it. In another context, I might have thought he was a painter. He sat with his back against the wall opposite me, beneath the closed-off window, his head in his folded arms, elbows propped on his bent knees. I knew he was listening to what the men outside were saying, but pretending not to; he didn't want to have to tell us. Hours ago I had stopped demanding he translate the words being spoken outside the door. After they boarded up the window, Riak had simply stopped talking. That Riak was terrified, when these were his people, was what scared me most of all.

The chill from the dirt floor seeped up my spine. I pulled my knees up to my chest and hugged them, rocking back and forth. Both of my sweaters were still in my hut, back at the compound.

I wanted to ask Riak if they were deciding which one of us to kill; the voices outside the door kept growing louder. Solomon had been driving, but all of us were in the truck. Likely as far as they were concerned, all three of us shared the guilt.

I looked over to where Solomon was lying on the floor, on his side with his knees drawn up to his chest. I wasn't sure if he was crying, but he had been moaning earlier. Just the other day he had been telling me how he sent his small wages home to his family every month.

I wondered if Jim had heard by now. I could see his face turning from sunburnt red to white, his eyes widening at the news. I pictured him standing out in the open, far away from the trees so he could get good reception, dialling number after number on his satellite phone, talking to head office in Nairobi, to the SPLA in Nairobi and Juba, the capital in the south, asking if they could help. Trying his damnedest to get us out of this situation before one of us, or all of us, got killed. It is the mandate of the SPLA to protect us, as long as we are bringing them aid. But sometimes things fall between the cracks. Accidents happen. Things spiral out of control.

Adut

2003, TURALEI, SOUTH SUDAN, IN THE MONTH OF NOVEMBER,

THE SEASON OF *ROOT*

∞∞∞∞∞∞∞∞∞∞∞∞∞∞∞∞∞∞∞∞∞∞∞∞∞∞

We walk. I carry the sack on my back, the one Father brought with him to Saleh's when you and he came to retrieve me. It is black and orange and has pockets in its front. It looks like it comes from America. Rith is wrapped in his sling on my front, and Adhar holds my hand as she tries to keep up, her tiny, bird-like fingers squeezing against my bones. She did not ask me this morning where it is that we travel to. Perhaps she has become accustomed to these journeys now, these departures from all she knows without warning.

As Adhar's grip slips in my hand, I wish inside of myself that we could have joined the group of women who left with Kwol this morning, for perhaps Abiong would have been there, and would have offered to carry Adhar on her shoulders. Or perhaps we would have been one of the lucky ones chosen to travel in the back of Miss Dee's lorry, especially when the *khawajas* saw how difficult it is to walk with these small children.

But we will arrive, of this I am certain. Perhaps we will have to rest under a tree on the way, and will not see Akoch until the light of tomorrow's day. And we will certainly arrive thirsty and hungry. But we will not have to hide in the reeds of the river and the bush during the day to escape the eyes of the *murahaleen,* as we did with my father on our way back, not so very long ago.

Inside of this sack is the plastic bottle filled with water that Father had brought with him to Saleh's. I never did ask him where he had found the things he brought with him. Thievery is not a thing we Dinka practice, especially a man like my father, a chief, who sat in his court under the big acacia tree when I was a child, and would decide on the punishment for those who thieved. As I told you before, *khawaja,* this war changes you. You do what you must. You become someone you did not, in your past life, imagine you could become.

After Auntie and the daughters set off to market this morning, I grabbed the sack I had hidden under Father's cot with our clothing already stowed away in it: Rith's jumper, the two adult-sized T-shirts I swaddle Rith in at nights, Adhar's and my skirts. We received these clothes from Auntie upon our arrival from up north. A group of Christian *khawajas* had come and handed out bags of clothing to people in the village just days before we arrived to Auntie Nyakiir's place. The clothes I had worn for the past eight years were torn and stained and thin enough to see through; I was so very happy when they showed me not one but two new skirts and tops for me to wear. And happy also to do away with the dress on Adhar's back, the one Saleh had given to her when it had become too small for his other daughter. I knew it was a waste, but days later, without telling anyone, I threw it in the cooking fire to burn away to ashes.

I put the rest of the cooked sorghum that I had made for the breakfast into Father's gourd, and then went to the borehole in the centre of town to fill the plastic bottle with water. The other women's eyes fell upon me in the queue as I filled the small bottle, while they stood there with their buckets and pails. As we walked back to the *tukal,* I glimpsed Abuk at the back of the line. She had her mad look upon her face, her eyes half-closed, her head jerking from side to side, looking for things the rest of us could not see. Perhaps this was the way she searched for her dead sons.

I wanted to avoid her crazy talk; I pretended I did not see her. I heard her loud cackle of laughter rise to the sky behind me and as I turned around I saw her pointing at me then, her mouth open in a wide circle, issuing forth her noisy cawing. I turned back and continued walking away.

Once back at the *tukals,* I shoved the gourd and the bottle of water into the sack with the clothes and set off. My heart was pounding. What if Achai had decided to come back to the *tukal* to rest that morning, as she sometimes did? Or what if Ringo saw me leave, with the children and this sack upon my back?

We came to the edge of the village with no prying questions landing upon us, and for this I was relieved. All the day there have been people scattered along this road, walking in both directions, young soldiers, women carrying baskets and babies, men with their whittled walking sticks. But thankfully I have seen no one I recognize.

If one of Auntie's customers saw me with my children travelling west, surely they would go straight to her shop to tell her. Auntie would guess I was going to Akoch. Would she send Achol after me? Or Abraham? I do not want to think of Auntie's anger; she has taken it upon herself to be my guardian since Father's death, and she means to be certain of my leaving with Ringo in just a few days. She has already bought the goat in the market for our leaving ceremony; when I left I saw him standing, tethered and fat, beside our other milkless goat in the garden by our hut. No, I cannot think of Auntie's anger now. How she will come back this evening to an empty hut, with no dinner prepared after their long day, and with all of us gone. Or how she will ask the neighbours if they know where I have gone, and they will tell her they have not seen me all the day. Or perhaps they will tell her I left in the morning, with an American bag upon my back.

I reach back and touch the front pockets of the knapsack. I cannot feel them through the thick fabric, but I know Father's necklace and feather are tucked in there. I will bury his precious possessions in his home. I will make peace with his spirit.

We come to the river Lol. There are two young boys who stand by the water beside their canoe. Neither of them wear clothing. The older one looks to be about ten years old. He approaches us.

"Mother, do you need a ride across?"

Indeed we do, but I have nothing to give these boys in return. I look at the water, which is being chopped up by a rising wind. I see several women crossing on their own, with their skirts hiked up, balancing their baskets on their heads with one hand, struggling against the current. These boys must have made some good business for themselves when the group of women led by Kwol crossed this morning. I wondered where Miss Dee and Miss Grace would have crossed in their lorry. I believe there is a bridge upstream for the purpose of these crossing vehicles, a bridge rebuilt not long ago. The women downstream have now given up on not getting their clothing wet; they hold their goods on their heads with both hands as they cross.

"Tell me, was there a group of women led by a tall young man who crossed here earlier this morning?"

The boy smiles. "Yes, Mother, and they had quite a time with their many bags of things. Some of them crossed on their own because it was taking too long to get everyone across in just one boat. The man, their leader, wanted them to make good time."

I continue to stare at the water. Its green wrinkles flash their winking thoughts to the sun. I sway a bit in the heat, thankful for the faint wind to blow my thoughts back into their right shape. For a memory has just come unbidden. Was this the place, this very spot here? Was it here that all of us women and children, tied in a line behind the horses, came to find the boys of our village that Father had sent out with the cattle weeks before?

"Miss." The boy speaks loudly, as though he believes I am deaf. Adhar leans her head against my leg, she is already tired from the walking.

"Ach, I do not have anything to give you for this journey across, Son." I look toward the women who now scramble up the opposite bank of the river, their clothing soaked through.

He smiles at me with all of his teeth, a wide smile that spreads across his small face. His eyes are lit up. "Miss, we take people across to get them to the other side, my brother and me." He points to the younger boy who is already getting the canoe into the water. "We accept what people will give. But if they have nothing," he shrugs, "we take them across anyway." He laughs. "My brother and I cut a *kwel* tree down and carved this boat ourselves. Our mother does not make enough for the fees to send us to the school, so we do this." He helps Adhar and me into the boat. "Someday, we will carve many boats, fine boats, and we will sell them. To fishermen."

I smile at his bold, young innocence. Fingers of light from the sun reach down and nestle in his hair.

I try to concentrate, put my mind firmly to the light in the boy's hair, his wide mouth with its many words, as he talks of his future plans. We start across the river. Adhar lays her head in my lap and listens to his stories. Rith's head rolls upon my shoulder in his watery sleep. How can this boy, who cannot even afford clothing, reach forward with his bright heart to a better future? But as I am thinking this the memory that is being launched by the river starts to take over. It is bulging at the edges, likening itself to one of my many nightmares. But unlike my nightmares, this is a too-clear memory of what happened on that day.

The water was this way, on that day. The sun beat upon us. The wrinkles in the water from the slight breeze winked at the sun then, too. I remember thinking this: how cruel the river was to wink, with all of us broken ones standing there, tethered. I wanted to drink in those cruel flashing ripples, quench the scorch in the soles of my feet, the scorch in my lungs from screaming at Khajami to go back home. And to drown my heart, its twisting sorrow. I wanted to walk into this water and drown. I wanted this water to end my life.

Instead I stood, tied at my wrists. The thick rope stopped up the main rush of blood, but slow drips from my wound kept leaking. I wished it would gush, pour out, take my life and stop the beats of my heart. I stared into the water with the others, tied and motionless, at this pause on our journey toward our new animal lives.

We watched the men get off their horses and drink, and then lead their horses to the water to drink as well. Some of the women rushed toward the water's edge, forcing the rest of us to lurch forward. But they were held back by the punches and kicks of the men. Were they wanting a drink of water only? Or did they too want this water to drown out their lives? I wonder that now as I gaze at this green surface and into the brown depths beneath, this whispering witness to that day.

Did the river also see when the boys of our village, the ones who had just gone through their rites of manhood, were brought out of the bush with their hands held behind their heads? Did it see the *murahaleen* on their high horses with their big guns? Did the river weep along with the mothers in our line when the *murahaleen* shot two of these boys from behind with no warning? Did the river drink up the tears of these wailing women who fell to its shore in their shrieking and grief at witnessing their young sons' executions?

The other boys, the ones who had remained alive by chance, were trussed up in ropes and flung onto the backs of the men's horses. Some of them had cried out at watching their brothers crumple to the ground. But so many of their faces remained as stones.

A few other *murahaleen* came out of the bush then, unheeding of the dead boys' bodies under their horses' hooves. The one in the lead carried a joyous smile on his face. He shouted in his strange Arabic, "Ay-yi!! We have found the cattle! So many! Over one hundred head, maybe two hundred!" The other men whooped and hollered at this news of their precious find.

I wonder if my father felt guilt at his decision to send those boys out. But *khawaja,* it is all a game of chance in this war. Who would have died and who would have lived, had they stayed behind with us? Only God knows this answer.

We reach the other side. The smaller brother gets out of the canoe and drags it up to the shore. Rith lifts up his head in a jerk, looks around, begins to wail. I shush him as we step out of the boat, and I thank the young boy. He stands to smile and wave at us, wishing us luck on our journey westward.

We walk a little ways to a large *kwel* tree with overhanging branches. Under it sit two women selling tea. One of them calls out.

"Sister! A cup of chai for your journey?"

I smile their way, yell back, "Ay, sorry, I have no *dinars* for this."

The older one laughs, waves her hand, beckons me. "Then come out of the sun with that screaming child, sit with us a bit, Sister."

I walk toward them and they make a space for me under the shade of the tree. I lean against the trunk and loosen the sling to allow Rith to suckle. Adhar leans into my arm and stares at the tin kettle, cracked cups, and the packets of tea laid out on the blanket. A fire burns nearby on which is set an iron grill to place the tea kettle. I take from the sack the plastic water bottle and give it to Adhar, who drinks from it greedily.

"Ay, that's enough now. Let's save some, love." I take the bottle from her and sip from it, wet the inside of my mouth, put it back in the sack.

The older woman's two eyebrows are raised up into a question. She has a plump face and dancing eyes, and she reminds me very much of Auntie Nyakiir before the raid. She motions to the sack. "You have received this from the Americans? Did they give this to you when they freed you from up north?" She jerks her chin toward Adhar and Rith. I almost tell her in that moment that yes, I was freed by a *khawaja*. But of course I cannot tell her how. It would shame my father in his grave. So I do not say anything. The beads of Father's necklace clack quietly together in the front pocket of the sack as I set it down so Adhar can lay her head on my lap.

Finally I say, "No, Mama, I escaped." At this she nods her head and clucks her tongue.

Some older men come by then and purchase cups of chai from her, talk to her about the recent rains. They talk too of the promise from the Sudanese People's Liberation Movement to build up the roads with the help of some money from foreigners. And they talk of the new foreigners in Akoch.

I lift my head. "How long ago did a group of women pass by this morning? Led by a young man?"

The older woman answers. "They were here not so long before you."

So we will not be so late after all. We can just rest a bit here before continuing on. Rith has finished feeding now and has fallen asleep again.

"Is it Akoch you are going to? To join them?" one of the elder men asks me. I look at him and see that he wears a necklace of beads, much like my father's. I wonder if he is a chief as well.

"Yes, I will join them in Akoch."

"This is good. My son is one of those who have been hired to help rebuild the *tukals* there. These women from Canada pay him honestly and on time. These are good *khawajas* to work for."

I nod my head and smile as I look down at his gnarled toes bunched up in his sandals. Something is happening that I cannot explain. Something inside of me is filling up, ever so slowly. A trickle of water, a simple stream, perhaps. Some of these cracks are growing shallower, closing in, as I sit here and talk amongst my people in this terrain so familiar. Their voices and the rhythms of their words are replenishing somewhat these old ruptures. But I think too of Auntie's face red with anger as she explains to Ringo that I have fled, and he must go back to the east and to his wives and children, alone.

As if reading my thoughts, the man asks, "Who accompanies you, daughter?"

"No one."

"Your husband is where?"

"My husband died in the war."

"Ay. Your father, then?"

"He died last week."

"Sorry." The man and the two women nod and look down at the ground.

"Ay, this war. It makes widows of all of us." The older woman pats my hand.

"My father was the chief of Akoch many years ago. Before it was destroyed." I do not know what in my body pushes me to speak this.

The man lifts his head to look at me. He says quietly, "I knew your father. He stayed on in his village after the village died. He stayed on for many years."

Immediately I regret saying anything. I do not want to bring shame to my father's name. For I know some people thought him to have gone mad after the raid, living alone in the village for so many years. I believe that when Father was able to retrieve us from up north, some of this madness which had been building in him through all his lonely years began to retreat from him. But I do not want to speak further, in case the question comes up of how it was he finally left.

This old man says to me, "He was a good chief. A good leader. He was respected by many. You should be proud." I nod and look away as the tears in my eyes threaten to spill down.

We arrive by nightfall. I have dragged Adhar along for the last couple of hours, forcing her to keep up. I did not want to have to sleep the night under a tree for fear the yellow-eyed ones might come upon us. Now she is exhausted and weepy.

I smell the ghosts of the day's cooking fires, now put to sleep until tomorrow. And I hear the women talking and laughing in their huts. I walk to the centre of the village, and look up at the blanket of stars spread out above me. Is this what they looked like, these tiny fires in the sky, the night I laid with my mother outside our hut, with her arm tucked under my neck, when I first met the Women? I turn around in a small circle and see that many more *tukals* have been built, and there is now a large compound off to the side, enclosed by a straw fence. In front of this is parked the women's lorry. This must be where the *khawajas* will stay.

Someone approaches in the dark. It is Kwol. "Sister Adut! We waited for you this morning." He does not sound pleased.

"I am sorry, Brother, I had to make the breakfast for my auntie and cousins before I left."

He clucks his tongue and shakes his head.

I look down to the ground and pretend to be shamed in front

of this boy, younger than me, for I know he has been asked by the *khawajas* to help lead us. Truthfully, my heart flaps in happiness at having arrived to my home, humming with some kind of life. I hide the small smile that plays on my lips.

"These *khawajas,* they respect time, and now so must we. They wrote down your name at the registration and when we called you this morning and you were not there, we waited for some time for you. Come, I will take you now to Miss Dee and Miss Grace."

We follow Kwol through the small opening in the grass fence and into the compound. There are three *tukals,* a large green building, and a latrine. Two long wooden tables sit in the centre of the yard, and beside them stands a canopy made from straw, which shelters pots and long wooden sticks for stirring. A white woman passes in front of us and smiles. I am not certain who she is because the darkness has now fallen completely, but it looks to be Miss Grace, from the day of the registration.

Kwol knocks on the door to the big building. There is a mesh screen with which to see through to the inside. The door squeaks on its hinges as it opens.

This looks to be a kitchen and an office together. There is a countertop piled with dishes, and a pot of rice and boiled chicken sit on a hotplate. The smell makes my mouth water and Adhar begins to whine.

Miss Dee sits at the large table in the centre of the room, with papers and a map spread out before her. She looks very tired. She looks to me and then smiles weakly at Adhar. At first I think that she is holding a writing pencil, but upon a second look I see it is a cigarette. The burning smell wafts our way. She puts it to her mouth and inhales, just like the Arab men who smoke their *cigaras,* or the elders who received the cigarettes from the soldiers passing through our village, so long ago now. Her eyes are half-closed as she looks up at Kwol with a question on her face, while the smoke builds a film between them. He speaks to her in English. She nods her head, then points to the food.

Kwol asks us to wait outside. He brings Adhar and me a bowl of rice and chicken each. We sit on the ground and gobble it down with our fingers. Though it is cold it tastes excellent, richly spiced. I want another bowl but know to not ask for this. Rith wakes up at the smell and grabs at the bowl with his hand. I put a few of the cooked grains in his mouth and he chews slowly, swallows them down. Kwol talks to the Kenyans in English until we have finished, and then he shows us to our hut.

Inside are three cots, and on one of them sits Abiong. She jumps up from her cot when she sees me. "Ah, Sister! How are you? How are you?" She shakes my hand. Kwol nods and leaves. "You made it! And with your little ones! What a journey! I was hoping you had not been stolen away! I asked Kwol if we could share the same hut."

The woman that Abiong was talking to in the queue on the day of the registration comes into the hut then. Abiong introduces her as her cousin, Neima. She points to Adhar and Rith. "And so who will care for these children while you work?"

I had not thought of this. I had assumed I could bring them to the lessons with me.

Abiong waves her hand as if to shoo away the thought. "Ay, never mind this! This will be discussed in the morning, when we meet with the *khawajas* for an orientation. Let us sleep now. It is late and we are all tired."

I do not know what an orientation is, but I am too tired to ask. As soon as we lie down, the sleep comes quickly in to take us.

"Hurry now, hurry, hurry!" Kwol hisses at me as I rush past the door of his *tukal* where he stands smacking his wrist with his index finger, as though he were wearing a watch, which he is not. I slip through the narrow opening of the tall grass fence into the *khawajas'* compound, dragging Adhar behind me by her wrist. I open the squeaking door of the main building and see Miss Grace standing before the other women who sit behind their sewing machines at the back of the room, behind the large table where Miss Dee can often be found with all of her papers spread out before her. Miss Grace turns around and looks at me sternly. In the first weeks, these *kha-wajas* always seemed to have a smile for all of us. Now they are no longer so ready with their smiles. The hot sun has set upon them, bringing out their impatience. At first Miss Grace was forgiving if any of us were late. Now she does not bother to hide her displeasure.

I sit at my machine and hand over a sleeping Rith to Adhar. She lays him down in the corner to play with the things Miss Grace gave to her on our first day here. *Grace* gave her these things. She has asked us to not call her *Miss,* as Kwol still insists upon doing.

Adhar had not seen such playthings as these before. When she finally understood these things were hers to use, she stared at Grace with wide, unbelieving eyes. There is a doll with long red hair and white skin, several books with big and colourful pictures in them, a wooden car with wheels that turn, and a long stick with a wheel attached to the end; it flies around in a fast circle if you blow on it. There are also many interlocking blocks of different colours, a tin can filled with a bright pink soft clay, and even a small blue blanket for the red-haired doll. The blanket is Adhar's favourite.

When Rith sleeps and Adhar does not have to walk him or play with him, she is happy to play in the corner by herself, surrounded by all her new toys. Other times she walks through the village with Rith swaddled in the doll's blanket, too small for his growing body. Other women have brought their children with them as well; Dee told us that morning at the orientation that they want to start a school here in Akoch so these children, *girls included,* she emphasized loudly, could become educated. My heart swelled with joy at the thought of Adhar receiving her schooling. She would perhaps be able to take care of me in my old age. I did not want my hopes to soar too high with this thought however, and so I tried to tuck it behind my other thoughts.

On our first day sitting down at the machines, I feared Miss Grace would see that I did not know how to sew. There were eight of us in the sewing group, and all of the others had experience with these machines. I only knew of what I had seen Tazket do, as I sat across from her on the floor of her small room, my back against the mud wall opposite, on those days when I felt I might crumble altogether. Many times I watched as Tazket slipped the fine piece of thread between her thin, wrinkled lips to wet it with the end of her tongue before poking it through the tiny hole of the long needle. I saw the action she made with her dry, brown feet bunched into her worn sandals. They pushed at the pedal again and again and this would make the needle dive into the cloth faster and faster. She would pull the garment toward her with her curled hands, steering the needle along its straight line down the cloth.

I could see in Grace's eyes soon enough that indeed she knew I had not used the big, clunky sewing machine before, but she was patient with me. On the first day, Grace explained to us with a mixture of her few words of Dinka and Arabic that we would be making uniforms for the newly built school in the nearby town of Wau. This surprised me; many of our schools had been destroyed in the war. I did not know whether to think of this new school as a sign of hope, or foolishness. Grace told us that Dee had spoken to the headmaster and he had agreed to hire us to do this. She told us we would all be receiving fifty thousand *dinars* for our work. I had never received any money for doing work before, but again I did not want this promise to raise my hopes up. And yet, I had found myself seeing in my mind the walk to the nearby market of Abin Dow to buy a new dress for Adhar, new pants for Rith. Perhaps even a new dress for myself.

The uniforms for the boys and girls are made from dark blue cloth, the colour of the sky in the distance before a rain. We are learning to stitch together the garments for the children in folds and pockets, perfect angles and corners. We must make many different sizes of these uniforms, for it is a big school with many students attending. Behind where Grace's sewing machine sits, there are two long pictures hung with tacks. They show the dotted outline of the boy's uniform and the girl's uniform, in all their separate pieces that are to come together.

Three other women and myself have been given the duty of sewing the girl's uniforms. The one I work on now is the size of a girl who would have been around my age when my moon blood first came to me. As I slip the cloth under the cool, silver foot and press down on the pedal, trying to follow the line the way it is shown on the wall behind Grace's table, I think of that night I first saw the Women. I wonder if the girl who wears this uniform will have received her womanhood rite yet, and if she will already have a husband who has spoken for her. Will her father allow her to go away to continue her education elsewhere, unsupervised, as I have heard some do now? Or does she come home after the school day to pound the grain for supper, cook for her family, and prepare to be a wife? Does she know that her schooling will stop once her marriage begins?

I am grateful to be able to spend my days in this cool room, not outside hunched under the hot sun and the demands of the heat, where Abiong and the others sow their large field of sorghum. Abiong comes back to the hut in the evenings and asks her cousin Neima to rub her neck. Sometimes Neima refuses, complaining of her own sore neck from pounding the grain in the kitchen, where she works. Adhar tries with her small hands to rub out Abiong's pain when Neima refuses.

Miss Dee sometimes joins the women in the field, picking up the long working hoe herself. When Abiong first told me of this I was shocked, for we have not seen a white person work like this. Only behind the windshields of their vehicles, or speaking under the shade of a tree is where we have seen these *khawajas,* using their words as their work. It does not seem right, says Neima, to see this white woman out there working and sweating. Is she not educated? Is she not showing herself to be lower than she is? We do not understand these white ones.

We have seen less and less of Kwol in this room lately, as he runs between Dee and Grace to translate for them, along with taking care of his other duties, such as making certain the men are progressing with building the *tukals*. I can see in his eyes, red with his fatigue, that he is already being worn down by this job. In Kwol's absence Grace has begun to use big movements with her arms and large expressions on her face to show us what she means for us to do. Otherwise, if we do not understand even then what it is she says, she has us stand around her in a tight circle as she displays on her own sewing machine at the front of the room what we should do.

The screen door creaks open and Dee appears before us. Her face is covered in a thin veil of sweat, and the skin on her arms is dusted with a light red from the dirt in the field. In her hand she carries the camera, a small, black box with a circle that comes out from it. On the other side of it is a square that allows you to see yourself after your picture has been taken, like a small, still mirror. Abiong told me that Dee often spends her time walking round the village taking pictures of everything, when she is not with them in the field or working across from us at the table, surrounded by her papers. The other day she took the picture of Abiong and the others in the field and then showed it to them afterwards in the still mirror. Abiong said the girls howled and laughed, for they could not believe this was how they looked. The next day many of them returned to the field with their hair plaited and their clothes washed.

Dee and Grace speak to each other rapidly in English, and then Grace motions for us to follow her outside. She arranges us under the large tree, in two rows of four. Grace kneels before us, the knee of her long pants digging into the dirt. Dee stands away facing us, raises up the camera box, and then says something in English. There is one small clicking sound. She looks at something on it, and then holds up the camera box again, smiles wide at us, in her way of trying to make all of us to smile. Some of the women laugh at her way of smiling to us and then the clicking sound makes itself heard again. She turns the camera over and looks at it, then walks toward us.

She holds the small box out to us and we crowd around it. Caught in the small square mirror, all of us still as trees, as though trapped inside the moment just before. Some of the women are laughing, others are smiling. My face is closed behind a straight mouth, serious. The plaits of my hair are pulled back tight and there is a shine coming off of my forehead. It surprises me to see that I no longer look like the girl who married Tobias, for this is how I still think of myself. Here in this small frame I see that, indeed, this life I have lived has shown itself on the outside too. For I do not see any joy in my body here as I stand beneath the overhanging leaves with my shoulders drawn together, as though to hide away inside of myself.

Just as we are about to gather back inside the sewing room, the sound for lunch clangs at our ears. Neima hits with the short steel rod at the inside of the metal triangle, which hangs from the main building. At this now-familiar sound, all of us stop our work to go to the middle of the *khawajas'* compound, where there is a long table with pots of cooked sorghum or rice, beans, and sometimes vegetables. All of this food comes to us in bags and tins from the plane that lands just outside our village every two weeks.

I scoop some cooked beans and mushy sorghum in two bowls and then go to sit under the acacia tree near the main building. Adhar runs to me with Rith in her arms. I put as much as will fit into the bowls, for I know we are only allowed one serving each meal. Nevertheless, the three meals each day is more than Adhar has ever eaten before. I am excited to see her already growing fatter. Soon Abiong comes to join us. As usual, she looks very tired. She does not say anything, but begins to gobble down her meal with her fingers.

"Is this the sorghum you have grown for us?" I know this is not true, but want to set my tired friend in a good mood.

She barely smiles. "No, it will be a time before our crop grows. Then it will be sold in the market. And then we will be paid for our labours."

I already knew this, for Abiong has told Neima and myself this several times. Abiong keeps her thoughts of the *dinars* she will be receiving close, to help her through her hot days in the field.

Abiong looks across the compound toward Neima, who is bringing to the table another large, steaming pot of beans from the lean-to where the women cook the food. She shakes her head. "How I wish for Neima's job. At least she can sneak some food she prepares into her mouth when no one is looking! Ay, she wishes to grow fat for her future husband!"

I immediately think of my time at Saleh's, when I snuck the food from the unwashed plates into my mouth, standing before the basin in the tiny cell, with my ears open for anyone coming near. I push this out of my mind at the sound of Abiong's throaty laugh. We have heard the many stories of Neima's childhood love, and his promise to her before her arrival here of his coming for her. She told us many times that she has been trying to fatten herself up, to make herself desirable as his wife. She too lost her first husband in the war. Now she seems very eager to marry this man, whom her father would not let her marry when she was a young girl. Before she had the chance to sire children from the husband her father had chosen for her, her husband died. Now with her father also gone in the war, she says, she is free to marry this man she has loved since she was young.

"Look at her rump, how it grows!" I look toward Neima, bent over the fire just outside the lean-to, stirring the sorghum in the large pot, and I see it is true. She has grown wider since she began her work as one of the cooks. Her hips begin to stretch the fabric of her skirt. "I will not listen to her complain of her job anymore! She widens for her husband; he will not stop smiling when he comes for her!" We laugh together and even Adhar laughs loudly with us, though I hope she does not understand our meaning behind these words.

Here I think of Ringo, and I try to see myself sitting in one of Ringo's huts in his compound, sewing clothes for his neighbours in his village, and being paid for it, but the picture will not come. I do not think Ringo would allow this, as he would not want his wife to make money while he does not. It has been three weeks now since my arrival to Akoch and there has been no sign of Auntie Nyakiir, kicking up dust behind her as she comes for me down the narrow road, a deep frown carved in her face, to scold me and tell me I must leave this place to go to the east to join Ringo and his other wives. Kwol walks rapidly toward us and for a moment I fear he comes to rebuke us for laughing too loudly.

He stops under the shade of the leaves. "Adut, there is a man here to see you."

The food immediately dries in my throat. I stop chewing and try to swallow it down.

"He is just outside." Kwol points to the narrow opening in the tall grass fence that leads outside to the *tukals* and the rest of the growing village. I continue to sit, trying to swallow the beans down my throat. Kwol's eyes grow impatient as I look at him, unmoving.

Abiong nudges my shoulder with her elbow. "Will you make your visitor wait in the sun, Sister?"

Abiong takes the bowl from my hand. I raise myself up with the help of the acacia tree, and wipe the dirt from my skirt. I begin to walk toward the opening in the fence, and as I feel Kwol's and Abiong's eyes upon my back, Ringo comes into view, where he stands tall and rigid just on the other side of the fence, waiting for me.

Not long after they took Adhar, Nyikoc came for me. The sound of the bars releasing from the jaws of the padlock was a dim, distant noise in my ears, as I lay in the centre of the stall curled into myself, knees to my chest, my hands covering my face. Soon I became aware that someone was standing over me. I did not care who it might be; it could have even been the servant returned with the machete, ordered by Head Wife to do away with me, to slice open my heart, like the sacrifice of a goat, as they would no longer need me now that they had gotten the child.

Nyikoc's voice was soft, quiet, as though he were talking to a cow about to give birth. "Adut. It is time to go back to your room now."

I did not care to hear these words. Could he not do me the kindness now of ending my life? I wished in my heart he carried with him the machete for this purpose. I stayed still where I was and I willed silently in my mind that he should leave, so that I could continue this sleep inside of myself, this pushing farther away into the darkness.

But Nyikoc stood there for a very long time. I had begun to think perhaps he had left without closing the door. Then I felt his long hands reach under me, cradling my neck and my knees before lifting me up and into his arms in one swift motion. The surprising strength of him carried me out of the stall and across the yard.

I kept my eyes shut but could smell the closed damp of my cell as we entered through the narrow doorway, could hear the ghosts of the slaves that were there before me whispering their secrets. I felt their happiness at my failure surround me like a veil, closing me off and away from the world. I understood now that they too had tried what I had tried. And they too had failed.

Nyikoc set me down gently on the blanket. The welts throbbed. I curled up into myself again with my face toward the wall, staying silent.

"Sleep well. I will return in the morning." Nyikoc's voice was unsteady and so quiet that if we had not been covered over with silence, I might not have heard him at all.

His footsteps made their quick, light sounds against the narrow tunnel as he walked away.

The next morning I awoke to the sounds of hammering. I lifted my head and saw the figure of Nyikoc just outside my door. I saw the thin sinew in his upper arm move with each strike of the mallet against the outside wall.

I got up and slowly walked toward him. I saw then that he was attaching hinges to the doorframe with nails. Against the wall beside him leaned a thick wooden door.

He stopped his pounding and looked at me. A trickle of sweat was curving its way from his forehead down to his lower jaw. "Head Wife has asked me to do this. So that you will not escape again."

He resumed his work, and the noise of the pounding reached through me, dulling my heartbeat. I walked back to the blanket, lay down upon it, turned to the wall again. I covered my ears with my hands but the pounding continued to press down on the beating of my heart.

When he was finally finished, Nyikoc entered my cell. I could feel his eyes looking down upon me. He spoke as though to an injured animal. "This door will be locked every night now. In case you again decide to leave us."

I could feel him sit himself down on the edge of the blanket then, as he continued to talk to my back. "Adut. Saleh is a good master, better than most. He ordered for your life to be spared. I am certain you came to this decision of leaving in a most hasty way. Perhaps ... you were not thinking clearly."

I knew in this moment that Nyikoc was trying to let me find my way out. He wanted there to be some excuse for my behaviour in order that his own mind be set at ease. I also wondered here if he was waiting for me to apologize to him for putting him in danger, for mentioning his name to the man in the market. Likely the boy did not bother to tell Khalid Nyikoc's name, however, bent as he was only on receiving money for his information. If he had, Nyikoc would have been punished by now also. But I could not apologize. Nyikoc sighed loudly in response to my silence, and his voice became hurried.

"You will have to arise soon, Adut. I will come to you with the dishes and the clothes for washing today. The cooks will want you to pound the *durra* for the dinner this evening as well."

It did not surprise me that I would be given more chores now, the difficult ones that the others did not want to do, to add to my punishment. The welts on my back throbbed with each slow shush of my heart. I tried to will away the pain, for I did not want to think, or remember. I did not want to be brought back into this world again, with Nyikoc and the others, and this damp cell where I had to do my chores from morning to night. And now I was without Adhar. I could not.

I heard Nyikoc get up off the blanket and leave down the corridor. Later, I heard him return; I heard him piling the dishes into the basin and heaping the dirty clothes in the corner with a soft *whump*. These chores waited for me as I continued to lie curled into myself with my face to the wall. I could feel Nyikoc's irritation grow each time he came into my cell and saw me in this same position.

As the cracks in the wall began to cast shadows from the late afternoon light, different-sounding steps came down the corridor toward me, steps I had not heard before. I recognized the cook's voice as she yelled at me from the doorway. Her words fired around the small room, snapping against the crumbling walls.

"*Abida!* Get up now, you lazy *sharmuta!* We need the *durra* to be pounded, these dishes must be washed for the dinner, what are you doing lying there? We give you food and shelter and you just lie there? Get up now! Or I will call Master Wife to come to you with another punishment!"

I did not move. I only breathed. Let her come, I thought. Let her come to take my life this time. She took a few quick steps toward where I lay and kicked me in the middle of my back with the heel of her sandal, one strong, swift kick. My body jerked forward and the welt she struck cried out raw and bloody to my insides. But still I did not make a sound or a motion to leave my place. I stayed lying with my face to the wall like a dead thing.

After a few moments I heard her walk back outside to the corridor, muttering to herself about lazy southerners.

Soon evening fell, and with it came a sleep alive and burning with images of Adhar and *tukals* on fire and horses looking down upon me with red, murderous eyes. At one point in my half-asleep state I heard Hassan come and lock the door from the outside, the new door that Nyikoc had fastened to the entrance of my cell that morning. The sound of the sliding bolt became the sound of Adhar's voice in my dream; she was calling for me. Over and over this sound echoed through my mind as I ran across the low rolling hills outside of the compound, searching everywhere wildly for her, with only the repeating thud of the bolt as her voice to follow. It was nighttime, and the few stars in the sky were not enough to light my way. I stumbled over my bare feet as I ran over the sandy hills, falling many times in the dark as I tried to find her. I needed to find her so that I could unlock her voice, I needed to hold her small, warm body in my arms. Though this sound continued to echo around and through me, I did not find her.

I awoke from my fitful sleep to the morning light bleeding through the window, painting itself muted and thick onto the wall in front of me. I had not moved in all this time; I could only hear what went on around me, could only see the mud wall in front of me with its deep uneven cracks. Shuffling steps echoed far down the corridor. I could hear them through the door, coming toward me. These were Tazket's steps. Had they sent her to come to appeal to me? Would it not be simpler to do away with me altogether?

The bolt slid across and she pulled open the heavy door with a grunt. She entered the room and began mumbling in her strange language. They were words I could not understand, yet their sounds washed over me like a cool cloth. She set a bucket down by the top of my head. The steam fingered my scalp, heating my hair and the skin underneath.

I heard her grunt again as she lowered her old, bent body down to the floor and seated herself on the blanket at my back. She laid her crooked hand on my shoulder; I flinched at the light pressure from her fingers on the tail end of one of the welts. Then she shook my shoulder, lightly, continuing to speak to me in her low voice in her words I could not understand. She tugged at my sleeve, then shook my shoulder again. I shrugged, trying to shake her hand away. She dropped a large piece of cloth in front of my face. It looked to be a crumpled piece of clothing. Without thinking, I reached out and put my hand on it. The material was thick and brown. Once again Tazket tugged at my sleeve, harder this time. Then she tugged at the bottom hem of my top, pulling it upwards. I began to understand what she wanted.

With great difficulty, I sat up. The welts screamed at me, stuck to the cloth with the blood that still oozed slowly from them. With Tazket's help I slowly peeled my top away from the sticky welts. This thin shirt that I had worn the past four years lay defeated and sad against the blue of the blanket. I sat hugging my knees to my chest, as Tazket sponged the long, deep welts on my back with the hot water from the bucket. I bit my lip, trying not to yell out. I did not want to bring anyone to my door to see Tazket helping me. I did not need to cause trouble for her. And here I thought of Aluel, who had sat in this same position in that place where they rounded us up so many years ago. Her eyes had been those of a frightened animal. To this day I have not heard of what happened to her. Father told me he believed she was still a slave up north. But we do not know where, or even if she is still alive.

When Tazket finished sponging my back, I let her pull the new brown top over my head, guiding my arms through the sleeves. I wanted to tell her that I did not need this top, that we Dinka women often went topless, unashamed, not like these women up north, who would cover everything, even their faces. I wanted the air to breathe its cool breath on my wounds. But I had understood early that in this compound it was a grave sin for a woman to be without her shirt; to show her breasts was something one must never do. This cloth was heavy and thick, blocking the air that my wounds longed for. It felt strange to wear this new clothing on my body.

She helped me to stand, and then Tazket gathered up the bucket in one hand and my ripped top in the other. As she prepared to leave, I lay back down in my position on my side, my face to the wall. Now her words became louder, faster, spiralling down to my body on the floor. She was trying to tell me something important. Of course I did not understand, though I could guess at what she was saying, for her voice sounded as Nyikoc's had when he had scolded me for not getting up and doing my work. Still, I did not move. I heard her set the bucket down, and again she shook my shoulder. My body rolled forward slightly in response. Then I heard her click her tongue. I imagined her shaking her head as she walked out of my cell and back down the corridor.

The day after this day began the same way. Nyikoc came in, dumped the dishes in the basin, threw the clothes in the corner of the room to be washed. I felt his displeasure growing at my refusal to move every time he entered, but he did not say a word to me. I also felt his fear for me; it was a choking mist that hovered between us. This behaviour of mine would get me killed, this we both knew. That afternoon, Nyikoc stayed in my cell after he dumped the dishes in the basin. I heard him pouring water he had gathered from the well into the basin. Then he began to wash the dishes himself.

Night fell again. I prayed for it to cover over me like a dark cloak, to press down upon my breath and to take me away from here and to the place of my ancestors. I knew these thoughts were nonsense, even as I tried to will it. But my mind was light, like a feather coming loose and trying to float away from my body altogether. I knew that the lack of food and water was encouraging me to truly believe that the night could do what it could not. If I could only fall into that dream state again I would be able to find Adhar by following her voice, following the sound of the deadbolt's thud.

I got up. The dark room swirled. I had heard Hassan come hours ago to lock the door. The heavy cloth of my new top scratched against my raw wounds. I walked to the window. On the corner of the basin was a bowl of rice and okra that Nyikoc had left earlier. I looked out into the night, beyond the stables, beyond the sandy low hills. To nothingness. How long ago it seemed that what lay beyond had been freedom. It seemed a century ago that I had walked those hills with Adhar on my back, the sand burning under my feet.

I do not know how long I stood there. The black night stared back at me, indifferent. It regarded me as nothing much, just another human being with a beating heart standing behind a thick pane of glass, staring out at it. After a long while I picked up the bowl of rice and okra and sat down on the blanket. I scooped up the cold rice with my fingers and put it to my mouth. Made myself chew, swallow it down my throat. It dropped down into my empty stomach, sickening me.

The next morning I was awoken by yelling. Head Wife's voice, in the kitchen. My heart beat wildly against my bones. But still I did not move. I was terrified she would come here to find me unmoving, and beat me once again, inflict welts on top of welts with her whip. I told myself I could endure more pain, and that death would kindly come for me soon to take me away from all of this completely. Then I heard a man's voice, quiet. Someone trying to calm her. She continued to scream in her rapid Arabic, but I could not make out her words. Other voices speaking now. The cook? Nyikoc? I could not tell with the thick door between myself and the rest of the house. I stayed with my face to the wall and cursed myself for eating the food Nyikoc brought. Cursed myself for allowing Tazket to attend to my wounds. If only no one would come to me, I could slowly die, be free of the prison of this world altogether. I cursed the food in my belly for giving my mind and body strength. I cursed it for letting me hear the voices, letting me feel the fear that Head Wife might come to punish me again. I told myself I would refuse to eat again when Nyikoc brought food.

The yelling stopped. I heard no more voices. I do not know how long I slept, while the sun poked his arms through the window above the basin. Finally I heard the deadbolt slide back and the door open. I did not know if I could take this sound of the heavy bolt much longer, linked as it was to my eternal search for my daughter in the dark, rolling hills.

Someone was standing beside the blanket looking down at me. I could tell by his breath after a few moments that it was Nyikoc.

But there was also another sound. It was not the sound of the deadbolt screaming shut but of someone else's breath, soft and light. Just before she spoke, the hovering mist lifted and vanished into the sun's light that swept through the thick glass of the window.

"Mama?" Adhar was there, in Nyikoc's arms. He put her down and she ran to me and nestled her small warm body tightly into me and held on, her tiny arms wrapped around my neck, her legs around my waist, and the tears that I did not know I had in my body any longer came down fast over my cheeks as I held her and refused to let her go.

Finally I pulled her from me, looked her over, felt her limbs, her head, her fingers. She was fine, unharmed. I looked up at Nyikoc. He had a small smile on his face.

"Master Saleh made Master Wife do this. You have him to thank. He would not allow Master Wife to sell her to another family, as were her plans."

Before he left, Nyikoc laid down a small bundle of cloth by the door. After some time I went over to it, picked it up, unfolded it. My old top, with the long rips now stitched and mended by Tazket, like furrows mending the soil of a newly planted field.

IX

APRIL 30, 2003, EL-MUGLAD, NORTH SUDAN

◇◇

The end is near. I can feel it.

The one-armed servant boy brought me food yesterday. A bowl of rice, a bowl of water. The bowls are ceramic, blue pictures of girls and boys in hats, running in the countryside, a countryside with hills and windmills. I considered the strange irony of this as I ate, gobbling the sticky rice down with my fingers. I've left some of the water, which sits, staring at me. It quivers in the bowl at my feet.

I think back to when I was so careful with the water I drank, making sure it was purified, or boiled. Since being locked in here I've drunk what's been given to me; I've had to. The thick thirst has obliterated any thoughts of illness. But not when I was locked in the hut; I remember that now.

We had probably been in the hut a day and a half before the old man came in. The sun had set and come up once, sharp stabs of light filtered through the crack under the door and between the boards of the window. It was just about to go down again when my eyes were blinded by the door opening. At first, I couldn't make him out. I assumed he was a prisoner too. Once my eyes adjusted, I saw him more clearly; he was hunched over on frail, bent legs, and his clothes looked like rags hanging off him. His T-shirt was so torn and full of holes that I wondered why he bothered wearing it. His hair was matted and twisted and there was a single, large feather stuck in it. There were noises coming out of his mouth; at first I thought he was speaking to Riak quietly in Dinka, even though his head was moving all about. Then I realized he was muttering to himself.

He held a leather flask, which he brought to Riak first. Riak lifted his head and reached out his long arm to take it. Solomon and I watched him take several gulps before wiping his mouth and handing the flask back to the old man. Then the old man shoved the flask right in front of my face. I took it, smelled it, put my lips to the mouth of the bottle. I needed moisture.

"Sandy." Riak's voice, warning me. Jim had told me a story about a girl who was at RESCUE before me. A young volunteer from Scotland, out to change the world, Jim said. "She got cocky, tried to fit in with the locals," he told me, his eyes blazing, "and she started drinking straight from the borehole. The borehole! Imagine. She would line up behind the other women with her bucket. At first I thought that she was just going to boil the water afterwards, that she was trying to prove some kind of point. But now I'm sure she was just going mad out here. She was young. She hadn't had a break in a while and this was her first time away from home." He took a swig of his Tusker and his face went serious. "Yeah, we sent her home. She was in the hospital for months, apparently. Almost died. Last I heard she's still not the same."

I could not risk illness on top of everything else. I would just need to wait and hope. I handed the flask to Solomon. As I watched him finish it off, I felt like crying. The old man shuffled closer to Solomon, staring at him dumbly, his legs bent like twigs. He snatched the flask from him and held on to it lightly, as though he were about to drop it. He stood there for some time, swaying back and forth, then he started yelling at Solomon and pointing at me. Riak interrupted and started talking to him in Dinka, gesturing to me with his arms. The old man seemed to ignore Riak, who I assumed was trying to tell him I couldn't drink the water he was giving me. He kept saying *khawaja* and *lir*. I knew these words meant "white person" and "water".

Then he came over to me and held the flask right up to my lips and spoke at me loudly in Dinka. Riak said something to him in a raised voice, and the old man lowered the flask. Water was dripping down the edges, making dark marks in the leather. Then the old man bent down with his face close to mine and peered into my eyes. Hundreds of lines ran along his face, tiny rivers. His mouth gaped open and his eyes were a watery grey, burnt out from the sun. I wondered briefly if he was blind. He stared at me until I looked away. Then he started talking to me in Dinka, in a soft voice, a cooing sound. When I looked at him again, his eyes looked like they were asking me something important. Pleading. Finally Riak said something to him again, and then he stopped talking. But he stayed there, close to my face, for what felt like several minutes. Then he straightened up quickly, and left. He came back again a couple of hours later with the flask. He walked in through the door and handed it straight to me. The leather was warm. He had boiled the water inside of it, probably over one of their fires they had burning outside.

I drank most of the bottle and poured the remaining drops onto the deep welts on my legs. The dust was clotted in the open wounds and clung to the dried blood. Pouring the warm water on the cuts stung like hell. This old man just stared at me with his huge, mad eyes the whole time I did this. When I handed him his empty flask, he grabbed my wrist and I screamed. Riak leaned forward and spoke to him like he would a child, and he let go of my wrist. One of the soldiers came in then and yelled at the old man, pushed him out the door.

After he left the second time, I asked Riak what it was that he had been saying to me. Riak said wearily, "He is asking you to help him. He is a crazy old man. The Arabs came through here years ago and killed his family. He's been all alone here ever since. Just ignore him. He won't hurt you."

"How do you know this?"

"It was what he said when he was asking you to help him."

"How could I possibly help him?"

"Never mind. I told you, he is mad. He is not who we need to worry about." Then Riak put his head back down on his forearms which were propped up on his knees. There was a long, heavy silence.

That is when the boys with the guns came in.

There was no warning; we heard them lift the post from the other side of the door, and then they were there, dragging Solomon away. Riak stood up, the top of his head mashing against the straw ceiling. Little flecks of yellow were scattered in his hair like crumbs. He was shouting at them in Dinka, screaming, pulling at the boys, at Solomon. Riak's limbs flailed, trying to stop what he couldn't.

One of the boys kicked Riak in the legs and stomach until he fell to the ground. This boy's eyes looked dead to me. The ones who dragged Solomon away couldn't have been more than fourteen years old. Their ribs poked out from under their thin shirts. The bones in their faces looked soft and unformed, far away still from being the faces of men.

Solomon stayed curled into himself as they dragged him away on the ground, leaving a trail of his body behind in the dust. He was crying, big, gulping dry sobs, but he wasn't thrashing about wildly like Riak. It was as though he knew. He was the driver.

Riak and I may have been spared, but we were not spared from hearing his cries when they dragged him away and barred the door behind them. Nor were we spared from hearing that single gun-shot. I waited to hear a scream or a cry to prove that Solomon was still alive. But no cry followed. They would have shot him directly in the head, at point blank range.

This water must come from a borehole — and it's making me sicker, I can feel it. It's getting harder to heave myself up onto the pail. I haven't passed any diarrhea in days. My urine is scant, dark-coloured, foul-smelling. My legs ache in my sleep.

No one is coming for me. The little girl hasn't come back since that first time, staring through the hole in the boards at me with her huge, innocent curiosity. Perhaps she has been warned to not visit the prisoner in the stall. I haven't seen Kufi-man in days. The last time he came in here, it was only to smirk at me. A warning. He means to destroy me. He tells me this by the way he looks at me, stares down at me. It is too clear.

The snake came up from his home again, today. But he wouldn't meet my eye. He wouldn't even greet me. He just slid his long black body past my feet and under the door of the stall, to the outside world. How easily he could leave — a heavy lock is nothing to him. I envy his freedom. He's used to me, he thinks I belong here. He won't help me either, now. I have become just another animal to him, unthreatening, a part of his scenery.

I think of Dad, and Geri. And Graham. And that I will never see them again. And Mom. My anger at her has been a bundle that I've carried in my chest all these years, tucked way inside. I was wrong to think that barricading her from my life would heal the distance she put between us. The bundle is still there. It hangs, heavy.

I imagine fat tears running down Geri's cheeks when she hears. I think of her chastising herself for not talking me into staying home and "facing the music." And Graham. I'll never get the chance to tell him off the way I wanted to. Or forgive him.

And Dad. I think of him smoking his rolled-up cigarettes,

squinting at the blue light coming off the television. Or does the television sit dark and mute now, while he spends all his time on the phone, calling the embassy, lawyers, Amanda at AFS? Trying, somehow, from within his small, square house, to get his daughter home?

I lead Ringo to a nearby tree outside of the compound. No one is around to see us; they are all inside the compound eating lunch, even the workers who build the *tukals*. The emptiness reminds me briefly of the time Father and I stopped by the village on our way down to Auntie's place in Turalei, except, of course, now there are new *tukals* and the *khawajas'* compound that demands to be seen. These new buildings smelling of a new life. Adhar runs out to where we are settling down under the tree. She has left Rith back with Abiong.

"Adhar, go to Neima and ask for Ringo a glass of water." Adhar stands before us, staring at Ringo with her eyes wide. Ringo sits himself down under the tree without a word. "Go now! He must be thirsty after his long walk!" She turns and runs back into the compound.

Besides the time Ringo came to me in Father's *tukal,* we have not been alone together. I sit away from him under the shade of the tree, looking down to the ground. Still he does not speak. Would he have me speak first? How can he not know this is not my place? I want to ask after Auntie and Achol and Achai, but I know they will be angry with me for betraying them as I have done with my leaving. I say nothing. One of the village's stray dogs comes to sniff at our feet. Ringo shoos him away, kicking his foot out at him. The dog yelps even though he has not been touched, and trundles away with his tail between his legs.

"My brother would be proud of you, Adut." He is not looking at me but down at his hands, which are trying unsuccessfully to mend a snapped twig. "Tobias told me a long time ago that you were his favourite."

I feel my face flush at these words. What secrets do men, brothers share?

He continues, "I always looked up to my brother. He was strong, brave. I wanted to be like him."

These words were a surprise. I felt them float around me before I allowed their weight to settle down into me. I waited. I did not know what to say in return.

"Your auntie guessed you had come here, back to your home. She was angry at first. She is still angry. But perhaps she also understands."

The image of Auntie walking down the road to Akoch to retrieve me comes clearly to my mind. "Do you understand that I cannot go with you?" My heart leaps up to my throat in my own surprise at my boldness.

"I think of what Tobias would have wanted. What I know is that he would not want you to suffer more than what you already have." Ringo continues to play with the snapped twig. It is tiny in his large hands. "If this is what you want, to be here, doing this, then..." He shrugs and reaches out his long arm toward the *khawajas'* compound, while still looking away from me.

And here, it is as though this is the first time that I see Ringo. Though he has five wives, his face is young, still unlined. He has the similar mouth and eye shape as my husband. His face is open, turned away for now from the other men who would push him to do his duty and take me as his wife.

Just then Adhar comes running to Ringo with a glass of water, which he accepts and drinks all at once.

Ringo hands the glass back to Adhar and stands. "I will take my leave now, Adut. I am going back to the east to join my family. Good luck to you."

I stand up, dust off my skirt. Adhar leans her head against my hip. "Thank you," I say, though this does not seem enough, not nearly enough.

Ringo simply nods and then turns, begins his long walk back to Turalei. His tall, broad back slowly recedes and then disappears behind the clutch of *tukals* that outline our new village.

The Women stopped coming to me for some time after my return, and in my anger at their refusal to warn me of Khalid's arrival in the town I did not summon them, even though Saleh returned to me in the nights. But as the days wore on I saw that perhaps my desperation for escape blinded me to their cryptic warning. One night I opened my eyes and they came to me in a rush, all of them, thirteen large women with their glistening eyes, sitting on their haunches, their huge skirts brushing the dirt around their large fire, their drooping, naked breasts, their chorus of voices in their sing-song unison. These voices quieted my heart, and scattered my anger to the air for the slave-ghosts to consume.

It was some years later, when I had almost given up on escape completely, that you came to me, with Father. This did not happen so very long ago, and still I wonder where you are. And here I think of Nyikoc, and I wonder if he is still alive, what punishment Saleh bestowed upon him for letting Father and I walk free. I believe it was Nyikoc's heart that leaped toward me for so many years that freed us, a decision he made in one moment. Did he regret this? Like war, love can make one do things that they otherwise would not do.

I was sleeping in my cell, my arm draped over Adhar to guard her from her nightwalks, when I heard the deadbolt slide back outside my door. I closed my eyes and moved away from Adhar, for I believed this was Saleh coming to me once again. I lay very still, waiting for him. But the figure stood above me for too long. I could hear his rapid breath, and here I opened my eyes and found Nyikoc looking down at me.

I sat up abruptly, put my hand to my throat. Why was he here? He would be punished if it was found that he had left his room in the night.

"Adut." I could not see his eyes but his voice was strange, not his own. As though what connected him to his own voice had been broken, and yet he was trying to use this voice still. "Come." He put his hand out for me to take. I took it and he helped me to stand.

"Nyikoc, what . . ."

"Bring the girl." He motioned down toward the sleeping Adhar. In my fatigue and my fright at this new Nyikoc, I paused, unmoving. I did not understand what he asked. He scooped Adhar up into his arms. She squawked quietly.

We stepped into the narrow passageway and walked out the open door into the cool night. Nyikoc began to walk quickly across the yard, with the sleeping Adhar draped over him. The well was bathed in moonlight. This walking out so boldly made me think too much of the night I escaped. Was Nyikoc giving me another chance at escape? This may sound crazy to you, but I did not feel in that moment that I was ready to go. I did not have food with me, or water. I was not certain of which way I should go to avoid the wrong eyes upon me. Was Nyikoc planning to escape with me? What if Khalid found us again? Surely if we were caught my life would not be spared a second time.

I looked around the yard for Hassan. Nyikoc walked quickly ahead. I scurried up beside him to ask him of Hassan. But before any words left my mouth, he said to me, "Hassan is out grazing the cattle with the others. Master Saleh asked me to keep watch on the yard." Nyikoc did not carry a gun. Of course Saleh would not risk giving a weapon to a slave. Nyikoc spoke so quietly that I had to strain to hear him. "I have been guarding the yard sometimes for a while now, as Master Saleh sends the other men to graze the cattle further south." He turned to look at me. "Master Saleh trusts me. Like a son." Again, he did not sound like the Nyikoc I knew. And then, just before we rounded the corner of the stable, Nyikoc said to me, "Adut. Tonight is your night to find your freedom." I saw his eyes shone with a certain fear. "This thing for which you have been waiting for so long."

We turned the corner and there you stood. And behind you my father, with a gun strapped across his frail, old back. To him I ran. But we did not embrace. He simply took my hand in his and held it for a moment. I was taken aback at his eyes, which had turned to a grey dust, and the lines in his face, now caverns. Was he with this gun forcing Nyikoc to set me free? Could you and Nyikoc not see that my father did not know how to operate this gun? I knew my father had never used a gun, and here I could see by the way he carried this weapon that it was the first time he had been so close to one. I stared deeply at him, trying to understand that this thin, old man with wild, shaking eyes, and carrying a gun, was my father. And here it was in his eyes I saw, without asking him, that the rest of our family was dead. That my Khajami was dead. I cannot remember if I said Khajami's name and then saw in those dusty eyes the answer I did not want to know. But it was in that moment that I fell to the ground. A crumpled, dry leaf falling from the top of a tree.

And it was you who helped me up again. I had never stood so close to a white person before this. I saw the scar on your forehead, and I thought of my wrist as I looked upon it. And I saw you look upon my wrist as you clamped your fingers over it to lift me. Your tired, frightened eyes met mine as you touched the thick scar that lay itself bare on my skin.

And then Nyikoc's voice again, so distant. "Go now, Adut, with your father. He has brought your payment." And here he pointed to you, *khawaja*.

So this was it. My father was not forcing Nyikoc after all. But was this not madness? Paying for my freedom with a white woman because he had no money? Would this *khawaja* replace me then, take up the residence in my cell, wash the dishes, fetch the water from the well, hang the clothes on the line? Be treated like an animal by the other servants? Have nightly visits from Saleh, bear him more children?

Had my father gone mad? And Nyikoc? What would Saleh do to him for setting me free and putting a white woman in my place?

Perhaps Nyikoc believed that this white woman's family would pay Saleh a lot of money to have her released, and this is why he agreed to do what my father asked. I hoped that this could be true. I came closer to Nyikoc, very near to his face. Under the sky of that night I could see his pain at seeing me go, but his decision had been made. He might face death, but he would have me gone. His face looked angry but he could not hide the pools in his eyes.

"You go now. Go home." It was a command. How could I say no to him? This was all I had wanted for eight long years. I turned to my father. Adhar was now awake, staring at this strange scene. She had come to me, clutching my hand in both of hers.

"Come." Father's voice was ancient, close to death, this I could already see. "Bring the little one. We shall go back home now." His eyes did not show surprise as they rested on my large stomach, which held Rith, waiting to soon be born. My father looked too strange with the new American backpack slung across his shoulder. I would find that it held food and a bottle to hold the water that we would gather at the rivers on the long and dangerous trek back home to the south. What a skill, what kind of desperate bravery for my father to have taken you up to the north, *khawaja,* unseen. With his gun my father must have forced you to hide along the way, in the reeds of the river, in the bushes at night with the wild ones near.

Then Nyikoc grasped your arm and led you to the stable. You looked back at me only one time. You were terrified, this was clear. You did not scream out, but your eyes were wide with their seeking to try to understand this thing that was being put upon you. You face was whiter than white, the colour of ashes. And yet you did not look angry, *khawaja.* Why is this? I wondered if there was a place deep inside of yourself where you had accepted to put your sadness in place of mine.

As Father and I stole away, I heard the heavy lock shut, a loud gnashing of teeth. Nyikoc had locked you in one of the stables. Was it the same one they locked me in four years ago after I tried to escape? And then Father and I left, and I did not look back, not at Nyikoc, not at the stables, not at Saleh's compound that I would not see again.

When did Nyikoc choose to do this thing? I learned later that messages had been coming from Father to the market man over the years. Nyikoc had been speaking to my father through the market man for all this time without my knowing. I believe that Nyikoc had not wanted to tell me he had heard from Father again, for fear I would again try to escape — he knew a second try might mean my death. But the communication with Nyikoc made Father desperate too, and when my father saw the chance of you arriving in his empty village, he took it. I believe he knew he was getting closer to death, and he saw you as his only opportunity to come for me.

I think of Nyikoc often and I wonder if Saleh spared him. And also I wonder if you have left that place. Did they make you a slave there? I cannot set the picture into my mind of you hanging the wash on the line, pink-skinned, with drops of sweat falling from your face onto the hard earth, while Saleh's children run around you chanting their cruel words and songs. Or perhaps your family from your rich country came to buy your freedom, after all.

And I have prayed, *khawaja,* that though I have spoken my story while the sun was above us, its power has reached you, across time and space, as my grandmother promised it could do. Perhaps it has saved you. Perhaps this story has somehow set you free.

After I left Saleh's place, the Women stopped coming to me. I have not seen them since. But I have hoped they stayed there, up in the north, watching over you from their fire in the sky. Giving you hope and strength on your way, as they did for me. These Women, this story. My gifts to you.

X

Sandra

MAY 4, 2003, SOMEWHERE OVER THE ATLANTIC OCEAN

The plane's engines rumble beneath me, around me. Most people on board are asleep. A baby has been crying for a couple of hours now. A tired-looking father shushes her, walking up and down the aisle carrying her in his arms. The woman beside me has been asleep since we left the tarmac, shutting out the noise and the cabin's activity with her eye mask and her bright yellow earplugs.

While she snores lightly, I look at the black night outside the small, cold window. Somewhere behind the darkness is the moon, floating and full. Listening to my thoughts, perhaps.

But are you still listening? Do you sit somewhere, waiting for the invisible storyteller to come to the end of her story? Have you noticed I stopped the story before it was finished? Did you hear me giving up, did you wonder at the sudden silence?

I realize now, as I hover between my home and yours, that I needed to believe you were listening. I needed you there, so I could make sense of the nightmare. My mind has carved its own illusions out of the air in order to survive.

But you know the rest of the story, don't you? Did your father, or maybe he was your grandfather — did he tell you? Did he tell you how he snuck into the hut the night after they shot Solomon?

I was lying in the hut as Solomon had been before they came to take him — curled up against the mud wall. Riak and I weren't speaking to each other; fear kept us mute, a thick wall between us. My eyes scanned the dirt on the floor where I lay on my side, my breath inching the tiny clumps toward the wall. Riak hid his face in his arms, opposite me.

The boys and men outside were loud that night — celebrating, it seemed. I didn't understand what they were saying, but I could tell they were drinking, probably the local drink, *marissa,* fermented sorghum. I was terrified that a drunk soldier would come in here and take me outside to rape me. I wanted to crawl over to Riak, wrap my arms around him in an effort to make the shaking inside my body stop. But I couldn't move from where I was.

The drunken shouting and laughing of the men was dying down. It was probably 2 or 3 a.m.; they were likely passed out now, in their tents. I heard one of the boys then, right outside our door, shouting to someone. I sat up, whispered hoarsely to Riak, "Is he going to come in here?"

I could only see Riak's outline in the dark. He lifted his head, slowly. His voice drifted over to me across the small space. "No, Sandra, do not worry. It is only the boy that they are putting outside the door to guard us."

Guard us from what, I wanted to ask. But instead I said, "They're all drunk right now, aren't they." It was more of a statement than a question.

"Yes." Riak whispered this, his voice projected down to the floor. His head was resting on his arms again.

My stomach felt like it was caving in on itself, I was so hungry. I lay back down, facing the wall.

I had drifted into sleep by the time he came in. I woke to the sound of the post being lifted up on the other side of the door, carefully, slowly. I sat up. When the door began creaking open, I scrambled over to where Riak was sitting and leaned against him. He put his body in front of me, guarding me from whoever was entering.

The old man stood in the doorway, his features indiscernible against the black night. He had a gun, and he was pointing the barrel of it toward us.

Riak and I put our hands out in front of us, making stop signs at the gun. Riak moved back a bit, against me, pushing me into the wall, and began speaking rapidly to him. At his voice, the old man entered quickly and pushed the barrel of the gun at Riak's head. Riak stopped talking. He barely breathed. I cowered behind him, trying to hide my body behind his.

The old man spoke to Riak in a fast, urgent whisper, with the barrel of the gun pushing into Riak's forehead. He was saying the same thing, over and over. A demand. Riak wasn't speaking back. Only blinking at the air in front of him as the barrel of the gun was being jabbed at his head.

Riak finally spoke quietly to me. He was being forced to; he didn't want to tell me what he was about to say. I had buried my head between his shoulder blades. I waited for the old man to press the trigger, for Riak's head to explode all over me, all over the hut.

"Sandra, he wants you to go. With him." He spit it out in a whisper.

"No!" I screamed it out, from behind Riak. Then the old man spoke in a rapid whisper again, pushing both of us back with the gun against Riak's head. He didn't like that I screamed. Riak spoke rapidly to him again, a pleading tone.

Riak whispered, "Sandra, please, he does not want us to yell. You must be quiet. You must be quiet or he will kill us both."

I couldn't believe that this old man was going to rape me. I had been so sure it was going to be one of the soldiers. He was so old, and looked so fragile, and small. I told myself that I would fight back, when he put down the gun. After he made me take my clothes off, he would have to put the gun down, at some point. My legs ached and I felt weak, but I knew I could fight back, hard, if I needed to.

Riak's breathing was loud. Our fear was a cocoon wrapping us tight inside it, and this old man with his gun was ripping it apart. To get at me.

I stood up. My legs shook, and I stumbled. The old man kept his gun on Riak, as if he knew Riak would fight for me once the gun was no longer pointing at him. He motioned for me to go out the door.

I stepped outside. My body was shaking all over; I wanted so badly for it to stop. I looked back at Riak. The old man was right behind me, still pointing the gun at Riak. I saw tears coming fast down Riak's face in the faint starlight. Powerless and sad. The old man closed the door, pushed down the post, locking Riak in.

I took another few steps into the abandoned village. It was completely quiet. I looked to my right. There was the boy guarding our hut, sleeping on the ground. Passed out. Just an adolescent boy. With no gun. Had this old man taken his gun from him?

I felt the gun's barrel at my back. He pushed at me with it, leading me somewhere. The night was so dark I was worried I would trip and fall, even as he pushed at me to hurry. We walked to the edge of the village, past the tents and the crumbled, decaying huts, to a truck. Was he going to try to do it in here, get on top of me in the bed of this truck, so I wouldn't have much room to fight back?

He opened the driver's door. With his gun he motioned for me to get in. I sat behind the steering wheel. The keys dangled from the ignition. I could just start the truck now, and drive away. I raised my hand to the ignition to start it, but the old man was already at the other door, opening it, pointing his gun at me. He was quick.

He saw what I was about to do. I lowered my hand. He sat in the passenger seat, closed his door, and with his gun he motioned at the keys. What the hell did he want me to do? Drive away? He motioned with his gun again, more urgently this time. He was getting impatient. It was dawning on me that he was having me steal this vehicle. Was he going to make me drive a ways away so he could rape me and then do away with me? I wouldn't do it. I stayed still.

I turned and looked him full in the face. He was blinking rapidly, his eyes had become huge round disks. It struck me that he looked terrified himself. He pushed the barrel of the gun into my upper arm and waved his hand at the keys again. He wanted me to start the truck.

I turned the ignition. The truck rumbled to life. The noise was deafening in the quiet of the black night. He looked over his shoulder out the back window, to see if anyone was coming. He jabbed the gun's barrel at me again, motioning with it for me to go. There was desperation in those eyes. He didn't want us to get caught.

I pushed the pedal to the floor.

We drove for hours in the dark on a narrow, bumpy dirt road. Morning arrived, and the old man still didn't take his gun from me; he rested the barrel lightly against my upper arm as I drove. He had the base of it cradled in both of his arms. He didn't close his eyes once from fatigue. His eyes were no longer moving all about, as they were when he first came into the hut; they travelled from the road to me and back, focused and calm.

We passed several other vehicles during the day, and many people walking on the road. We drove through a few villages. The men and women on the road always waved to us. I never waved back. I knew I couldn't stop and scream for help with this gun against me. Besides, who would help me up here?

As we travelled further north, there were fewer villages, and fewer people on the road. The land up here started to have an abandoned feeling. I had a sense we were getting close to the front lines, where most of the fighting happened. Where was he taking me? What did he want with me?

I wanted to talk to him, to ask him where we were going. In the light of the day I began to be less scared of him. I saw that he was crazy, but I believed that he wouldn't harm me. His eyes were not angry; they were sad grey pools.

I had watched the gas gauge move slowly toward empty as we drove. Finally the engine began to splutter. We were in the middle of nowhere, and it was near sundown. What would we do now? I pulled over to the side of the road. The old man got out of the truck, and with the gun still strapped across his back he hoisted a jerry can from the flatbed and poured fuel into the tank. Perhaps he wasn't as mad as I had thought at first; he must have known when we left the village that there was extra gas in the back of the truck. He had planned this.

I really had to go to the bathroom. The land was flat and spare of trees or bush. There was nothing to hide behind. I wished I was wearing my skirt, so I could just hike it up right here and go beside the vehicle. I walked around to the back of the truck, and the old man watched me intently. When I squatted out of sight, he didn't follow me with his gun. He must have known I had to go, after all this time. It took me forever, I was so anxious, but I finally finished and then climbed back in the driver's seat.

He fed me from Riak's backpack; when had he stolen this? He took out the bottle of water, now full, a tin of fish, and some bread. I was grateful that Riak had thought to take some food from the kitchen at the compound before we left. He handed me pieces of bread and slippery fish and the bottle of water to take sips from. I drove with one hand and ate with the other.

We crossed four rivers, all of them with narrow, rickety bridges that I was terrified wouldn't hold the truck. But they did.

When we ran out of gas a second time it was dark. I pulled over to the side of the road again. My legs were starting to throb from the cuts, and my thighs and hands were vibrating from driving for so long over the bumpy, narrow trail. We both stepped out of the truck. I needed to stretch. As I was bending over, trying to touch my toes to release the cramps in the back of my legs, he came up behind me, motioning with his gun again. We were going to walk. Obviously there was no more fuel.

We walked in the dark, on the road, for what must have been several hours. This old man didn't utter a word or a sound to me. I was getting so tired. I hadn't slept in more than a day; my adrenaline had kept me going all this time, but now I was beginning to fade fast. I sat down on the road. What the hell did he want with me? What was he going to do? I was starting to get really scared again. I thought being with him was probably safer than being around the drunk soldiers who killed Solomon, but I couldn't stop thinking of Riak. And I wanted to know what this old guy wanted with me. He let me sit for a minute or two before pushing at me with the gun again. I got up, continued walking for a while — but soon I sat down again on the road, exhausted. I couldn't keep going, I was too tired. And scared, and in pain. There wasn't anything left in me that could make me keep on going. He prodded at me with his gun to get back up again. I started to plead with him, crying, asking him what it was he meant to do with me, even though I knew he couldn't understand my words.

Finally I got up. I couldn't walk fast, but he didn't push at me with his gun to move faster. I forced my feet to move, one ahead of the other. I was so tired I had to make myself think about it, or my body would just take over again and I would collapse. But I kept putting one foot in front of the other; perhaps a half hour later we came upon the place where you were. He had known exactly where to go, this old man. And no one had seen us; we hadn't come across anyone in the dark.

When I first saw you with the little girl — the girl so thin, her face an open, terrified question — I still didn't understand. I could see that you were pregnant. I wondered later how you were going to walk back to the south with your little one and another child in your belly.

Why am I not angry at you? Were you the woman in the photograph after all? Was it really you the gods had planned for me to meet? Perhaps. Your eyes weren't angry, like hers. They were bewildered. Sad. I helped you up when you fell, likely because of your shock at seeing us there. My fingers touched your scar, a smooth half-moon on your wrist. I didn't strike out at you, or the man, or the boy. I didn't scream. I was tired. I could not see the future.

Not until the servant boy grabbed my arm to take me with him into the barn did I understand. I was being traded. My freedom for yours. My fear shot up then in a rush, tired and hungry but totally alive. But still I didn't scream. I didn't struggle against this boy. I didn't want to be shot, or hurt.

This fear is still inside of me. When you have so much fear for so long you end up carrying it with you, no matter where you are, no matter how safe you make your world. It's still there, curled up and ready to strike.

I spent two weeks in that stall. I had given up, finally, had decided I would no longer eat the food brought to me. I would curl up in the corner and lay down to sleep, let my confused dreams take me where they would. When the one-armed servant came to retrieve the bowls from outside the door, I was there, waiting. As he gathered the bowls in his one hand, I tucked the folded article through the hole in the bottom of the door, presenting it to him. A gift in exchange for the food he had brought to me. I didn't understand why he continued to bring me food; I was pretty sure he lost his arm because of me.

I would no longer need the article anyway; my ritual wasn't working. The stone fell where it wanted, and it had nothing to do with what would happen that day. It foretold nothing. The woman in the photo could not help me; she might not even be alive. The reality of it all had come at me with such a force that it had knocked me into my corner in retreat — I finally saw, much too late, how I had re-made her image into my own fantasy as a way to mend a broken heart.

The boy paused a long time before taking the article from me. I could see him through the hole, staring at it, this piece of folded, coloured paper. He winced every few seconds, breathing hard. His face shone with sweat. Finally, he set the bowls down and took it from my hand, so gently that I thought he might drop it. But he didn't. Instead he opened it with his fingers. It took him a long time. I watched him as he looked at the pictures — women and young boys and girls dressed in rags, like him. Tired and angry. Broken. And the pictures of the white people, looking red and hot, wearing hats and hiking boots, carrying water bottles, knapsacks. He lifted his eyes to meet mine. They were so empty. I wanted, in those long moments, to fill them for him. But I didn't know what I would fill them with as I was already so empty myself.

Then he disappeared, and I could no longer see his face. I turned around to take the two steps back to my corner, ready to move into dreamland, to curl up into myself, to die.

And then, the sound of the padlock, a heavy click. Was he coming in here? I waited. The stall door creaked open, just a crack. He stood behind the door. I knew he was there. Was he waiting for me? I heard his footsteps cross the boards, and then the barn door sliding open.

I stood, looking at the open door. My fear planted me in the centre of that stall for I don't know how long. One minute, two?

Finally, I edged out of the stall and into the barn. I was terrified that Kufi-man would catch me, grab me, do I don't know what to me. Dust hung in the light that seeped through the cracks in the walls. Just a bunch of empty stalls and a wooden floor smattered with hay — nothing more. I moved out through the barn door into the open air. It was very warm, and quiet. The one-armed boy was walking ahead, slowly. He had moved out of the yard and was heading for a series of low hills beyond. There was no one else around.

I tried to run after him, but my throbbing legs wouldn't let me. I hobbled as quickly as I could, keeping him in my line of sight. Night was about to fall; I didn't want to be left alone out here. His thin, loping figure was getting smaller. I began to panic, tried to run again, but found I couldn't. I knew I would need to stop for a break soon. I looked back at the barn in the distance. I could see a part of it through the opening in the tall fence that enclosed the yard, and behind it there was a long, low, grey house. The yard looked empty. No one had seen us leave.

I shouted at the boy, "Hey!" My voice broke the air, crashed through the quiet. He stopped, turned round to look at me. Though he was far away and I couldn't see his face, I could tell by his stance that he didn't want me to yell again. That this was imperative. Very slowly, he lifted his finger to his mouth. I nodded my head in response. I hoped he could see that I understood.

We walked for a long time. The mysterious noises that crept around the hills terrified me. This time there was no man with a gun to protect me from a wild animal, from the night. My fear kept me walking through the pain in my legs. Strangely, I felt more frightened walking in these hills than I did locked up in that stall. My breathing was loud and quick, deafening to my own ears. I worried that I was making too much noise, that my obvious terror would get us found by someone or something that we didn't want to find us.

The shape of the one-armed servant became smaller and smaller ahead of me. I wanted so badly to shout at him again, but I didn't dare. The night and the hills were swallowing him, and he was about to leave my sight altogether.

I sat down on the hard, sandy earth. I couldn't go on. My mouth was so dry I couldn't swallow properly. Why did I leave, why did I follow him? I should have stayed in the stall, curled up, and gone to sleep. I couldn't take this anymore. I couldn't take all of this walking in the night in the middle of Africa, open prey to animals and kidnappers and madmen. What the hell was I doing here? Why did I come here at all? I should have just stayed in Toronto, slinging beer to drunken university students, hitting the nightclubs with Geri, embracing my new single life. That life would have been simpler. There would have been less pain, less scarring, in the end. I made a horrible mistake coming here. And now no one knew where I was. I was totally lost. I knew then that I would die.

I heard his unbalanced, shuffling gait before I saw him. He stood before me, just far enough away so I could see him in the dark. He stood there a long time. I noticed he was swaying slightly. When he was this close I could hear his breath rattling in his chest. It looked as if he was in a lot of pain. But he didn't say anything, he didn't make any noise, didn't gesture. After a few minutes I stood up. He turned around and began walking again. I followed him.

After some time I saw him stop again. When I caught up to him I saw that he had sat down in front of some bushes. He gestured for me to sit as well. His stump reeked like a small dead animal. Decaying. I lay down beside him, turned away, covered my nose with my arm. Exhausted, I slept.

I awoke to a noise. I opened my eyes, looked around me; I was next to a road, and I could see in the distance a truck barrelling toward me. Plumes of dust trailed behind the truck, choking the early morning air. For a brief moment I wondered if I should stay hidden. With great difficulty I stood up. I needed water, soon. My insides were scratchy, dry. Sharp waves of pain rode through my stomach. I looked down at the bushes, and all around me. The one-armed boy was gone.

I walked toward the road. I couldn't think properly. I stood and faced the oncoming truck. It slowed down, stopped. Two men peered out at me from the front window. Two women and a girl with abayas covering their heads were in the back flatbed, leaning over the siderails, looking down at me. The man in the driver's seat opened the door, stepped out of the truck, approached me.

"Miss?" He stared, looking me up and down, my bare, swollen legs, my dirty skin.

"Please help." It's all I remember saying before collapsing.

I woke up in a hospital. I found out later that the family in the truck who had found me drove all the way to Khartoum to drop me off here. A three-hour drive? More, perhaps; at least six if you count both ways. They left without giving their name or forwarding address.

When I first awoke, a man was looking over me. His hair was closely shorn, and he wore glasses and a small smile on his face. His eyes were a clear green. He introduced himself as Dr. Mohamed.

"You are very lucky, Miss. You see this?" He pointed to the IV machine hooked into my arm. "These are antibiotics going into your blood. To stop the infection in your legs." Even now I could feel them throbbing. "And this other line, in your other arm, it is hydrating you. You were very close to not making it. What were you doing out there, all alone?"

I closed my eyes. How could I begin to tell him the whole story?

"It is all right. You do not need to tell me. But the police will be here soon, demanding some answers. Be prepared. They have been here already, asking many questions." The furrowed line in his forehead seemed to possess concern. "The nurse will also be in here soon, to feed you."

He paused. It looked like he wanted to say more. But instead he offered his small, worried smile again, and left.

I woke once more, this time to a woman looking down at me. Her hair was covered with a black, filmy scarf. Her face was a kind oval. "Hello, hello? Are you awake?"

"Yes." I could barely speak.

"Here, drink this." She aimed a straw toward my mouth. I drank from it obediently. It tasted chalky. I must have made a face, for she said, "Do not worry, this is good for you. Full of vitamins."

I took another sip and lay back on the pillow. It was amazing how tired I was.

I asked her, "Please, could you do me a favour? It's very important." Her eyes examined mine. "Please." With all my strength I leaned forward and pressed my fingers into her forearm. "Can you get me a pen and a piece of paper? I'd like you to call someone for me."

The NIF, the National Islamic Front, came soon after: four men in beige uniforms and caps. They closed my hospital room door behind them. The one who did most of the talking had a sparse moustache playing along his upper lip. They were in my room for three hours, maybe four. Clearly they had given orders to the staff to not disturb us; no one came through the door in that whole time.

Their questions pummelled me. "Why were you in our country illegally? Are you a spy for the SPLA? Who sent you? How much are they paying you?"

I don't know how many times I told them that I didn't understand what they were talking about. That I worked for a small Canadian organization and had been taken prisoner by rebels when our truck ran out of gas. And I had let my ID card expire; I didn't have it with me. This is as far as they would let me get in my story. They wouldn't let me finish.

"What organization? There are no Canadian organizations in Sudan. What rebels do you speak of? Who were they? Where are these rebels?"

I tried to answer but they wouldn't listen to what I said. The man with the moustache would interrupt and then come back at me with the same questions, over and over. I needed them to leave; finally, I started falling asleep in the middle of the interrogation. But every time I nodded off, the man with the moustache would put his face an inch from mine and yell the same questions again, over and over, forcing me to jolt awake.

Finally, he stood straight above me, "You will be discharged soon. And then you will come with us. For more questioning." Then they left, and closed the door behind them.

The next morning I woke to Jim's hovering, ruddy face. There was moisture in his eyes. I was so happy at the sight of him I started to cry, even though I was sure he must have been very, very angry with me. Instead he leaned down and gave me a tight hug. "Please stop ... you're hurting me," I grunted.

"Sorry, sorry." He stood up and took my hand. "Girl, you are thin. So thin. God." He shook his head. "You are goddamn lucky. A lucky white girl, you hear me? That whole ID business, letting it expire, what the fuck were you thinking? Never mind, never mind ... it probably wouldn't have done you much good where you were anyways ... How the hell did you get all the way up there? What the hell did that old man want with you? Where did he take you to? Where did you stay?"

Jim's eyes sharpened in at me. His breath stank of instant coffee. I opened my mouth to speak, but nothing would come. I pressed down on my lips with my fingertips instead. I could feel my eyes filling up.

Jim shook his head back and forth, vigorously, like a dog shaking off water. "Never mind, never mind. There's lots of time for that later. But you're okay. You're okay right? You're ... unharmed?" His words probed. I knew what he meant.

"I'm unharmed." I saw his shoulders visibly relax. Then his voice started climbing again.

"You are bloody lucky girl, *first*, that that kind family brought you here, and *second*, that that nurse called me ... or else you would be headed to a safehouse for months of interrogation. And no one would know where you were, for months. Do you know how they torture people here? Never mind, never mind. I have been to both embassies, and I just lost my job 'cause of you, lass. But you're going home."

"What? Jim ..."

"Hey, don't worry. It's time for me to go anyway. RESCUE is none too happy with me for not keeping better tabs on you and letting your ID card expire. And they blame me for you three being out after curfew and ending up prisoners." I couldn't believe I had waited until now to ask. "Riak?"

"He's okay. We came for him the day after that old guy kidnapped you. We had gotten word from some SPLA spies who had been following that rebel army that you guys were being held there. They just let Riak go, they didn't even accept a bribe. We were going to pay them in cattle. But I think they were ready to move — probably had gotten wind the SPLA was on their tail." Jim paused, looked out the window. "Solomon . . ."

I looked out the window too. The grey sky was sunk down over the smoggy city.

"RESCUE and AFS sent his family in Kenya some money." Jim was silent for a long time.

"I'm sorry." The words sounded so petty in light of what happened, what was owed; but they were all I had.

"Your flight has been booked. You're going home. I talked to Amanda, who got a hold of your Dad for you."

Amanda. Dad. Were these people still in my world? It was all so strange.

I didn't know what to say, how to thank him, how to explain anything. "When am I leaving?"

"A hell of a lot sooner than you should, according to your doctor. But we have to get you out of here, girl. The government in the north is talking forcible expulsion here."

"What?" I was trying to compute everything.

"You're not allowed back in the country. Ever. They think you're a spy. They think anyone's a spy who's down south and not a southerner. Especially if you don't have ID to prove what you're doing down there. So we have to get you out of here. You're leaving tomorrow."

Jim escorted me out of the hospital and to the airport early the next morning, flashing his paperwork at all the officials. In the airport, he let me use his cellphone to call home.

Dad's voice sounded shaky at first, uncertain. "Sandra? Oh my God. Sandra." I couldn't talk. I couldn't get any words out. "Get home, will you? Just get home." His voice cracked. There was a long silence.

Then Dad spoke again, filling the silence with his foreign voice. "Your mom has been calling me every day. She's going to fly up here to see you when you get back. I hope that's okay. Oh, and Graham's called, about five or six times, I think."

Graham. I couldn't think about Graham right now. I didn't say it to him on the phone then, but I already knew that I would be leaving Toronto and moving back to Halifax, moving in with Dad. For a while. I wanted to sit with him in the evenings and watch the blue light flickering off the television set. Let him make me eggs on toast, the same breakfast he made me every single morning after Mom left, even when I complained at the monotony of it.

The woman beside me has woken up, taken off her eye mask. She turns to me, smiles contentedly. She had a good sleep. I want to tell her that I usually don't look like this. I'm not usually this skinny, or sickly looking. But I don't. I smile back. I turn to the window. I still can't see the moon. Only the black.

The sound of the gunshot that killed Solomon has faded. It no longer ricochets off the walls of my bones, but now hums quietly, trailing away. Hearing that shot cracked something open in me; something important became fragmented and broke away. If I close my eyes, I can see it — a lonely red moon floating above the dust and the broken huts, against the wide black sky. I remember thinking, after they killed Solomon, that I needed to get it back, before I go home. But that red moon part of me is still floating somewhere out there, above the desert. Now it belongs to Africa.

And there is an image that won't leave me.

It's burned into my mind above the other images. I couldn't have seen it, because I was sleeping, but it has haunted me since I woke up in the hospital.

It is night. The low hills are awash in moonlight. The one-armed boy is walking away from me, walking south, leaving me where we stopped at the bushes beside the road. The article is clasped in his one hand. The dirty bandage dangles, swaying with each step, from the stump of his other arm. I watch his ambling frame get smaller, until the hills finally absorb him.

But just before he passes over the horizon, I see a group of women who seem to walk out of nowhere to join him. They surround him, as if to hold him up should he fall. There are many of them, a procession of older women. They look like Dinka women, shirtless, their long skirts brushing the hard sand. They are singing a song, all of them singing together. I cannot see the one-armed boy's face. But I can see his smooth back, just before he passes over, his protruding shoulder blades, clipped wings. It seems less rigid, his back.

He seems happy, cloaked in their presence, listening to their song. And the stars above him, they look to be raining down, gently, like a fine mist. Bringing their light down, creating around him a bodily halo. It is as if these women somehow brought him this light from the night sky. As if they came to him solely to give him their song and these stars.

Adut

2004, AKOCH, SOUTH SUDAN, IN THE MONTH OF JANUARY,

THE SEASON OF *ROOT*

I wake Abiong by whispering her name loudly in her ear. Her eyes are tired slits, angry at my waking of her.

"What is it?" Her voice is rough with sleep as she sits up to look at me closely. "Is something wrong?"

"I need your help."

We walk out under the stars now. The night is black, but everything feels as though it is filled with light, my heart, the sky, the Women's eyes above me. I cannot see them but I feel them there, I know they must be there. The tiny fires in the sky have shaken Abiong awake. I look up to those small fires and I smile, wondering which ones the Women sit behind now. Why does it not seem so very long ago that I was a young girl who received her first moon blood? It could have been yesterday; the memories of all that has happened between now and then fade under this full night sky.

Abiong does not speak as she follows me to the edge of the village. As though she knows that what I am to do demands our silence. I stop at the clearing just past the line of newly built *tukals*. I close my eyes and I remember the old cattle byre that was here before the northerners came. We kept our cattle inside here in the nights; I can still summon their smell, the sweet smell of hay, their snuffling sounds, the freshly cut trees and grass and dried mud which held the byre together. I walk with my eyes closed to where I imagine the door to the byre to be, my feet tracing the large circular foundation. I feel Abiong's eyes upon me; she wonders at this unknown path I am carving in the dirt with my feet, but she follows me anyway.

I reach the entrance. The cattle low at me, asking me in their way to take them out to the river Kiir for water. Their long tails slap at their flanks; the show bull's bell tinkles. I want to stand in the centre of them, I want to reach out and pat the beautiful ones, the red ones and the black and white ones. Instead I turn my back to the wide open entrance and leave them to their soft night noises.

I kneel down and dig in the hard dirt with my fingers. Without saying anything, Abiong kneels down beside me and begins digging as well. After a few minutes, we have created a shallow hole. I take Father's necklace from around my neck and place it in the hole. Then I take the feather that I had stuck in the waist of my skirt and place it on top of the necklace. In that moment, I feel Father standing among the cattle. When I turn around to look for him I see only shadows. But I know, *khawaja*. I know he is watching me, and that he is pleased.

Abiong and I scoop the loose dirt over the necklace and the feather to cover up the hole. I stand up and turn toward the entrance, saying a silent goodbye to the cattle. I promise them in my mind that I will take them out to the river some day. But not tonight.

Then I walk back to our *tukal,* to my sleeping children, to my new life, with Abiong at my back.

The following books aided me in my research: *Dinka Cosmology, The Dinka of the Sudan,* and *The Dinka and their Songs,* by Francis Mading Deng; *War and Slavery in Sudan* by Jok Madut Jok; and *Divinity and Experience: The Religion of the Dinka* by Godfrey Lienhardt. Thank you to Waveland Press for permission to reprint an excerpt from *The Dinka of the Sudan* by Francis Mading Deng (Prospect Heights, Illinois: Holt, Rinehart and Winston, Inc., 1972).

A huge thank you to Jane Roy and Glen Pearson: your open arms and generosity gave me the opportunity to do the research I needed. I am indebted.

To GOAL and all the people in Twic County, Sudan, who saw my vision and helped me along the way: thank you for offering me food and shelter, and for doing your very best to protect me while I stayed with you.

To the Ring family: thank you for sharing your lives, your home, your hearts, and your stories with me. Peter, Adut, Aluel, Anita, my gratitude to all of you is enormous.

To all my peers and instructors at UBC: thank you for showing me what it takes to become a writer. To my workshop colleagues, thank you for offering your deep and invaluable insight. To Catherine Bush and Lisa Moore, your ability to see and believe in the potential of a novel from mere words sweated over on a page is a rare thing indeed, and how grateful and lucky I am that both of you have this in spades. Your sage guidance and wisdom was the reason this book was born. I truly don't know how to properly thank you. For Stefan and Vicky, thank you for your keen eyes and for your friendship that has continued beyond the workshop. And thank you, Miss Vicky, for caring about this story enough to take the time to make it more than it was, again and again.

To my editors, Don LePan, Robyn Read, and Sarah Ivany: thank you for taking a chance on this story in an industry fraught with peril; I have been struck, again and again, by your ability to free a better story from what is on the page, by your love of literature, and by your tenacity in the midst of constant change. My gratitude to all of you is never-ending.

To my parents: though you questioned and worried at every step of my journey, thank you for your enduring support. It was essential. To my sister, Nannette, thank you for your belief. To my nephews, Noah and Isaac, and my niece, Emily: you cannot know the refuge you gave me when I returned home from Africa the second time, unmoored and culture-shocked seemingly beyond repair. Your childish joy was my balm until I could again emerge.

To Jok Madut Jok: thank you for sharing your breadth of knowledge with me, for your patience, and your willingness to answer my mountain of questions from wherever you happened to be in the midst of your incredibly busy life. To Regina: thank you for your patience and your knowledge and, especially, your friendship. You can see in every chapter how what you have taught me about your culture has been entwined.

To Helena and her family in Turalei: thank you for feeding me and taking care of me when I was sick, for helping me when I needed it, for simply letting me live with you and be beside you so I could understand your lives, even though we could not communicate through language. To my brave and helpful translators, Alor Arop and Mangok Zacharia Atem, quite simply, this book could not have happened without you. Thank you for pushing beyond your boundaries in your already fraught lives to answer my questions, for leading me to person after person and village after village for photographs and interviews so that this book, which you believed in simply because I was writing it, could get published. To one of my heroes, Mama Victoria: thank you for the days-long interview about Dinka culture and for generously sharing your vast knowledge in a huge gesture of kindness. My gratitude and respect is enormous for all of you; thank you for your friendship, for enfolding me into the fabric of your lives.

And finally, to my son, Gabriel: though it is almost impossible to not become blinded by atrocities such as slavery and war that are beset by and upon humanity, through your dimply smile and profound joy I am reminded daily that there is still so much love in this world. Thank you from the very bottom of my heart.

MELANIE SCHNELL grew up on a farm in southeastern Saskatchewan and has lived in Regina, Vancouver, Toronto, Boston, Colombia, Thailand, Kenya, and Sudan. She has a Master of Fine Arts degree in Creative Writing from the University of British Columbia and has written for television, magazines, and journals across Canada. *While The Sun Is Above Us* is her first novel.